The Lynchers

Also by John Edgar Wideman

A Glance Away
Hurry Home
Damballah
Hiding Place
Sent for You Yesterday
Brothers and Keepers

John Edgar Wideman

THE LYNCHERS

An Owl Book
Henry Holt and Company   New York

Published by Henry Holt and Company, Inc.,
521 Fifth Avenue, New York, New York 10175.
Published simultaneously in Canada.

Library of Congress Cataloging-in-Publication Data
Wideman, John Edgar.
The lynchers.
"An Owl book."
I. Title.
PS3573.I26L9   1986   813'.54   86-9851
ISBN 0-8050-0118-2 (pbk.)

First published in hardcover by Harcourt Brace Jovanovich, Inc., in 1973.
First Owl Book Edition—1986
Printed in the United States of America
10 9 8 7 6 5 4 3 2 1

ISBN 0-8050-0118-2

*To Hiram Haydn—
bless the affinities*

The author wishes to acknowledge Herbert Aptheker's collection *A Documentary History of the Negro People in the United States* (New York: Citadel Press, 1951), which served as the source for many of the quotations in this novel's "Matter Prefatory."

The Lynchers

Matter Prefatory

And entering in [a river], we see
a number of blacke soules,
Whose likelinesse seem'd men to be,
but all as blacke as coles.
Their Captaine comes to me
as naked as my naile,
Not having witte or honestie
to cover once his taile.

"The First Voyage of Robert Baker to Guinie . . . 1562"

Everye white will have its blacke,
And everye sweete its soure.

Thomas Percy, *Reliques of Ancient English Poetry*, 1765

I Would Willingly Whisper to You The Strength of Your Country and The State of Your Militia; Which on The foot it Now Stands is so Imaginary A Defence, That we Cannot too Cautiously Conceal it from our Neighbours and our Slaves, nor too Earnestly Pray That Neither The Lust of Dominion, nor The Desire of freedom May Stir those people to any Attempts The Latter Sort (I mean our Negro's) by Their Dayly Encrease Seem to be The Most Dangerous; And the Tryals of Last Aprill Court may shew that we are not to Depend on Either their Stupidity, or that Babel of Languages among 'em; freedom Wears a Cap which Can Without a Tongue, Call Togather all those who Long to Shake off the fetters of Slavery and as Such an Insurrection would surely be attended with Most Dreadfull Consequences so I Think we Cannot be too Early in providing Against it, both by putting our Selves in a better posture of Defence and by Making a Law to prevent The Consultation of Those Negros.

Governor Alexander Spotswood, 1710

3

And while we are, as I may call it, Scouring our Planet, by clearing America of Woods, and so making this Side of our Globe reflect a brighter Light to the Eyes of Inhabitants in Mars or Venus, why should we in the Sight of Superior Beings, darken its People? Why increase the Sons of Africa, by Planting them in America, where we have so fair an Opportunity, by excluding all Blacks and Tawneys, of increasing the lovely White and Red? But perhaps I am partial to the Complexion of my Country.

Benjamin Franklin, 1751

They import so many Negros hither, that I fear this Colony will some time or other be confirmed by the Name of New Guinea.

Colonel William Byrd, 1736

Ibos pend' cor' a yo (Ibos hang themselves)

Old Haitian saying

From New London [Connecticut], Feb. 20th past. By certain Information from a Gentleman we are assured, that some Weeks ago to the Westward of that place, a very remarkable thing fell out, (which we here relate as a caveat for all Negroes medling for the future with any white Women, least they fare with the like Treatment,) and it is this, A Negro Man met abroad an English Woman, which he accosted to lye with, stooping down, fearing none behind him, a Man observing his Design, took out his Knife, before the Negro was aware, cut off all his unruly parts smack and smooth, the Negro Jumpt up roaring and run for his Life; the Black now an Eunuch is alive and like to recover of his Wounds and doubtless cured from any more such Wicked Attempts.

Boston News-Letter, March 3, 1718

I'll tell you 'nother funny joke 'bout Henry Johnson. He had to clean up most of the time. So Mrs. Newton's dress was hanging in the room up on the wall, and when he come out he said to old Uncle Jerry, he said: "Jerry, guess what I

4

done." And Jerry said: "What?" And Uncle Henry said: "I put my hand under Old Mistress' dress." Uncle Jerry said: "What did she say?" Uncle Henry say: "She didn't say nothing." So Uncle Jerry 'cided he'd try it. So he went dragging on in the house. Set down on the floor by Old Mistress. After while he run his hand up under her dress, and Old Master jumped up and jumped on Jerry and like to beat him to death. Jerry went out crying and got out and called Henry. He said: "Henry, I thought you said you put your hand under Old Mistress' dress and she didn't say nothing." Uncle Henry said: "I did and she didn't say nothing." Jerry said: "I put my hand under her dress, and Old Master like to beat me to death." Uncle Henry said: "You crazy thing, her dress was hanging up on the wall when I put my hand up under it."

From *Lay My Burden Down*, B. A. Botkin, ed.

In fact the only weapon of self defense that I could use successfully was that of deception.

Henry Bibb, *Narrative*

. . . I remember Mammy told me about one master who almost starved his slaves. Mighty stingy, I reckon he was.

Some of them slaves was so poorly thin they ribs would kinda rustle against each other like corn stalks a-drying in the hot winds. But they gets even one hog-killing time, and it was funny, too, Mammy said.

They was seven hogs, fat and ready for fall hog-killing time. Just the day before Old Master told off they was to be killed, something happened to all them porkers. One of the field boys found them and come a-telling the master: "The hogs is all died, now they won't be any meats for the winter."

When the master gets to where at the hogs is laying, they's a lot of Negroes standing round looking sorrow-eyed at the wasted meat. The master asks: "What's the illness with 'em?"

"Malitis," they tells him, and they acts like they don't want to touch the hogs. Master says to dress them anyway for they ain't no more meat on the place.

5

He says to keep all the meat for the slave families, but that's because he's afraid to eat it hisself account of the hogs' got malitis.

"Don't you all know what is malitis?" Mammy would ask the children when she was telling of the seven fat hogs and seventy lean slaves. And she would laugh, remembering how they fooled Old Master so's to get all them good meats.

"One of the strongest Negroes got up early in the morning," Mammy would explain, "long 'fore the rising horn called the slaves from their cabins. He skitted to the hog pen with a heavy mallet in his hand. When he tapped Mister Hog 'tween the eyes with that mallet, 'malitis' set in mighty quick, but it was a uncommon 'disease,' even with hungry Negroes around all the time."

From *Lay My Burden Down*, B. A. Botkin, ed.

Dear Brother: . . . It was a sense of the wrongs which we have suffered that prompted the noble but unfortunate Captain John Brown and his associates to attempt to give freedom to a small number, at least, of those who are now held by cruel and unjust laws, and by no less cruel and unjust men. To this freedom they were entitled by every known principle of justice and humanity, and for the enjoyment of it God created them. And now, dear brother, could I die in a more noble cause? Could I, brother, die in a manner and for a cause which would induce true and honest men more to honor me, and the angels more readily to receive me to their happy home of everlasting joy above? I imagine that I hear you, and all of you, mother, father, sisters and brothers, say —"No, there is not a cause for which we, with less sorrow, could see you die." Believe me when I tell you, that though shut up in prison and under sentence of death, I have spent some very happy hours here. And were it not that I know that the hearts of those to whom I am attached by the nearest and most enduring ties of blood-relationship—yea, by the closest and strongest ties that God has instituted—will be filled with sorrow, I would almost as lief die now as at any

time, for I feel that I am now prepared to meet my Maker.
. . .

John Copeland, fugitive slave captured with
John Brown at Harpers Ferry, 1859

Petition from Kentucky Negroes, March 25th, 1871

To the senate and house of Representatives in Congress assembled: We the Colored Citizens of Frankfort and vicinity do this day memorialize your honorable bodies upon the condition of affairs now existing in this the state of Kentucky.

We would respectfully state that life, liberty and property are unprotected among the colored race of this state. Organized Bands of desperate and lawless men mainly composed of soldiers of the late Rebel Armies Armed disciplined and disguised and bound by Oath and secret obligations have by force terror and violence subverted all civil society among Colored people, thus utterly rendering insecure the safety of persons and property, overthrowing all those rights which arc the primary basis and objects of the Government which are expressly guaranteed to us by the Constitution of the United States as amended; We believe you are not familiar with the description of the Ku Klux Klans riding nightly over the country going from County to County and in the County towns spreading terror wherever they go, by robbing whipping ravishing and killing our people without provocation, compelling Colored people to brake the ice and bathe in the Chilly waters of the Kentucky River. . . . We appeal to you as law abiding citizens to enact some laws that will protect us. And that will enable us to exercise the rights of citizens. We see that the senators from this state denies there being organized Bands of desperaders in the state, for information we lay before you a number of violent acts occured during his Administration. . . .

1. A mob visited Harrodsburg in Mercer County to take from jail a man name Robertson, Nov. 14, 1867.

2. Smith attacked and whipped by regulation in Zelun County Nov. 1867.

3. Colored school house burned by incendiaries in Breckinridge Dec. 24, 1867.

4. A Negro Jim Macklin taken from jail in Frankfort and hung by mob January 28, 1868.

5. Sam Davis hung by mob in Harrodsburg May 28, 1868.

6. Wm. Pierce hung by a mob in Christian July 12, 1868.

7. Geo. Roger hung by a mob in Bradsfordsville Martin County July 11, 1868.

8. Colored school Exhibition at Midway attacked by a mob July 31, 1868.

9. Seven persons ordered to leave their homes at Standford, Ky. Aug. 7, 1868.

10. Silas Woodford age sixty badly beaten by disguised mob. Mary Smith Curtis and Margaret Mosby also badly beaten, near Keene Jessamine County Aug. 1868.

11. Cabe Fields shot—and killed by disguised men near Keene Jessamine County Aug, 3, 1868.

12. James Gaines expelled from Anderson by Ku Klux Aug. 1868.

13. James Parker killed by Ku Klux Pulaski, Aug. 1868.

14. Noah Blankenship shipped by a mob in Pulaski County Aug. 1868.

15. Negroes attacked robbed and driven from Summerville in Green County Aug. 21, 1868.

16. William Gibson and John Gibson hung by a mob in Washington County Aug. 1868.

17. F. H. Montford hung by a mob near Cogers landing in Jessamine County Aug. 28, 1868.

18. Wm. Glassgow killed by a mob in Warren County Sep. 5, 1868.

19. Negro hung by a mob Sept. 1868.

20. Two Negros beaten by Ku Klux in Anderson County Sept. 11, 1868.

21. Mob attacked house of Oliver Stone in Fayette County Sept. 11, 1868.

22. Mob attacked Cumins house in Pulaski County.

Cumins his daughter and a man name Adams killed in the attack Sept. 18, 1868.

23. U.S. Marshall Meriwether attacked captured and beaten with death in Larue County by mob Sept. 1868.

24. Richardson house attacked in Conishville by mob and Crasban killed Sept. 28, 1868.

25. Mob attacks Negro cabin at hanging forks in Lincoln County, John Mosteran killed & Cash & Coffey killed Sept. 1869.

26. Terry Laws & James Ryan hung by mob at Nicholasville Oct. 26, 1868.

27. Attack on Negro cabin in Spencer County—a woman outraged Dec. 1868.

28. Two Negroes shot by Ku Klux at Sulphur Springs in Union County, Dec. 1868.

29. Negro shot at Morganfield Union County, Dec. 1868.

30. Mob visited Edwin Burris house in Mercer County, January, 1869.

31. William Parker whipped by Ku Klux in Lincoln County Jan. 20/69.

32. Mob attacked and fired into house of Jesse Davises in Lincoln County Jan. 20, 1868.

33. Spears taken from his room at Harrodsburg by disguise men Jan. 19, 1869.

34. Albert Bradford killed by disguise men in Scott County, Jan. 20, 1869.

35. Ku Klux whipped boy at Standford March 12, 1869.

36. Mob attacked Frank Bournes house in Jessamine County. Roberts killed March 1869.

37. Geo Bratcher hung by mob on sugar creek in Garrard County March 30, 1869.

38. John Penny hung by a mob at Nevada Mercer county May 29, 1869.

39. Ku Klux whipped Lucien Green in Lincoln county June 1869.

40. Miller whipped by Ku Klux in Madison county July 2, 1869.

41. Chas Henderson shot & his wife killed by mob on silver creek Madison county July 1869.

42. Mob decoy from Harrodsburg and hangs Geo Bolling July 17, 1869.

43. Disguise band visited home of I. C. Vanarsdall and T. J. Vanarsdall in Mercer county July 18/69.

44. Mob attack Ronsey's house in Casey county three men and one woman killed July 1869.

45. James Crowders hung by mob near Lebanon Merion county Aug. 9, 1869.

46. Mob tar and feather a citizen of Cynthiana in Harrison county Aug. 1869.

47. Mob whipped and bruised a Negro in Davis county Sept. 1869.

48. Ku Klux burn colored meeting-house in Carrol county Sept. 1869.

49. Ku Klux whipped a Negro at John Carmin's in Fayette county Sept. 1869.

50. Wiley Gevens killed by Ku Klux at Dixon Webster county Oct. 1869.

51. Geo Rose killed by Ku Klux near Kirkville in Madison county Oct. 18, 1869.

52. Ku Klux ordered Wallace Sinkhorn to leave his home near Parkville Boyle county Oct. 1869.

53. Man named Shepherd shot by mob near Parksville Oct. 1869.

54. Regulator killed Geo Tanhely in Lincoln county Nov. 2, 1869.

55. Ku Klux attacked Frank Searcy house in Madison county one man shot Nov. 1869.

56. Searcy hung by mob Madison county at Richmond Nov. 4, 1869.

57. Ku Klux killed Robt Mershon daughter shot Nov. 1869.

58. Mob whipped Pope Hall and Willett in Washington county Nov. 1869.

59. Regulators whipped Cooper in Palaski County Nov. 1869.

60. Ku Klux ruffians outraged Negroes in Hickman county Nov. 20, 1869.

61. Mob take two Negroes from jail Richmond Madison county one hung one whipped Dec. 12, 1869.

62. Two Negroes killed by mob while in civil custody near Mayfield Graves county Dec. 1869.

63. Allen Cooper killed by Ku Klux in Adair county Dec. 24, 1869.

64. Negroes whipped while on Scott's farm in Franklin county Dec. 1869.

65. Mob hung Chas Fields in Fayette county Jan. 20, 1870.

66. Mob took two men from Springfield jail and hung them Jan. 31, 1870.

67. Ku Klux whipped two Negroes in Madison county Feb. 1870.

68. Simms hung by mob near Kingston Madison county Feb. 1870.

69. Mob hung up, then whipped Douglass Rodes near Kingston Madison county February 1870.

70. Mob takes Fielding Waller from jail at Winchester Feb. 19th, 1870.

71. R. L. Byrom hung by mob at Richmond Feb. 18th. 1870.

72. Perry hung by mob near Lancaster Garrard County April 5th, 70.

73. Negro hung by mob at Crab-orchard Lincoln county Apr. 6th, 1870.

74. Mob rescue prisoner from Summerset jail Apr. 5, 1870.

75. Mob attacked A. Owen's house in Lincoln county Hyatt killed and Saunders shot Apr. 1870.

76. Mob releases five prisoners from Federal Officers in Bullitt county Apr. 11th, 1870.

77. Sam Lambert shot & hung by mob in Mercer county Apr. 11th, 1870.

78. Mob attacks William Palmer house in Clark County William Hart killed Apr. 1870.

79. Three men hung by mob near Gloscow Warren county May 1870.

80. John Redman killed by Ku Klux in Adair county May 1870.

81. William Sheldon Pleasanton Parker Daniel Parker Willis Parker hung by mob in Laurel county May 14th, 1870.

82. Ku Klux visited Negro cabins at Deak's Mill Franklin county robbed and maltreated inmates May 14th, 1870.

83. Negro's school house burned by incendiaries in Christain county May 1870.

84. Negro hung by mob at Greenville Muhlenburgh county May 1870.

85. Colored school house on Glen creek in Woodford county burned by incendiaries June 4th, 1870.

86. Ku Klux visited Negro cabin robbing and maltreating inmates on Sand Riffle in Hay county June 10, 1870.

87. Mob attacked Jail in Whitely County two men shot June 1870.

88. Election riot at Harrodsburg four persons killed Aug. 4, 1870.

89. Property burned by incendiaries in Woodford County Aug. 8, 1870.

90. Turpin & Parker killed by mob at Versailles Aug. 10, 1870.

91. Richard Brown's house attacked by Ku Klux, in Hay.

92. Simpson Grubbs killed by a band of men in Montgomery county Aug. 1870.

93. Jacob See rescued from Mt. Sterling jail by mob Sept. 1870.

94. Frank Timberlake hung by a mob at Flemingburg Fleming county Sept. 1870.

95. John Simes shot & his wife murdered by Ku Klux in Hay county Sept. 1870.

96. Oliver Williams hung by Ku Klux in Madison county Sept. 1870.

97. Ku Klux visited cabins of colored people robbed and

maltreated inmates at Havey Mill Franklin county.

98. A mob abducted Hicks from Lancaster Oct. 1870.

99. Howard Gilbert shot by Ku Klux in Madison county Oct. 9th, 1870.

100. Ku Klux drive colored people Bald-Knob Franklin county Oct. 1870.

101. Two Negroes shot on Harrison Blanton's farm near Frankfort Dec. 6th, 1870.

102. Two Negroes killed in Fayette county while in civil custody Dec. 18, 1870.

103. Howard Million murdered by Ku Klux in Fayette county Dec. 1870.

104. John Dickerson driven from his home in Hay county and his daughter ravished Dec. 12, 1870.

105. A Negro named George hung by a mob at Cynthiana Harrison county Dec. 1870.

106. Negro killed by Ku Klux near Ashland Fayette county January 7th, 1871.

107. A Negro named Hall whipped and shot near Shelbyville Shelby county Jan. 17, 1871.

108. Ku Klux visited Negro cabin at Stamping Ground in Scott county force (White) & Ku Klux killed two Negroes killed in self defense.

109. Negro killed by Ku Klux in Hay county January 14, 1871.

110. Negro church & school house in Scott county [burned?] Jan. 13, 1871.

111. Ku Klux maltreated Demar his two sons and Joseph Allen in Franklin Jan. 1871.

112. Dr. Johnson whipped by Ku Klux in Magoffin county Dec. 1871.

113. Property burned by incendiaries in Fayette county Jan. 21, 1871.

114. Attack on mail agent—North Benson Jan. 26, 1871.

115. Winston Hawkins fence burned and notice over his door not come home any more April 2, 1871.

116. Ku Klux to the number of two hundred in February

came into Frankfort and rescued from jail one Scroggins that was in civil custody for shooting and killing one colored man named Steader Trumbo.

On Lynching

. . . The crime which these usurpers of courts of law and juries profess to punish is the most revolting and shocking of any this side of murder. This they know is the best excuse, and it appeals at once and promptly to a prejudice which prevails at the North as well as the South. Hence we have for any act of lawless violence the same excuse—an outrage by a Negro upon some white woman. It is a notable fact, also, that it is not with them the immorality or the enormity of the crime itself that arouses popular wrath, but the emphasis is put upon the race and color of the parties to it. Here, and not there, is the ground of indignation and abhorrence. The appeal is not to the moral sense but to the well-known hatred of one class to another. . . .

For 200 years or more white men have in the South committed this offense against black women, and the fact has excited little attention, even at the North, except among Abolitionists; which circumstance demonstrates that the horror now excited is not for the crime itself, but that it is based on the reversal of color in the participants. . . .

Now where rests the responsibility for the lynch law prevalent in the South? It is evident that it is not entirely with the ignorant mob. The men who break open jails and with bloody hands destroy human life are not alone responsible. These are not the men who make public sentiment. They are simply the hangmen, not the court, judge, or jury. They simply obey the public sentiment of the South—the sentiment created by wealth and respectability, by the press and pulpit. A change in public sentiment can be easily effected by these forces whenever they shall elect to make the effort. Let the press and the pulpit of the South unite their power against the cruelty, disgrace and shame that is settling like a mantle of fire upon these lynch-law states, and lynch law itself will soon cease to exist.

Nor is the South alone responsible for this burning shame and menace to our free institutions. Wherever contempt of race prevails, whether against African, Indian or Mongolian, countenance and support are given to the present peculiar treatment of the Negro in the South. The finger of scorn at the North is correlated to the dagger of the assassin at the South. The sin against the Negro is both sectional and national; and until the voice of the North shall be heard in emphatic condemnation and withering reproach against these continued ruthless mob law murders, it will remain equally involved with the South in this common crime.

Frederick Douglass, 1892

I was struck by a question a little boy asked me, which ran about this way—"Why does the American Negro come from America to fight us when we are much friend to him and have not done anything to him? He is all the same as me, and me all the same as you. Why don't you fight those people in America that burn the Negroes, that made a beast of you, that took the child from its mother's side and sold it?"

William Simms, May 11, 1901, during Filipino Insurrection

. . . More than 500 persons stood by and looked on while the Negro was slowly burned to a crisp. A few women were scattered among the crowd of Arkansas planters, who directed the grewsome work of avenging the death of O. T. Craig and his daughter, Mrs. C. P. Williamson.

Not once did the slayer beg for mercy despite the fact that he suffered one of the most horrible deaths imaginable. With the Negro chained to a log, members of the mob placed a small pile of leaves around his feet. Gasoline was then poured on the leaves, and the carrying out of the death sentence was under way.

Inch by inch the Negro was fairly cooked to death. Every few minutes fresh leaves were tossed on the funeral pyre until the blaze had passed the Negro's waist. . . . Even after the

15

flesh had dropped away from his legs and the flames were leaping toward his face, Lowry retained consciousness. Not once did he whimper or beg for mercy. Once or twice he attempted to pick up the hot ashes in his hands and thrust them into his mouth in order to hasten death.

Each time the ashes were kicked out of his reach by a member of the mob. . . .

As the flames were eating away his abdomen, a member of the mob stepped forward and saturated the body with gasoline. It was then only a few minutes until the Negro had been reduced to ashes. . . .

Memphis Press, January 27, 1921

I watched a Negro burned at the stake at Rocky Ford, Miss., Sunday afternoon. I watched an angry mob chain him to an iron stake. I watched them pile wood around his helpless body. I watched them pour gasoline on this wood. And I watched three men set this wood on fire.

I stood in a crowd of 600 people as the flames gradually crept nearer and nearer to the helpless Negro. I watched the blaze climb higher and higher encircling him without mercy. I heard his cry of agony as the flames reached him and set his clothing on fire.

"Oh, God; Oh, God!" he shouted. "I didn't do it! Have mercy!" The blaze leaped higher. The Negro struggled. He kicked the chain loose from his ankles but it held his waist and neck against the iron post that was becoming red with the intense heat.

"Have mercy, I didn't do it! I didn't do it!" he shouted again.

. . . Nowhere was there a sign of mercy among the members of the mob, nor did they seem to regret the horrible thing they had done. The Negro had supposedly sinned against their race, and he died a death of torture.

Soon he became quiet. There was no doubt that he was dead. The flames jumped and leaped above his head. An odour of burning flesh reached my nostrils. Through the leaping blaze I could see the Negro sagging and supported by the chains. . . .

16

. . . The mob walked away. In the vanguard of the mob I noticed a woman. She seemed to be rather young, yet it is hard to tell about women of her type; strong and healthy, apparently a woman of the country. She walked with a firm, even stride. She was beautiful in a way. . . .

"I'm hungry," someone complained. "Let's get something to eat." . . .

"Gov. Whitfield won't have a lick of luck with any investigation of the burning of Jim Ivy." So declared William N. Bradshaw, of Union County, Mississippi, admittedly a member of the mob that for forty-eight hours sought the Negro accused of criminally assaulting a white girl near Rocky Ford, Miss., Friday morning in a statement to the *News-Scimitar* this morning. "And furthermore," he continued, "not an officer in Union County or any of the neighboring counties will point out any member of the crowd. Why, if he did, the best thing for him to do would be to jump into an airplane headed for Germany—quick. Sure the officers know who were there. Everybody down there knows everything else. We're all neighbors and neighbors' neighbors." . . .

Memphis *News-Scimitar*, September 1925

When the two Negroes were captured, they were tied to trees and while the funeral pyres were being prepared they were forced to suffer the most fiendish tortures. The blacks were forced to hold out their hands while one finger at a time was chopped off. The fingers were distributed as souvenirs. The ears of the murderers were cut off. Holbert was beaten severely, his skull was fractured, and one of his eyes, knocked out with a stick, hung by a shred from the socket. . . . The most excruciating form of punishment consisted in the use of a large corkscrew in the hands of some of the mob. This instrument was bored into the flesh of the man and woman, in the arms, legs and body, and then pulled out, the spirals tearing out big pieces of raw, quivering flesh every time it was withdrawn.

Vicksburg, Mississippi, *Evening Post*

I had rationalized my environment, but it had rejected me in the name of colour prejudice. Since there was no understanding on the basis of reason, I threw myself into the arms of the irrational. I became irrational up to my neck . . . the tom-tom drummed out my cosmic mission . . . I found, not my origin, but the origin. I wedded the world! The white man has never understood this magical substitution. He desires the world and wants it for himself alone. He considers himself predestined to rule the world. He has made it useful to himself. But here are values which do not submit to his rule. Like a sorcerer I steal from the white man a certain world which he cannot identify. . . . Above the plantations and the banana trees I gently set the true world. The essence of the world was my property. . . . The white man suddenly had the impression that I was eluding him and taking something with me. They turned out my pockets but found there only familiar things. But now I had a secret. And if they questioned me, I murmured to myself . . .

Frantz Fanon, Black Skin, White Masks, 1952

Every organization, then, involves a discipline of activity, but our interest here is that at some level every organization also involves a discipline of being—an obligation to be of a given character and to dwell in a given world. And my object here is to examine a special kind of absenteeism, a defaulting not from prescribed activity but from prescribed being.

Erving Goffman, Asylums, 1961

Slavery was the worst days was ever seed in the world. They was things past telling, but I got the scars on my old body to show to this day. I seed worse than what happened to me. I seed them put the men and women in the stock with they hands screwed down through holes in the board and they feets tied together and they naked behinds to the world. Solomon the overseer beat them with a big whip and Massa look on. The niggers better not stop in the fields when they hear them yelling. They cut the flesh 'most to the bones, and some they was when they taken them out of stock and put them on the beds, they never got up again.

When a nigger died, they let his folks come out the fields to see him afore he died. They buried him the same day, take a big plank and bust it with a ax in the middle 'nough to bend it back, and put the dead nigger in betwixt it. They'd cart them down to the graveyard on the place and not bury them deep 'nough that buzzards wouldn't come circling around. Niggers mourns now, but in them days they wasn't no time for mourning.

The conch shell blowed afore daylight, and all hands better git out for roll call, or Solomon bust the door down and git them out. It was work hard, git beatings, and half-fed. They brung the victuals and water to the fields on a slide pulled by a old mule. Plenty times they was only a half barrel water and it stale and hot, for all us niggers on the hottest days. Mostly we ate pickled pork and corn bread and peas and beans and 'taters. They never was as much as we needed.

The times I hated most was picking cotton when the frost was on the bolls. My hands git sore and crack open and bleed. We'd have a little fire in the fields, and iffen the ones with tender hands couldn't stand it no longer, we'd run and warm our hands a little bit. When I could steal a 'tater, I used to slip it in the ashes, and when I'd run to the fire I'd take it out and eat it on the sly.

In the cabins it was nice and warm. They was built of pine boarding, and they was one long row of them up the hill back of the big house. Near one side of the cabins was a fireplace. They'd bring in two-three big logs and put on the fire, and they'd last near a week. The beds was made out of puncheons fitted in holes bored in the wall, and planks laid 'cross them poles. We had ticking mattresses filled with corn shucks. Sometimes the men build chairs at night. We didn't know much 'bout having nothing, though.

Sometimes Massa let niggers have a little patch. They'd raise 'taters or goobers. They liked to have them to help fill out on the victuals. 'Taters roasted in the ashes was the best-tasting eating I ever had. I could die better satisfied to have just one more 'tater roasted in hot ashes. The niggers had to work the patches at night and dig the 'taters and goobers at night. Then if they wanted to sell any in town, they'd have to git a pass to go. They had to go at night, 'cause they couldn't ever spare a hand from the fields.

Once in a while they'd give us a little piece of Saturday evening to wash out clothes in the branch. We hanged them out on the ground in the woods to dry. They was a place to wash clothes from the well, but they was so many niggers all couldn't git round to it on Sundays. When they'd git through with the clothes on Saturday evenings, the niggers which sold they goobers and 'taters brung fiddles and guitars and come out and play. The others clap they hands and stomp they feet and we young-uns cut a step round. I was plenty biggity and liked to cut a step. . . .

In them days I weared shirts, like all the young-uns. They had collars and come below the knees and was split up the sides. That's all we weared in hot weather. The men weared jeans and the women gingham. Shoes was the worstest trouble. We weared rough russets when it got cold, and it seem powerful strange they'd never git them to fit. Once when I was a young gal, they got me a new pair and all brass studs in the toes. They was too little for me, but I had to wear them. The brass trimmings cut into my ankles and them places got miserable bad. I rubs tallow in them sore places and wrops rags round them and my sores got worser and worser. The scars are there to this day.

I wasn't sick much, though. Some the niggers had chills and fever a lot, but they hadn't discovered so many diseases then as now. Massa give sick niggers ipecac and asafetida and oil and turpentine and black fever pills.

They was a cabin called the spinning-house and two looms and two spinning wheels going all the time. It took plenty sewing to make all the things for a place so big. Once Massa goes to Baton Rouge and brung back a yaller gal dressed in fine style. She was a seamster nigger. He builds her a house 'way from the quarters, and she done fine sewing for the whites. Us niggers knowed the doctor took a black woman quick as he did a white and took any on his place he wanted, and he took them often. But mostly the children born on the place looked like niggers. Aunt Cheyney always say four of hers was Massa's, but he didn't give them no mind. But this yaller gal breeds so fast and gits a mess of white young-uns. She larnt them fine manners and combs out they hair.

Oncet two of them goes down the hill to the dollhouse, where the Missy's children am playing. They wants to go in the dollhouse and one the Missy's boys say, "That's for white children." They say, "We ain't no niggers, 'cause we got the same daddy you has, and he comes to see us near every day and fotches us clothes and things from town." They is fussing, and Missy is listening out her chamber window. She heard them white niggers say, "He is our daddy and we call him daddy when he comes to our house to see our mama."

When Massa come home that evening, his wife hardly say nothing to him, and he ask her what the matter, and she tells him, "Since you asks me, I'm studying in my mind 'bout them white young-uns of that yaller nigger wench from Baton Rouge." He say, "Now, honey, I fotches that gal just for you, 'cause she a fine seamster." She say, "It look kind of funny they got the same kind of hair and eyes as my children, and they got a nose look like yours." He say, "Honey, you just paying 'tention to talk of little children that ain't got no mind to what they say." She say, "Over in Mississippi I got a home and plenty with my daddy, and I got that in my mind."

Well, she didn't never leave, and Massa bought her a fine, new span of surrey horses. But she don't never have no more children, and she ain't so cordial with the Massa. That yaller gal has more white young-uns, but they don't never go down the hill no more to the big house.

Aunt Cheyney was just out of bed with a suckling baby one time, and she run away. Some say that was 'nother baby of Massa's breeding. She don't come to the house to nurse her baby, so they misses her and Old Solomon gits the nigger hounds and takes her trail. They gits near her and she grabs a limb and tries to hist herself in a tree, but them dogs grab her and pull her down. The men hollers them onto her, and the dogs tore her naked and et the breasts plumb off her body. She got well and lived to be a old woman, but 'nother woman has to suck her baby, and she ain't got no sign of breasts no more.

They give all the niggers fresh meat on Christmas and a plug tobacco all round. The highest cotton-picker gits a suit of clothes, and all the women what had twins that year gits a outfitting of clothes for the twins, and a double, warm blanket.

Seems like after I got bigger, I 'member more and more niggers run away. They's 'most always cotched. Massa used to hire out his niggers for wage hands. One time he hired me and a nigger boy, Turner, to work for some ornery white trash, name of Kidd. One day Turner goes off and don't come back. Old Man Kidd say I knowed 'bout it, and he tied my wrists together and stripped me. He hanged me by the wrists from a limb on a tree and spraddled my legs round the trunk and tied my feet together. Then he beat me. He beat me worser than I ever been beat before, and I faints dead away. When I come to I'm in bed. I didn't care so much iffen I died.

I didn't know 'bout the passing of time, but Miss Dora come to me. Some white folks done git word to her. Mr. Kidd tries to talk hisself out of it, but Miss Dora fotches me home when I'm well 'nough to move. She took me in a cart and my maw takes care of me. Massa looks me over good and says I'll git well, but I'm ruint for breeding children.

After while I taken a notion to marry and Massa and Missy marries us same as all the niggers. They stands inside the house with a broom held crosswise of the door and we stands outside. Missy puts a little wreath on my head they kept there, and we steps over the broom into the house.

22

Now, that's all they was to the marrying. After freedom I gits married and has it put in the book by a preacher.

. . . My husband and me farmed round for times, and then I done housework and cooking for many years. I come to Dallas and cooked for seven year for one white family. My husband died years ago. I guess Miss Dora been dead these long years. I always kept my years by Miss Dora's years, 'count we is born so close.

I been blind and 'most helpless for five year. I'm gitting mighty enfeebling, and I ain't walked outside the door for a long time back. I sets and 'members the times in the world. I 'members 'bout the days of slavery, and I don't 'lieve they ever gwine have slaves no more on this earth. I think God done took that burden offen his black children, and I'm aiming to praise Him for it to His face in the days of glory what ain't so far off.

Mary Reynolds, Louisiana, from Lay My Burden Down,
B. A. Botkin, ed.

Part

1

SOMEWHERE he was singing. Pure, effortless tenor rising to the mellowest, highest note possible a sweet tenor ever sang. *Nearer, nearer my God to thee* shaping his lips. His eyes closed, head tilted so that the nape of his neck sank into the white choir robe and his throat from which music issued curved thick and fluted from stiff white collar to outthrust chin. Yet he did not strain, could have been sleeping, so easily, smoothly did he form the notes. Then it was gone, the rest of the choir sweeping up his solo in their gusts of rich chanting.

She saw him sprawled in the soft chair, mouth open, head flung back, pasted to that perpetual grease spot on the slipcover. The rug did not quite reach the corners of the room and two legs of the soft chair dug knurled toes into the linoleum. His arms dangling where they had slipped from the thin, tattered arms of the chair, one big hand empty and from the other, inching as fingers relaxed, a brightly colored paperback book. She stood motionless until the book slapped against the scarred border of linoleum. He did not stir and she stepped noiselessly from the room.

When he awakened his neck hurt and his eyes watered, blinking into focus. The necessity of a gunfighter's eternal vigilance jostled into his thoughts and he wished he could be like the Pecos Kid, one eye always open when he slept. A surge of good feeling, of warmth reminded him he had done something well, or had something pleasant to anticipate. Orin Wilkerson recalled the climbing, the crystal note. But when he grunted up from the chair, clumsy sections of himself clattering and bumping like freight cars shuddering into motion behind a steam engine, he knew music had been left behind. No rhythm to his footsteps as he shook the

cocoon of sleep from his body. Dust and smoke and moss
sliding down. In piles at his feet. You want to wipe the sleep
fog from your skin the way you dry yourself with a warm
towel after a shower. Work shoes still on his feet weighing as
much as they do at the end of the day, though this day is
barely beginning.

He is suddenly cold, a swift, enveloping chill. Door or
window open he knows, though he can't see it. He would call
her but if it is morning she may be asleep and perhaps she
slept right through and I can tell her any lie, choose the
decent hour I came in and just too tired so went to sleep
downstairs on the couch. Even as he forms a probable fiction
he knows she will be sitting in the kitchen, aware of everything.

And she is and she asks why did he bother to come home
for the hour he did. He wants more from her. He wants her
calling him out of his name, calling him *Sweetman,* treating
him like he's still in the street or like she wants him gone.
He shivers again in the draft, his voice aching the no sleep,
the endless fog hours reeling inside him, wasted and still to
come that he must set in order for the small woman drinking
coffee at a gimpy table. Does the table tremble too in the
same chill waves that pass over his flesh, is it cup rattling
against saucer that he hears chattering inside his jaw. She
stirs her coffee very slowly, spoon the elongated fin of a
meandering shark circling its prey in the brown liquid. Some
slops into the saucer, mutes the bone rattle.

—Don't lie to me. He thought she would repeat the phrase.
Please, don't lie to me, the *please* a softening, a breach he
could enter and take her wronged softness, but she did not
admit him did not repeat or request, demanded simply, once,
that he not lie. And he couldn't. But circled the small kitchen
in his work shoes, saying nothing, avoiding her eyes, careful
not to step on land mines, or over sheer cliffs, tentative till
he found a safe path through the blue and gray squares of
linoleum, then repeating his steps exactly, not stepping on a
crack, not breaking his mother's back, circling till he realized

28

he was a spoon held in orbit by a giant fist whose knuckles were going white. And each time the hand forced him deeper into the floor, scoring the faded covering, burning down through lathes and plaster and beams, opening a hole to hell, a lopsided oval through which his wife would tumble with him.

In the kitchen a silent, curdling postponement. Pocked walls breathing sourly, patient mirrors of everything and if peeled layer by layer paint to paper to paper to paint to paint you would see old lives crowded as saints in the catacombs. Their children's hand prints crawling up the wall. The low border when it was a third leg to hold them up, the grease streaks from the boys' slicked down heads as they leaned back cockily on spindly legged chairs sneaking smokes and trading lies around the kitchen table, up near crease of ceiling and wa l, splash of roach where she told Thomas not to squash them even if he could reach that high. Once blue, once yellow, hopelessly white, blue again, now the rosette paper meant for somebody's living room. All layers seemed to hover near the surface, dark ghosts scratching through the faded blush of roses. The walls would never be disguised again. They would regress now, shedding skin after skin, betraying the past.

She realized how easily it could all disappear. Everywhere in the neighborhood buildings were being torn down. A wall could look so pitiful when everything around it had been stripped away. No ceiling, floors missing, no outer walls to protect its pink or blue from the bleaching sun. A room was just space, just emptiness bounded by paint and plaster.

Standing in the emptiness she liked to call *her* kitchen, where she reigned if nowhere else. Cooking and serving their meals. First two to feed, a neat ritual she could give herself to wholly, chiding him playfully to remember to bless the food, then three, a quiet settling down together, boy an image of his father, so pleased with himself, so grown when his seat hiked by a pile of cushions and phone books was pulled to the table, four, five, finally six, four, three, two again . . .

29

sometimes, but not the same two, not the same sleepiness, the anticipation, the gently fumbling progress through the dishes, the down hill glide of simple chores always easing toward the bed they shared. Not a circle. Not the same two. A steep hill you climb then tumble down. One.

If she would only cry. Orin wanted her to be the girl sobbing, the rich damp earth in which he had first planted his seed. Not spring but deep winter, snow clouding the mounds of garbage heaped on the curb. Rooftops stayed prettier longer than the rest, gleaming white crust unbroken by tires or footsteps though it too would gray in the fine, clinging soot constantly rained from thunderheads huddling blackly over the city. Summer hot in the room because furnace either overheated or sent nothing except pops and grunts up through its pipes. One day the room covered with soot, every surface, the edges of the oval picture frame with its sepia portrait of a moustachioed black man, doilies set out on the coffee table, in shoes under the bed, coating the waxy looking plastic flowers she had arranged in a water pitcher. She cried. And it was hell hot in November and we got as naked as we could, finally alone, finally together someplace where we didn't have to worry about somebody's footsteps or a door flung open. You are my sunshine. She was a stranger to me in her flesh, the places shaped by bones close under the skin, springy hair in the heat frizzled and damp on her head and curling thickly, innocently from her belly. Lighter places the sun never touched where veins showed, and the skin though mottled was one piece, a covering over flesh and bones that did not break into sections the way clothes make women breasts and waist and ass and legs but moulded one whole curving animal moving together, brown and supple.

It rained between us, stinging hot, cold, sweet, sour rain we trapped between our bodies, that we drank deeply into all the openings of our flesh. Rain dance an oozing sluggish rhythm then heat lightning and thunderclaps and tropical downpour threatening to wash us away, tugging our island to pieces, whipping up the sea that lapped icily like shadows. Her sobbing in peace, contentment and release as we lay side by side on our wet backs staring up at the blazing sun and a blue sky through which white clouds rushed. Smouldering, only hands touching, utter stillness until once every thousand years a huge cool drop of rain spattered against our nakedness and we shuddered. Then we were Mr. and Mrs. Wilkerson. If I had seen these walls and floors, the loneliness tottering from her womb, the years which her thighs flapping like tired pigeon wings opened and closed, the dark passage, time and time and endless hours, could I have seen her sitting in this kitchen her body either aged not at all or decaying flabby under the robe twenty years too soon would I have been so young once, so eager to enter and take her hand and walk on, keep walking and whistling and children laughing unseen in the corners and stumbling and walking in the darkness still while her ghost drinks coffee and there is nothing to say that is not a lie because I began so young and cager and she . . .

She leans, one hand holding the robe to her chest, and reaches toward the radio. Wrist is thin and ashy. He remembers the cold. He has removed neither the second sweater nor the quilted jacket, feels instinctively for the duck billed cap and when it is not there scratches loudly in the nappy thick hair above his ear. He feels silly, countrified, one monkey picking another's fleas from its red behind. As if the hat on or off made a difference. Little boy's hat he wore each morning to war with the rats. Cap should have been there so he could sweep it off and bow low in one elegant gesture. Honey, I begs your pardon, I shorely do ladychile I shorely does ma Lady Honey Lamb lighting up her regal frailness, wrapping her bright shoulders in furs and pulling lace up around her delicate throat, I do declare I don't know what got into me Honey Lady forgettin a thing like that. Prince Beauregard down on one knee, her pale hand withheld then graciously, haltingly tendered while the heavy lashes subtly flutter, dark butterflies above her lowered eyes.

All's well ending well. To be forgiven after the worse.

But ain't coming this morning in this kitchen ain't no need standing around waiting neither.

−You might as well take this. Something in your belly besides whatever rot you've been drinking all night. No way to take the mug of coffee she poured but in a fighting mood the way she'll fling it at you so catch her eyes an instant as you glare over your shoulder hard and mean like staring down a dog you just kicked and making sure he has no notion of sneaking back to his feet and coming at your heels Just the head swiveling round on the tight neck. Hadn't even heard her move from her chair but she is beside the stove pouring hot water from tin pan into the hulking mug. Steam. All those stories about mean nigger bitches throwing boiling water on the cool daddies who did them wrong. But she fills the cup and sets the pan back on a burner. Her body still has curves and soft places but you wouldn't believe it seeing her wrapped in that robe. Robe looks dirty. Like she cooks in it or sits around all day drinking. Know it's not. Just washed and ironed so many times color whipped out of it. Yellow or white or tan.

Mug is on the table. Me on one side, her standing across on the other. As far as she's going cup says sitting there like a bomb or a rat she's caught but don't want to pull from the trap so leaves it out for me to throw away.

−Woman, why don't you get a new robe. His eyes are lowered though he is almost shouting. Better pick it up by the handle or burn my fingers. Steam.

Her back is to him. She takes up little space but seems crowded between table and the stove which she now faces. Oven is probably on, she's probably standing there so the heat can run up under her night clothes. Her shoulders are shaking. Even through all the sweaters and jacket he can feel the cold. Maybe she is laughing. He looks down into the blackness with its aura of curling steam. Careful not to spill, to hold it steady and put one foot after the other carefully out of the kitchen back to the chair for ten minutes of blow-

32

ing and sipping and feeling the tickle of warmth worm
through him before he hits the streets again.

• • •

—So I took the wife downtown to see The Prime of Miss
Jean Brodie. Wasn't much else playing just shoot em ups and
the usual cops and robbers bullshit and I heard about this
movie being pretty good all about lesbians and what not it
was rated X so I thought mize well let the wife get out we got
clean my old lady looking nice as she wants to we jumped
in the car and went to see Jean Brodie. Movie was something
else. Full of people we had to sit where the usher took us.
Two old white ladies sitting behind us running off at the
mouth through the whole damn thing. I got tired and turned
around a few times but the old hens kept cackling getting
all excited humming and tsch-tsching during the finger fucking scenes when the broads naked and laying on each other.
Let me tell you now I was steady digging that action on the
screen and I didn't need no silly old white ladies clucking
in my ear like they didn't know people played sticky finger.
Lights went on and my old lady goes to the powder room
them bitches still jabbering behind my seat I started to get up
and tell them something but I hear *Are you ready to go* one
bitch up the other kneeing hell out my seat the bitch finally
gets up turns her broad backside right up against my head
and cuts loose. Blat. Easy and loud like it was nothing farting up against the back of my head. Lawd. Barupp. Loud
just like that. Now you know. Man, I couldn't move. Just sat
there not believing she had done it. Lights on and everything.
Natural as if she was saying good-bye. Cuts loose on my
head and said *let's go* to the other white lady and went on
about their business. Talk about a nigger being hot. I was so
mad I couldn't do nothing but sit there. Nasty old heifer.
Barupp. I had to tell my old lady when she got back. She

cracked up laughing all over the place but I didn't see a damned thing funny behind that action.

–Sweetman you look like somebody done farted on you this morning.

–Go on nigger, I'm tired and evil today.

–You getting too old to take care of business all night and work all day.

–Hysterectomy—that means they ain't got nothing inside. Her function is pissing and that's all. Fucking's over with.

–You wrong man. Today, you're wrong.

–Naw, they take all her insides out. Sensation and what not but ain't good for nothing but pissing.

–Who you telling. I used to go with one. She fuck you to death. Better than ever.

–You talking about a partial.

–What you call a dildo.

–In France some cats making them. Whatyoucallit, what models in the windows. Matchikins.

–Mannequins.

–Yeah. I saw in a movie where he making them with hair and skin that feels like the real thing.

–You have to be a weird cat to lay on something like that. I'd rather jerk off it come to that.

–Some weird shit.

–Buy anything in them stores back of Market Street. Dildoes in any shape and size. And color.

–One, she had fixed up real nice. You know like a handle grip she musta had twelve rubbers wrapped around it. Before I started messing with this trash I worked in a gas station. You run into all sorts of strange bitches working in a station. Bitches out there get hold of the old man's car running around doing they business burn up all his gas and ain't got no money. White broad in a fifty-nine Caddy convertible. Fill it up check the oil and water. So I do it up nice. Gas and two quarts oil. Wipe down all the windows. Come to seven dollars and forty-two cents. Went round to the driver's side and she just sitting there. I guess you want some money.

Rolls down the window cutting her eyes at me staring big as day. Then she say I don't have a dime. Lawd. I knew what's coming next. White bitch don't even blink when she say But I got plenty cock. And I'm thinking seven dollars and forty-two cents you better got a whole lot of cock. I drives her into the garage and pulls down the door. Bitch already had her drawers off and laying across the back seat. I knocked it out and she scooted round the side to pee. Whiles she gone I still thinking bout my seven dollars and forty-two cents. Naw, I wasn't finished. Hard as my money comes. She switches back I turns out the light and we in that Caddy again taking care of business. You know when she drove outa that station she hand me seven dollars and forty-two cents just as nice as you please.

–Some strange shit out there in the world. Some weird bitches.

–Weird ain't the word. Let me tell you about this other bitch. Always be some change behind the seats and on the floor. Two, three dollars every time she bring it in. Her old man own the factory across from the station. You know the place I mean. Right on down the street. She bring it in almost once a week to be washed. A white Lincoln. She leaves it so I means to check it out good. I found some dimes and quarters down in the seat so I said shit go on and do it right I had the seats out the muthafucka and copped a five dollar bill. I was searching my ass off and had about nine dollars and some change. Decided I try to get in the glove compartment. I'm fiddling around struggling and prising till I got the muthafucka open. Man, I didn't know what it was. Looked like a handlebar grip offen a bicycle. This bitch musta had twelve rubbers wrapped around it. I commenced to thinking and said to myself she jugging herself with that thing.

–A dildo. What you call a dildo. I saw a bitch doing herself with one. She was into a weird thing. See her all the time up in her window. You know it was up on the third floor so I couldn't see nothing but her head and shoulders.

I couldn't tell what she was doing. But she was always there and always had that one arm going and gazing off into space. I could just see the shoulder from my window so I didn't pay it no mind. Figured she's shucking peas or squeezing margarine. Just sitting in her window with that shoulder I noticed always going up and down. I got to wondering more and more about this shit so one day while my mama was out shopping I sneaked up on the roof and crossed over two, three more so's I could look right down into her room.

—And I shore nuff gonna question her about that tool she had fixed up soon as she came back for her car. But I got busy with one another thing round there and missed asking her. Took me till next week fore I got to it but I asked her what she doing with that grip. Seems her old man ain't no good. Lawd. I told her ain't no need to be doing all that. You got a good man standing right here ready. I tore that pussy up. You better believe it. Her old man had to take her down to Florida. Moved out his building across the street. She got hot pants behind that action I put on her. Man's gonna need a chain to keep her home wherever he goes.

—The bitch got her legs cocked up wide as hell on the bed and working away at herself with a dildo.

—Be some hard work.

—It might be hard but she working that thing good and seemed to be liking it all right. All the time gazing out the window.

—That's damn hard work.

—Some weird bitches out here.

—You run into the damndest shit working in a station. Sometimes I don't know why I quit to come on this garbage job.

—Bitches out here is something, man.

—Riding to work about five thirty and it was cold's a muthafucka. Hawk was whipping them streets to death. I was on my way to work minding my business. Bitch scared me. Jumping out from behind a parked car. I had stopped for a light. Had my radio on and heater going I was all warm and couldn't care less. Heard tapping on my window. Bitch shocked shit outa me. So I rolls down the window. Grinning with her bad teeth she says How far down you going, Daddy. How far you going, girl. Get on in. Thought the bitch going to work. Bitch wasn't going nowhere. You know she was out there cold as it was hustling in the morning.

—Man, you oughta give the broad a few dollars and send her off that corner. Hustling at that hour. That's a hard up broad.

—I took er on down the station. Went in the garage and got her up on the lift.

—Childress, you lying now.

—If I'm lying, I'm flying and my feet sure ain't got no wings. I'm telling you just like it is, Sweetman.

—On the lift.

—Shit yeah. Drive on the platform and hike the muthafucka right up. Get that bitch up in the air and knock out that pussy.

—You crazy, man. You go on knocking it out and you gonna rock the boat. Capsize the mothafucka and you, car and broad hit the floor.

—Naw. I know that lift. Locked our ass tight in there we do all the rockin we want.

—Gotta rock a hell of a lot to bring a car down off one of those pneumatic jacks.

—After a while we ease on down. I takes her for some breakfast and the bitch be telling me how hungry she been and shit.

—Man, you saw that woman out there freezing you ought to give her a few dollars and sent her home.

—We finished eating and I say good-bye girl and don't you know the bitch start hemming and hawing and talking some off the wall shit. I . . . I . . . I thought you was going to give me something. Damn. Told her I did give her something.

—That's what you shoulda told her.

—I give her something, warmed up her behind real nice and bought the bitch breakfast besides. I told her you better go on girl, get out my face with that gimme something shit. Hustling in the cold at that hour.

—Was she clean.

—You damn right she clean. Rode up on the lift and spread them legs. She was real clean.

—Shit. Childress, all you know is your motherfucking dick ain't dripping yet.

—That was years ago, man. When I was working in a gas station. I'm still flying high hard and clean and that trifling whore probably dead by now.

—Good old days in the barracks. People with funky asses and feet who don't like to wash. Scrub them with lye soap and dry them in burlap. Stings for days. They remember that shower. One cat was good at picking out farts. Everybody be sleeping away and it be dark as a muthafucka, cats steady snoring and braaack somebody cut loose. If they find the Johnson out he goes. Don't matter how cold it be outside. But it be dark in the barracks, couldn't see shit. DePetrie could find the Johnson in the dark. I'd tap him and he'd still be half sleep and we lay there quiet till the cat popped again and DePetrie say it come from there pointing in the pitch black. Find that Johnson and out his ass would go.

—There be some cats can't help it. This boy he have the kind of feet be sweating all the time. Behind all the perspiring the cat have some funky dogs. But he keep his self clean and nobody say nothing to him. But them non-washing dudes. Out they go. Everybody jump on they ass. The lieutenant come in talking shit no passes cause the joint funky. You know you got some hot dudes. Whip on them that don't keep they ass clean.

—DePetrie find him and out the Johnson go. When you pulling duty and be walking outside the barracks you can hear it all night. Cats be in there blasting away. Hot dogs, potato chips, eggs, beer, and if they had beans in the Mess Hall, good gawd amighty. Blasting away. Barupp. Braack.

—Barupp. I couldn't believe the nasty old heifer. Got up

out her seat put her ass in the aisle and cut loose as much as if to say *Blatt. I'm going now. Good-bye, Mr. Nigger.*

—How you know the bitch was clean.

—It's best in the dark. You got to do it when it's dark . . .

—Like digging jazz.

Why you think people like it dark when they listen to jazz. Somebody had asked me that in Harold's. In the middle of all the nasty talk they did each morning. Like nobody really ready to git out of bed yet and they are still there dreaming all the pussy they've had or smelling and fingering their bodies or the body they've caught for the night. Coming to Harold's for some extra sleep. Talk and whiskey a woolly gray blanket over their heads. To each his own. But why should it be dark. First of all the dude that said it just knew he was right. People want it dark. Need it dark. And you don't dance either. Almost solemn as a sanctified church. But, hell. That ain't so solemn. Shoutin and signifyin and prayin loud enough to be heard in the street. I would have liked to hear Harold answer. Come up with some of his three years at Morgan State these are the facts of the matter shit. He'd be wrong but at least you have to beat him down and think before you open your mouth or he'll make a fool of you and everybody laughing till you can see somebody getting terrible quiet and tight jawed and then it's time to beat on somebody else. Even in the morning these dudes will fight. Fact is they probably fight sooner in the morning. Everybody still sleepy or sleeping and running down what they want to be not what they are. Like don't rap on my man's new coat if he been working like a dog to get the coins together even if he looks like a damn fool in it. After he starts cursing it himself, talking about how much it cost and wishes he had his coins back then you can beat on him. But these cats still dreaming at Harold's in the morning.

Because maybe jazz dreaming too. Or those listening dreaming of leather coats and big cars and fat thighed sisters. Don't know what a man playing jazz could be thinking. Does he want the lights out? I remember the piano player Childress knew and he came on down to the bar and we all had a drink. Just jiving. The cat was stone folks. Natural and we're rapping like I known him my whole life. Only thing his eyes redder than any eyes I've seen. And he blinks. Take the cover off a skillet with two eggs frying and see them kinda soupy running together before they firm up only these eggs was a pinky red bloodshot and each time he blinks top's off that skillet somebody turned off the fire because they are just sitting there undone and getting no better. He must have seen me looking. Said bitch broke my motherfucking shades. And I understood everything. How jazz men always on the go always moving from town to town and probably have plenty women but keep none of them actually happy so when he calls or knocks on the door the woman feels good but she is mad too because she knows here he is and something real nice is going to happen but sure as morning the nigger will be gone and god knows when he'll be back but sorry assed bitch that I am I'll get up and fix him something to eat and be hurt when he leaves and let him take enough of me with him I'll open the door next time and be opening it for him when others knock or call and them running through me like water because I'm waiting for him and he may not even come back but so good when he does I could kill him. So after he's been good and then getting ready to go she smashes the gold rimmed dark glasses to the floor. Her nail catches in his cheek when she rips them from his face. He knows it has to come to this and no way to change it because this is just the way it has to be if you move from town to town and try to have a little something going each place. But the bitch ain't supposed to fuck with my things. But this is the way it has to be so he doesn't really try to hurt her bad. He blots the sting on his cheek with an open palm and quick like an answer to the trumpet's riff same hand slaps her to the bed. She thinks for a second she is in hell, that the devil is standing over her, eyeless, his stare is so vacant. She thinks he will lean down and scrape his eyes from the back of the broken glasses, and paste them into the rawness above his cheeks. Watching that

40

act worse than the death. But he blinks, doesn't even look down because he knows what he'll see, crumpled on the floor. No sense in saving the jagged pieces. The way it has to be he just walks out saying nothing the way he came.

I am staring at his eyes and he has nothing to say except what he did. After all some things are plainly out of your hands so they are just there and people being what they are can't help noticing. You say a few words and they either understand or no sense in trying to say more. *I coulda killed that silly whore.* And tomorrow you'll find new shades in this city or another city and there will be nothing to say.

Childress said he had met the piano man in a bar one night. They just started to talk. The cat wasn't jamming just sitting at the bar. Childress didn't know him from Adam but they talked for a long time. Sees him now every time he's in town. The cat's real together. He's been around. One of the best at his trade. Childress didn't know much about music except that some of it got to him especially near the end of the night at the Vets and he thought he was over with some mamma, but since he had talked with the jazz cat Childress say he into his music. Dug the way the piano man played no matter what he played or who he was jamming with. And Childress didn't make a big deal behind knowing the cat. I mean he didn't *I want you to meet my man* loud enough for the whole place to hear and back slapping and tugging at the piano man's elbow like he was some fine bitch Childress was turning out. They both just kind of slid off to the side of the bandstand, at a corner of the bar where the waitress sets her tray and nobody sits. Tight with Childress and Childress say *this is Sweetman my main man*—everything's okay and I'm talking with them.

Cat was from the South. And he laughed about the home folks and country ways. Childress had only been there during the war but they understood one another about how you had to laugh at some of the shit or be dead or crazy. But they didn't talk that much. One would say something and they'd laugh or grunt or make some other noise or repeat a word

41

several times each taking a turn and doing something a little different with how he says it. They didn't want to be in one another's way so lots of space between sounds. Just the bar noise to fill in and little ripples of music from the jukebox somebody had turned on when the set was over. The light wasn't very good anywhere but it was almost black where we stood. Childress and the cat seemed to get far away. Not like they tried to make me feel I shouldn't be with them. It was like I was slipping into a deep thing someplace they might take me but where I'd be alone. I remembered how Childress talked about the cat's music. I thought about moving so fast nobody could see you pass but to you the moving would be very slow, drifting more than anything else, like in water or a scrap of paper sailing. Listening to jazz in the dark. The waitress made her order. Funny stuff like frozen daiquiris, lady fingers, sloe gin fizzes, and it had never seemed so funny until just then. Little kids running to the ice cream truck. Half of them ain't got a damned cent but they's running as fast as the pickaninnies that have dimes in their fists. Candy ice cream cake. And the bell tinkling and some Jew or dago in a frowsy white coat parceling out the goodies. I could see that summer day and me racing with the others and worried somebody would snatch my money or whatever I bought. Right in front of my eyes though I was deep somewhere in the talk of Childress and the jazz man, deep as in a black woods but a summer day I could look at floating like a balloon or closed in a glass ball. The kind you turn upside down and snow falls over the little church and people inside the glass. Snow drifting down lazy. You shake it and down again just as lazy over the house and people.

—She got a nice pair of tits.

—Yeah I was digging.

A small light below the level of the bar haloed the spot where the waitress paid her bills and picked up her orders. I didn't need to look to see her features then her tight white blouse modeled in the glow. His voice made both. Two smoked circles of glass had grown over the jazz man's eyes.

42

They were home again. I did not see them but I knew shades patched the rawness, that he needed them and they slide into place as real as the waitress switching her tail away from the arc of light.

But I be damned if I know. Badass jazz blowing cats traveling from town to town shooting down the locals, doing what they can do best blowing away, gunfighters only not at high noon but doing their fighting in the dark when all the lights out. Time I was in Camden trying to get into something my man Childress and me stopped for a taste in some little hole in the wall. Drinking gin in the middle of the afternoon getting friendly and loud talking with all these strange dudes after a while you get lost could be West Hell or Camden or round the corner from your crib for all you know niggers and gin kind of insinuating wrapping you round till you comfortable and floating with whatever place you be. Sitting there talking away and before you know it you been to New York City and Frisco and Deetroit and Chicago and China and West Hell and back all round the world drinking gin messing with white folks and cutting niggers and somebody smoking a reefer in the toilet good Nam grass a young dude with a black beret slanted on his head and the dude talking a funny game going to change the world you begin to believe his hat is straight and him leaning forty-five degrees he has a purple hand the bones sharp and the skin of his fingers like crusty canvas over tent poles offering you a toke on his shit you take it from him and drag the way it's supposed to be dragged though you don't like tobacco and only smoke once in a great while raggedy weeds like he's offering the dude running down his revolutionary game like you still there when you pull the door closed after you step into the midnight bar everybody bigger than when you left they are moving faster and their voices gathered in a box somewhere' near the ceiling that weaves them all together into a riff chasing the juke.

And the riff is people passing me like they going to a fire. Black faces blurring into white. Horns and plate glass windows and sad-eyed mannequins dead for fifty years staring at their own stiff reflections. You thought you were the lizard scuttling fast as four legs could carry you but the others without even trying leave you behind or high heel tramp their way right through you. You are jazz being played in some dark room. In the late afternoon street, sidewalks glinting a shower of golden flecks that swim before your eyes, sin kisses, you are a ghost losing his way. Somebody bumps you and you want to crumple where you are. Be another spot of spit, sweat or wine staining the sidewalk, flat on your back looking up pant legs and mini-skirts. Smell the soft underbellies of the bloodhounds chasing you. A cop is exploding in the middle of an intersection. At any moment the brass and blue and icy leather will tear apart the thick body puffing itself up to hold them together. I can see his belly straining to reach the billows of blue serge.

Because somebody is asking me last week how I am today and they are getting an answer. A lame, wrong answer but the social worker knowingly shakes her head and believes it, and here I am ass over ears bumping along chased by a gorilla riff.

So it must be the dark that does it. Darkness necessary. Like Childress said not so much that the cat was famous or supposed to be the best at what he was doing but that he knew the cat and that's what he heard when he listened.

● ● ●

Outside Harold's, city still dark or at least not light yet. We flowed out into our cars. Fuzzy edges still pretty much like they were when we went in to have our morning drink.

—Later, you badass bunch of sanitary engineers.

You have to go over a bridge to get to the depot. As a matter of fact the depot is kind of under the bridge you go over. Always in the shadow of the bridge so sometimes like you are going into a cave. The crews would be rolling in all at once thirty, thirty-five minutes before the trucks had to go out. Day didn't start till half hour after punch-in time. Union got us thirty minutes for changing, getting the equipment together. A good crew could get a truck ready in ten minutes and most came to work dressed to go so after punching in we had twenty minutes to bullshit and pass around a taste if anybody brought one. You could tell where people was at by the taste they offered around. Like Clarence bring a fifth of Bali Hai once or twice a month and be doing good then one day up he jumps with a pint of Cutty Sark you know he either done left his old lady again or hit the numbers or both if he come along with something top shelf for a couple days in a row.

When is this shit gonna cease. Orin Wilkerson swore softly under his breath. Somebody had killed the pregnant movie star. All that good, white pussy doing nobody any good anymore. A damned shame. Somebody crazy did it. Must of been to look at her fine as she was and in the condition she was and cut her down. Goddamnit. He saw them scurrying around him. The men he saw each morning. He thought he knew them. The way you know Clarence or Clisby who has that Continental he loves and nothing else in the world. But you see them hustling and bustling round here these last ten minutes, cursing, all those raggedy clothes they wear like space suits or second stiff, greasy skins they all look pretty much alike. Then again before the rush they all talk the same shit. Drinking and fucking and how badass they are or whatever team in whatever sport they are following on T.V. Some just sit quiet though. And some only speak when asked but when they put in their two cents you know they're happy to get it out and all they needed was an opening. I think I know them. Can call most names. Then I try to image one of these sorry assed dudes with a knife in his hand going to carve up some white movie star. Standing in her big living room where she paid more for a rug than he can for an automobile, where a picture tacked over the fireplace would buy the whole house in which he's renting three rooms.

I can't figure it out. Had to be somebody just like one of these. Or me. Not that half these niggers ain't stone crazy.

Got to be a little crazy to be out here before the sun even up wrestling with garbage cans and chasing rats. Or doing whatever you have to do day after day to keep food in your mouth and the Man from taking away every stick you got including the roof over your head.

All that ain't crazy as you have to be to get in a car and drive up to somebody's big house and cut them up like you would chickens on Saturday night.

Paper tries to make a story of it. Tell what was done, who did it how many bodies and ages and how much money but you take all the pieces and it still don't add up. Still don't tell me how one of these men I see every morning walking around me and laughing and shouting and drunk and getting in my way could do it. And it has to be one like them. Unless an altogether different kind of people in the world. Kind that can breathe in your face and shake your hand and talk the shit you do while really they never stop scheming and hating and looking for the chance to pull some woman's drawers down and slice her up.

I know there's people crazy sick. I mean so bad nothing you can do but keep them locked up. But too much is going on. And gets weirder every day. And the ones they catch seem hardly different except they did the thing that makes the newspaper full of blood. Getting so that strange shit is regular as rain. Nothing more to do about it than you can about rain. Stay indoors when you think it's coming.

–Let's make it.

–Hit the road, Jack.

–Do your dreaming with your arms wrapped around some fine garbage can. They be smelling good this morning. Make your joint hard.

–Let's make this run, youall. No time to be bullshittin.

• • •

Not quite dawn. Morning an echo over the city. Not an echo idly repeating, but drawing into itself all senses and details of the hour and returning them sea changed, unaccountably harmonious. Steep hill to climb, sharp right at the crest you are on the bridge under whose arching shadow we gather six days a week. Caught in a web of steel and concrete, sharp angles, the hurtling, whiney thrust of the machine. Somebody in the cab is fresh from a woman. Among the other odors of three large men cramped in a small space that special, sweet stink every so often pricks a nostril open.

–Poontang. Don't want to catch none of you niggers sniffing at his fingers.

River below. City panoramaed on all sides. Lights are warm. Not the high yellow or icy coal of night or the blank, sun blinded glare of day. Somewhere in between. Everything mellowed. As if after being together so long, silhouettes and sky had worn down the harsh, cutting edges of their conjunction. Dawn middle ground. Time Orin liked best particularly here on bridges, bridges which at this hour did not pace businesslike over the void but merged the shifting masses of water land and sky. And time. He never looked at his watch when the truck began its run. The motor turned over when the time clock at the depot reached precisely the half hour and he would mechanically glance at its bland, white face once to admire the synchronization. Then time left him as it seemed to leave the echoing stillness of the city. Since it was not night and not day and all he could hear see smell and touch confirmed some floating middle ground he felt no need to measure the transition, to rush away from its gliding fullness.

Did the others know how far away they were? That this bubble had left time and might never be trapped again. The motor would sputter and cough in the thin air. Rainbow fish would ripple past the windows. He wondered how a fly felt resting in the damp vault of an immense cathedral. A flea in the belly of a whale.

–If you want to sleep go right ahead. But I ain't gonna listen to your snoring. Cat's gonna come in here smelling of pussy, dreaming and snoring like just cause I'm driving I'm the only one with a job.

47

The vehicle clattered at the end of the bridge. Steel plates used to reinforce the bridge surface had been loosened by the pressure of heavy traffic and flapped when struck. Jolt and crash were no more inevitable than Childress:

—The muthafuckas gonna come clean apart one of these days.

Broad snout bloody with the last crumpled barricade the truck and crew highball to their rendezvous with the sleeping city.

• • •

It was March. Long afternoon walks that begin in warm sunshine end in shivering, rapid steps home again toward the indoors. Three men had talked in the park till the sun's waning and a chill wind sweeping off the river had driven them out of the bare trees to a bus stop. The park had been deserted. Ground snow blotted, still stiff, crunching underfoot when you stepped from the gray path beside the river. Grays and browns, dull city colors reflected in the water.

The men continued to argue as they waited beside a trembling aluminum pole festooned with bus route numbers. The city's avenues were broad, exposed, good for pomp and circumstance parades, for displaying monumental architecture, good for cannoneers to sight down in the best Napoleonic tradition. Bad for people whose clothes are thin and few. As the men talked their bodies shuttled in the wind.

—Hey Littleman, how come I got to be tween you and the wind every time you start to say something.

—Stand where you please, Saunders.

—I'd get behind you cept you don't make much of a windbreaker.

—Your mama breaks wind.

—How come little dudes always the first to jump bad and call the dozens. Must be cause they know they's put on earth to get they asses kicked.

—Every dog has his day. And the earth keeps turning, the days keep changing.

—I could say something about the dog that had you, since you started that mama stuff. But I don't play the dozens. Dogs and days. Listen to him, Wilco. Littleman thinks he might get lucky some day and whip somebody. That's why he tries so hard to fuck with people. Playing percentages. Figures if he gets whipped enough times he's due one of these days to get him a win.

Thomas Wilkerson wanted to speak. Say words which would dull the cutting edge of the talk. Talk had been brutal all afternoon. Pick. Pick. Pick. Both men on tangents of anger connected only when one decided to strike out at the other. Always tense when they spoke of the plan, but today circling through the gaunt trees of the park, never really warm under the deceiving blue of the March sky, his companions had seemed ready to explode. Littleman absolutely committed to the plan, teasing and slashing at the others with the authority his readiness gave to him. Saunders resentful because Littleman had something he needed badly and would relinquish it only on his own terms, terms Saunders must submit to. Wilkerson still fumbling, unable to see the plan except as a joke or enormous threat. So Littleman piped and they paid. And the chill air made them brittle as glass as they bumped awkwardly in the music he played. Wilkerson wanted words to make them all laugh, forget a moment the violence that drew them together. But Littleman spoke first.

—Still just like kids. Still shy away as soon as we get to a serious issue and I ask a question that puts your backs to the wall.

—I wasn't the one started playing the dozens.

—It was a fool like you who invented the dozens. Some darky done with his cotton picking, picking his nose and toes and had nothing better to do than insult the fool darky lying next to him in Mr. Charlie's hog pen.

—You sure don't like niggers do you?

—What am I.

—A sorry assed, runty nigger who don't like hisself.

—The hawk is a bitch. I'll give somebody bus fare if they stand between me and that wind. Wilkerson knew his words weren't enough. A flickering match in the wind's bluster.

—What about Littleman, Mr. Hall, here. You gonna give him a whole fare for covering only half your chest. Course if he didn't have that bear rug on his chin, he could ride for kiddie fare.

—Leave him alone now. You don't know how far to carry a thing, Saunders.

—Everythin's gonna be all right. I surely don't need you to tell me how far to carry anything. I got hands and feet good enough to get me out anyplace my mouth puts me. Which is more than I can say bout some folks.

—Saunders, you know it's my pity for you that keeps me from smashing your skull. Several times today you asked to die. But I see myself in you, that meanness in you and in myself I can't do a thing about. But the meanness may be useful, after all. It saved your life today. Be grateful . . . be grateful . . .

—Littleman's getting hysterical.

It wouldn't go any further. Saunders' voice was subdued as he spoke and a barely audible *only funning anyhow* meant nothing else needed to be said. Wilkerson was learning. If they were going to talk about killing they had to believe in each other as killers. Which meant they had to recognize the point you don't push a man past. Perhaps with the others it was always a ritual of testing, rubbing the raw, morbid places which had to be ready when the time to kill came. Wilkerson could not believe that he was ready. If he had wounds the others could prod, he had managed to conceal their seriousness, even from himself. When they talked of the plan he gave his assent not as a killer, but as one who was beginning to understand why the others must kill. And why he must choose to aid them.

Gray pole quivered ringing hollow as the little man rapped its base with his cane. Height of a twelve year old, heavy

50

head and shoulders done in a heroic manner then stick legs added by a clumsy apprentice.

–Let us forget the diversion. Let me return to the question you wanted to hide from.

Littleman's skin was that lightish brown that gets ashy in the cold. Eyes glazed too, wet in the cold, wide as if blinking were a sign of weakness. Rigid, distant as if he were not responsible for his voice or the light tapping of the cane which punctuated his words.

Bus wheezed to a stop beside them. There were clicks, jingles, rumbles, hot, stale breath in the face. Scattered seats were available and each man found a place, a silence among strangers.

• • •

Graham Rice lived in the basement. Two rooms and a kitchenette that shared crumbling brick outer walls with sixty other units of various sizes and shapes known collectively as the Terrace Apartments. Since words and particularly names fascinated Rice, he had developed the habit of looking for meaning behind, within or because of the patterns of words which confronted him in his everyday life. Words could reveal the significance of the past, prefigure the future, make a running commentary on Rice's present existence. The word science Rice had perfected was his history, religion and consolation. His own name was a mystery to be studied, a node at which countless lines converged. Rice. White food. White on rice. Rice of weddings. Soul food and Chinese food. Rice paddies. The East. The South. Uncle Ben. Ho Chi Minh. The Rice Bowl. Machine guns. Football games. Etcetera, etcetera he thought always some new consideration. Tentatively he had decoded these bare outlines of a plot: that rice was the sustenance of the poor man, the oppressed; that it was white because it came from the white man, the crumbs from his table, so much lotus for blacks and Chinamen to fight over while in fact both groups were themselves being consumed by the white devils' trickery. And Graham Rice was a vehicle, a manifestation of this knowledge of duplicity and oppression. In the very kernel of his being he understood exploitation and as a new Rice, a conscious, revolutionary Rice he would feed his knowledge to the masses, in fact become food for their souls. Graham was just a slave name, literally a cracker name, bestowed in ignorance to degrade and confuse him.

Living in the Terrace Apartments worried Rice. Not because of the building's deathly calm, its smell of old newspapers, not because he had to hide from the tenants while doing their dirty work, not because a Jew owned it, but because Rice could make nothing out of the name. Its significance utterly eluded him. None of its connotations or denotations aroused the slightest reverberations in the eighth sense he had developed. Even the obvious made no sense. No Terraces decorated the brick walls and the building's shape was an undifferentiated flat roofed box. The nothing name wasn't an overwhelming difficulty, more like the just discernible murmur in a tooth, the pre-critical worrisomeness that says things will get much worse, indeed.

Rice had forgotten to buy a new box of rice. When he turned Uncle Ben on his head, a short whisper of cascading grains barely covered the bottom of a cup. A few darker, fatter particles had also settled to the bottom of the package and speckled the tiny bit of remaining rice.

Shit.

Chicken and no rice. The wooden cabinet above the sink was easy to assay. Salt, pepper, flour, lard and hot sauce. Beans and sugar in pudgy, rolled-top bags. Not even a can of soup.

Shit.

Rice broke the tape and folded back the bloody paper. Chicken by itself. Wrinkled, yellowish skin looked forlorn, needing a cushion of rice and a blanket of brown gravy. Chicken was to last three days but without rice to pad this evening meal, the bird would only last two. Just won't cook more than a breast and wing tonight. That way it'll have to last. I won't be able to pick at it in the icebox. It was a small dead bird when you got to cutting it up and thinking how each piece is gonna look floured and crispy. Good thing I got those six extra wings.

Doorbell made him jump. It seemed a response to the sawing incision he began down the center of the breast.

Heavy, loose handled door scratched open finding its customary furrow in the kitchen linoleum. The three men arguing loudly carried Rice with them into the center of the room.

–Who you gonna cut. Rice saw he still had the knife in his hand. The chicken was back in the box, but the knife with its lacy, serrated edge proclaimed him guilty.

–I was turning a screw. Fixing the light switch just as you came in.

–That's a pointy knife for turning screws. Saunders winked at Littleman and Wilkerson.

–Little screws.

–I bet they is. Don't let us interrupt, brother, go on do what you doing. Just come to get out of the cold. Saunders rubbed his hands together.

–Cold.

–Yeah, the hawk. You know like he's flying high. It's a bitch out there. And speaking of hawks and such things, you ain't seen none in here, have you?

–What.

–I mean hawks, pigeons, ducks, chickens, birds one thing another like that.

–The man's busy. Didn't he tell you. Why don't you look for yourself and leave Rice alone.

–Hey.

–Hey is right. Look what Butcher Brown done laid down.

–Saunders, that's my dinner.

–All of this. Paper rattled, the plump chicken was undone.

–Shit.

–Now you wouldn't send these hungry brothers back into the cold just so you could hoard this bird for another week or two. You know that ain't right. You know that bird needs to be in our bellies tonight and not sitting lonely in your icebox. Littleman was already rummaging in the refrigerator.

–You know Littleman can cook up some chicken. Com'on Rice. Put some tunes on. We ain't come empty handed. Got some stuff that goes good with chicken. Goes good with any damn thing.

–Gentlmen, I accept the office of Steward as well as Cook. You will be delighted to learn I have uncovered a cache of Rolling Rock Premium Beer to lubricate our repast. And half a dozen succulent, virgin angel wings.

–Shit.

• • •

They sprawled greasy mouthed and high as if the floor was the seat of an enormous, steep sided chair and a giant hand had helped them slide gently down the green walls to join two stereo speakers and a rack of paperbacks leaning between them. One of the books was spread-eagled over Wilkerson's groin. In between snores he muttered in the direction of a copy of *Believe It or Not*. Thelonious in San Francisco dropped quietly, painfully onto the machine. After the glare of Archie Shepp's ear and throat filling insistence, it seemed you could count to ten between each note Monk chose to touch. To Littleman Monk playing in this quiet, thoughtful mood was what classic meant. Knowing where you're going, how to get there, and being in no hurry. Patient, pure, simple notes saying *I am here because this is where I belong and nothing else would do*. Angela and that summer five years ago in Atlantic City. She'd go as far as the head of the stairs each morning, naked under her black raincoat, hair messy, sleepy-eyed. Little skinny girl playing grownup in her mama's clothes. Golden skin and black coat saying good-bye honey don't be home late honey and watching me make my cripple ass way tapping down the steps. I think she believed I might fall and she'd have to come and dust me off, straighten the little man up and point him in the right direction. We bought two records and made love to them that whole summer. She told me she could play the Rachmaninoff or anything if she practiced and I believed her as we moved to that music or Monk Alone which I thought would be harder to play the way he did because it was just him and some way he made the piano feel like she made me feel and no one since the same way.

Rice still had a wing to eat. It was only right he thought, his prerogative he thought to take the first, last and as many pieces in between as he could. So he was there with his plate as Littleman turned out the crisp, golden brown nuggets. Meat white and juicy when you bite inside. Saunders made the white meat red with hot sauce. Ate the skin first, peeled it like he was skinning a piece of wild game and then saturated the exposed flesh so it looked as if skin had been flayed. If uncouth meant anything it described to Rice the black, loud talking man who ate his chicken like a beast. Rice didn't want that last wing but he knew Saunders had been ready to pounce. Almost a responsibility so Rice spoke up and claimed his right. And Saunders bad-talked him anyway.

I'll eat it after this Rice promised himself reaching to take the smoke Wilkerson held toward him. A long greedy drag, I got almost as much as Saunders could suck up into those pig nostrils of his.

–The nigger won't eat it. Just took it for spite. But Lenny Saunders am too clean to be bothered. Flying too clean.

Wilkerson knew the music by heart. At least it seemed he could run ten bars ahead of Monk, hearing the music once as he sped past it and a second totally different pattern of sound when the notes caught him and bathed his curled

55

body. Or backward, hiding till the music knew he had escaped and rhythms waited for him to resume the chase.

Monk died into Reflections. Last cut, last record on the stack.

Littleman flopped onto his belly. Wilkerson's eyes tracked across the bare floor. Dust balls, a safety pin, islands where the film of dust had not been disturbed. Littleman miraculously made whole, a normal man from this angle on the floor because his legs disappeared somewhere behind the thick shoulders. I am a fish sidling across the floor, a merman belly scrunching my way to where the restored Littleman has risen up to his elbows and challenges me with thundering eyes and swaying fist to arm wrestle.

—Thomas Wilkerson come give my ego a lift. Their open palms met, a violent, exaggerated thud. Clenched fingers were knots pulled tighter and tighter.

And if I could whip the little dude in this game, would I? But that's not the question, it's not holding back but seeing how long I can survive. Languor goes out of both, smoke glaze replaced by sweat, chicken, beer, pot, funky sweat which is a sheen then melts and collects, then dribbles as faces contort and shake. Littleman's beard is a live thing, a shaggy sponge drinking moisture from his face. But lips are laughing are sputtering when sweat seeps through moustache and black eyes tell Wilkerson exactly how much they are winning. Wilkerson begins to groan, to cry aloud, something part despair, part shouting down of Littleman's grunting, the machine-like pants that slowly form themselves into a word, *down, down.* Wilkerson heard the panting of dogs and women in labor, saw thighs grinding and buttocks bouncing smelled his own sweet farts and felt the soft parting, the rapturous release. Hmmmmm.

—Timber, timber, motherfucker. Slowly at first a tall tree in the wind, then strengthless but still erect, Max Schmeling after the Brown Bomber delivered, a wall slammed broadside by the black demolition ball, all stays gone, brief pitiful totter, maybe, maybe you won't die after all, then down,

56

down for good, good and hard, knuckles rapping on the bare floor, *down, down* Littleman still panting as if the rhythm and strength would not leave him, as if the victory were only partial, as if the hand embraced so tightly by his iron must be driven through the floor, driven to some subterranean rendezvous with *Down.*

The others had watched silently, not knowing how to be stirred, Rice nibbling at the wing, Saunders flexing his forearm as the balance teetered one way or the other. On his feet Saunders felt he had moved too quickly, covered an immense distance at too fast a pace. His knees wobbled, he was getting angry, half afraid to look down at his legs because he knew they would be naked, the knobby knees shaking, his pants down around his ankles. They all laughed at him. Everybody in the stands, the same bitches who had squealed every time he galloped to the finish line first. But here he was, one bad day, his guts bringing up stale wine onto the cinders, his cool busted because he had roared out too soon, responded to their cheers and burnt out in the first 220 of the city championship quarter mile race. Riggy got me. That stiffening death at the back of the thighs, that lead tightening the calves so you can't lift them just hobble on like a Buick is sitting on your shoulders, just stagger to that tape that ain't no more cause all the mothers with they silk asses and cardboard numbers burned past you and took your win away. Last race. You bend till finally had to go on one knee. Cinders biting into the skin but don't matter would bury my face in that shit if I could. Everybody saw my knees shaking and so damned funny I lost, only once but I lost, I lost they will always say the big one.

Saunders felt the queasiness pass. Better now, leap from down to up must be delicately negotiated, he took four slow, short steps and bent, pushing the stack of records up the shaft again and the first disc plopped down and began to spin. The tone arm jerked and floated, deliberate, aloof, settling easy as a bee in a sunflower. Music made. Jazz Messengers doing it. Columbia Avenue, South Street, the Jungle,

57

Senorita ohh laa la all mixed up in one bag. Staring at his stockinged feet Saunders watched them do quarter time an intricate cha cha step. The moves. He saw black sock transformed to spit shined patent leather. Square toed, buckled, perforated with intricate designs. Eyes doing double take from her brown ankles to hips and down again to his partner's red high heels following his lead. Moves. Catch her eyes hiding under drooping lashes, wink.

Saunders dat datted the staccato signature of Blakey's Cubano Chant. Trinidad by way of the Gold Coast. A naked brown girl, high breasts and fat butt wiggled to the rhythm. In her hands golden bananas that rattled like marimbas when she shook.

—I'm hungry again. Littleman was a grotesque puppet leaned against the wall, half a man bent in the middle with doll legs splayed in front of him that would never move unless someone tugged the invisible strings. Hand across high damp forehead his eyes dismissed Saunders' plaint even as lips buried in the beard answered:

—Chickee all gone, beer gone, joints all rolled and gone to heaven. Party's over.

Rice chewed cautiously, shifting the dry mouthful of chicken as best he could without allowing his cheeks to puff. He was afraid the wad he maneuvered might contain bones. Chicken bones could kill you. You don't even give them to dogs because the bones split and splinter like glass, become spears inside your soft guts. He wanted to get the mush down as fast as he could. He knew Saunders watched him, would abuse him for such a sloppy last ditch mouthful, so he had to get it down quickly. But he didn't want to die. They all were regarding him now. Accusing, stern faces. Eaten his chicken and now they were ready to hurt him for having his share of what *all* belonged to him.

Molars ground something hard. Bites tongue trying to dislodge the brittle morsel from the pack. Should I spit in my hand when I get it. Saunders. Bones.

Bones mean . . .

–Well, are you with us or not. Business time. It was Saunders' voice, crisply, impatiently, the way Littleman could ice his words.

Rice coughed, shavings of chicken flesh gulped and sprayed as Saunders whacked his hand down twice on the host's back.

–Little in-die-gest-nion, das all bothering the man. He ready to take care o business.

–Saunders, why do you try so hard to be a nigger, a sambo black ass field ignorant darky.

–What are you, Littleman? You want I should Speaka da Engleesh like a good wop, or sing Danny boy, or put ski on the ass end of all my words. Do you want me hunki-fied or spickified or maybe through my long Jew nose or like a Kennedy or collitch professor. I talk like your people, like your mother and mine been talking a long time. Is that what you don't like. Is you uptight with them.

–I thought we were ready for business. Wilkerson shouted to be heard.

–We've been through it all ten times in the park. I'll tell Rice what we've decided.

–I thought I . . . Rice was defeated but he could speak again squeezing the fistful of chicken balled in a sodden napkin.

–Wait a minute, Rice. Listen first. You'll get your say just like we promised.

On the floor again only this time ringed in a tight closed circle in the center of the room.

– . . . the crucial thing is to insure ourselves against fail-ure the most likely kind of failure and we've all agreed that the human factor, the four of us and what we must each do will put tremendous pressures on all of us. Therefore . . .

(run it down, brother)

Therefore we must build safeguards into the plan, minimize the possibility of individual cop-out by maximizing the cer-tainty that the one who fails cannot hurt the others and will himself be absolutely dealt with . . .

59

Wilkerson listened closely. The cloak and dagger intrigue, Littleman's lapses into grade B spy movie language at first amused him, but now as words and imagination drew closer to action, he had grown hypersensitive to nuances he hadn't dreamed existed. The wrong words could contaminate everything. He remembered making fun of Rice's notions. But the deed did have some magic relationship to the words. That was why Littleman was so angry in the park, why he became pedantic in his references to what they were doing. What they said they were doing was what the act would be. It had to be precise, it had to be *lynching a white cop.*

Lynch. Wilkerson remembered how he had laughed, had believed Littleman would laugh at the joke with him. But now he knew better. Littleman had never uttered the word *lynch* in jest. After Littleman had decided to recruit the others, each step had been carefully calculated. What seemed an idle, stray comment would be picked up later, embellished, repeated ten times in the space of a few days. Some lewd or comical suggestion would gradually lose its ridiculousness, establish itself in the meandering reality of their talks.

—What this town needs is a good old fashioned lynching. The real thing. With all the trimmings. It would be like going to church. Puts things in their proper perspective. Reminding everybody of who they are, where they stand. Divides the world simple and pure. Good or bad. Oppressors and oppressed. Black or white. Things tend to get a little fuzzy here in the big city. We need ritual. A spectacular.

—And they could put it on satellite T.V.

—In living color.

—Now I'm not talking about grabbing just any old body and stringing him up to the nearest lamp post. That's not it at all. We must learn to do a thing correctly, with style for immediate appeal and depth for the deep thinkers, the ones who concern themselves with history and tradition. I mean a formal lynching. With all the trimmings. And that's a world away from the crudities of your poor white vigilante

60

necktie parties. I would eschew that western model, go to the South where tradition means something.

—When I talk about lynching, I'm talking about power. Down home the ones with the power are smart enough to know that people are hopelessly forgetful. Give them a little wine, a woman and from one day to the next they can't keep it in their heads that they are on earth to serve and die. The woolly heads even forget whose earth it is. Here's where power comes in. Power must always be absolute. When it's not absolute it's something weaker, imitating power. Which means if you have power in a situation you can do anything you want to those whom you have made powerless. You must be prepared to assert your power brutally and arbitrarily if it is to remain pure. In fact you must periodically expose the fundamental basis of your relationship to the powerless. The most forceful and dramatic means are most effective. If it's a man over his woman, he beats her because she bats an eyelash; if it's a king over a subject people he systematically slaughters their first born. A master exercises droit de seigneur with the women of his slaves. The white citizens of Talladega Mississippi lynch a black boy. And so it goes.

—What could be more dramatic? A great artist must have conceived the first lynching. As a failed poet myself I envy his sweet touch, the sure hand that could extricate a satisfying, stable form from the raw fantasies of his peers.

—Mr. Neegro, swinging in the breeze. You recall now, charred blacker than you ever were in life, pea brain boiled away, monkey bowels carved to souvenirs, you recall now with nothing else to do but dangle in your cherished idleness, who gives and who takes away. Who made you in darkness and who can come in the black hour of the wolf to unmake you. Forked log swaying in the heavy air, black pendulum tolling power, power, power. White power.

—You better believe that poor lynched darky blinks his message like a lighthouse through the misty countryside. Beware. Nigger beware. If the whim took us, we would bur-

61

den every tree in Dixie. In our dealings with you we are
constrained only by the limits of our imagination. Imagination which we possess in abundance, fertile, subtle, co-ercive.
Witness your brother, our sport with him, how we make
poetry from our power.

Littleman rambling on till the outrageous and plausible
were linked in his metaphors. Often Wilkerson could walk
away with a slightly condescending smile, amused because
he had found the ravings of a madman so entertaining. But
he knew a sharp razor did much of its work before the flesh
felt its bite. His suspicions became increasingly palpable, he
felt himself awakening from a deep sleep, stunned and helpless.

—You know I'm right. One lynched nigger more or less
doesn't change anything. The symbol matters, the ritual. The
point is to get it all out front. To say this is the way things
really are. Will stay forever.

—Nothing is co-incidental. There are no accidents involved. All tactics and all roles are ordained within the master scheme. A passion play is what it's like. Only more
engrossing because with each enactment a fresh sufferer is
delivered to the mob. Real blood. Undignified screams and
writhing. Maybe even more holy and sanctified since each
actor is bound to his role not by some compact with a distant, abstract deity, but by the same circumstances which
tie man to wife, children to families, families to the community which they have created. When Rastus burns there
is a communal hard-on. Whites right, standing tall. Pine
tree straight, snow clean, gleaming big and power swollen
like an Empire State Building right here in lil ole Talladega,
population: white—7,000; mules and niggers—8,000 minus
one.

—Power. Neck stretching power.

—Cops standing around watching. Every damn body in the
town knowing the open secret. Nobody from the outside
knowing more than they can decipher from the mutilated,
swaying corpse when they come upon it in the woods. No

one must ever be prosecuted. Complicity. Conspiracy. From the littlest towhead red neck in progress to the fattest, cigar smoking most respectable cracker in the big house on the hill.

–What poetry.

–Do you think niggers could ever get themselves together enough to do a lynching in the grand manner?

–You know if it was done right, if tradition, nuance, imagination were consulted, the victim would have to be a white cop.

–And in the middle of the afternoon. And everybody standing around. Not looking at the beast but eating chicken from picnic baskets, sitting on fences munching watermelon. Dancing, singing, playing ball. Blasé as could be.

–In a big city. With black cops all around. Music blaring from the record shops. No white faces in sight.

–You wouldn't take his clothes off. Nobody would give a damn about seeing his pot belly and flabby ass. Leave him in his obscene blue uniform. Pour a sack of flour over his head while the noose is being fitted. He'd be sweating so much the flour would stick like it does to a wet chicken breast you're dipping to fry. Pasty, dough face screaming for John Wayne and the Texas Rangers to rescue him. Bleating Mercy boys, begging for mother, marines, yelling that the Jews did it. Red eyes vainly searching for some of his best friends out there in the crowd.

–Cart him away in a white sack with Nigger lover stenciled in eight inch letters. Throw it on the garbage heap at the city dump.

• • •

When Wilkerson left the others in Rice's apartment he had welcomed the cutting bitterness of the wind. It hurt him, defined him as Thomas Wilkerson, an old friend he has known for ages, a nice fellow whose eyes sting in the cold, whose hands and feet get numb even though he walks fast along the dark streets. Wilkerson could deal with the cold. No matter how badly the hawk whipped him it was like Littleman's hand, the reassuring challenge of flesh on flesh.

Thomas Wilkerson reflected upon Thomas Wilkerson, remembered there had been for him many nights like this cold March one. Time collapses and all those Tom Wilkersons stand side by side, compare notes, forget how many years had intervened between the lanky, self-conscious boy and this last lanky, shivering Wilkerson. How could he continue to work at what had been given him. His father's slow suicide. The deadening ache the Sweetman had become for his mother. How could he explain to the others what time had done. Perhaps he should listen and they could tell him. When you were thirteen the nappy headed kid began to say in his man-boy voice you thought nothing of stealin empties from behind Klein's store and cashing them in to get money and pay the girls for taking their drawers down so you could look. And the melange of voices began to tattle, scold and accuse, a babel of times and places that restored Thomas Wilkerson to himself.

Because once through the door and into the street he had been a stranger, some foul afterbirth of the smoke and talk and bloody promises compacted in Rice's apartment. The others would probably stay, sleeping on Rice's floor the way they often made themselves at home in Wilkerson's front room. But he had to get out. Escape. Leave the room though he knew he couldn't shake off Littleman's words.

—It's not as impossible as you might think. All the elements are present. The oppressors occupying army in their blue and white skins. Our people finally awakening to the nitty gritty of their situation with hundreds of years of anger and frustration to purge. In fact the dice are loaded in our favor. All we have to do is set the game in motion. Sevens will fall for us all day.

Streets were dark. Most houses seemed to have no curtains, just drawn shades, smoke gray over the windows or cat eye yellow where the odd light still burned. Nothing of spring in the night air. The hint of change he had felt in the park had died. Winter squatted with the finality of the first snowfall.

—*Pick a day. Preferably a holiday that has special meaning for black folk. Sure enough there will be some kind of memorial program. Most likely to commemorate a martyrdom since the best black men have all gone that way. Now suppose on this spring or summer day, has to be warm to bring our folks out, there is more cause than usual for the community to be hateful toward the Man. Suspicious, let's say, of some outrage. Perhaps a sexual crime. Maybe a white cop beat up on one of the whores that pay him protection. Let's say this rancor is in the air and nobody has seen the woman for a day or two. You know how that would be the number one topic. How everybody would build their own version of the story. How after telling lies all around about what they know and saw and how they heard about it before anybody else, the storytellers would have to believe the tales themselves. Then a story appears on the front page of the Black Dispatch. Mutilated body found. Think of the turnout for what would ordinarily be a jive little program where a few Toms get high puffing out one another's sails. People would be in the streets. You could be sure that every hustling organization would want some of the action. Try to get a speaker on the platform to run down their answer. It would be an event. Snicks and Muslims and Rams. Every damn body wanting to capitalize one more time on some poor bitch they wouldn't have given a Band-aid to if she walked by bleeding at the throat. So here's all these hot, bothered niggers. Waiting for a chance to bust loose. Hoping for a speaker to say the word they need to catch fire. Of course whiskey will be going around in some quarters. The young boys will be sweating through their head rags. The good Naacp brethren who sponsored the service in the first place will be looking for ways to slip through the edge of the mob and move their automobiles. A goddamn regular Fourth of July powder keg just waiting.*

Wilkerson had wished for some ghost of the high to gently becloud him. Or Monk's music to seep from one of the cold windows. Only Littleman's words came hard and brittle like sleet in the chill air.

—*Imagine just for an instant, if we could channel all that energy. Get to the people before the fever dissipates. Reach them before they explode into each other and bring the ambulances, fire engines and paddy wagons down on their heads. Suppose that for once we could put before their eyes the real villain. Now I don't mean some long winded string of epithets, no screaming condemnation of men far away and safe. Not hoarse words or silly puppet gyrations on a speaker's platform but the real thing. The criminal delivered up to them.*

—*Here's the one. This particular white man in his bold blue hunting suit is the one you all been talking about and looking for. No you haven't read in the white papers what he did to Clara Mae. Not news when some part time pimp cop slices up a black woman. (Crowd gasps) After all he's white, he's the Man. He's been serving her black meat to his customers all along. (Glory) She was his property. He had absolute power over her to do as he pleased. And he did as he pleased. Cut her the way you would a dead chicken. Why, I don't know. Not my business to ask why. He's the Man. (Motherfucking man) Why shouldn't he leave Clara Mae soaking in her blood. He paid rent to the landlord on Clearwater Street where we found her. Clara Mae owed him everything and it was his right to take back what he wanted. So he killed her and left her lying in her blood till the rotten black meat began to stink and her neighbors opened the door. (God rest her soul)*

—*Here he is. You won't see his name in the newspapers. Nor Clara Mae's name. Same old story, people. The Man gives and the Man takes away. This is not a guilty man. He's the judge and jury and we could hardly expect him to convict himself. I say he ought to go free. His hands are white. His eyes are blue. If that's not innocent I don't know what is . . .*

—*And the voice goes on signifying, insinuating. It's like a prayer meeting. Some old sister in the amen corner shouting back at the speaker. Blood of the lamb. Somebody weeping Oh god hunkies did it to my sister too. The walleyed junkies getting nervous at all the heat and rage they feel building around them. Picture it.*

—Then the speaker says something like . . . Go on brothers and sisters. Ain't nothing happening here. I thought we had a criminal, a guilty man, but we all know which color is right.

—Somebody dumps the sack of flour on the cop.

—Everybody go on. Mind your own business, people. Party. Nothing's going on. I thought I saw a white man next to me. A white man who had slaughtered a black woman after feasting on her body like a beast. But I don't see nothing. I don't see anything at all.

—Speaker's eyes roving the crowd. The black cops feel his gaze touching them. He peers through their blue shrouds. Burning through the ice. Entering like a camel through the needle's eye, weighed with the mass of black bodies encrusting his words.

—I see nothing at all.

—Crowd has begun to drift apart. They see and don't see. Clots of people form, seemingly intent on some business of eating or singing or talking which brought them together. But the platform is the still center of the constellations.

—From it the speaker's voice is almost an apologetic drone. Dully urging his audience to ignore him. Forgive his presumption. His mistake. At times his words are curdled in terrified screams from the throat of a man who cannot understand he no longer exists.

—Finally no voice rides above the crowd. Things are like they always are on a normal, loud Saturday afternoon in the neighborhood. Speaker has disappeared. His ghostly mistake hangs unnoticed, a piece of lumpy laundry twisting in slow, diminishing arcs.

The shower of words passed. Real or unreal, outside or inside it drenched him and shivers twitched from head to toe till nothing remained but the cold night and Thomas Wilkerson, shoulders hunched, head down, on his way home remembering himself.

Wilkerson recalls a bird he had seen in the park. Plump, red breasted bouncing from branch to branch, top of a bare tree quivering as if its dry limbs just weren't ready to endure spring so soon. Sky had been clear and blue at noon. Simple blue charged with brightness, cracked into intricate designs if you peered up through the naked branches. Those images come and go, do not displace the voice and smoke and grease popping.

On his bed Wilkerson reads for as long as he is able. *Gavrila Ivolgin.* Ganya. It is impossible to keep up with the Russian names. He turns down a page, three creases, the way the kids begin folding jack-in-the-boxes. Just before sleep comes he repeats the page numbers, hazily attempting to reconstruct what he will underline the next day when he has his hands on a pencil.

He had still many years of playing the fool before him. A profound and continual realization of his own mediocrity and, at the same time, an irresistible desire to convince himself that he was a man of the most independent mind, had rankled in his heart ever since his boyhood. He was a young man of envious and impulsive desires, and he seemed to have been born with overwrought nerves. He mistook the impulsiveness of his desires for strength. In his passionate desire to excel, he was sometimes ready to take the most reckless risks; but as soon as the moment for taking such a risk came, our hero was always too sensible to take it. That drove him to despair. He would perhaps have made up his mind, given the chance, to do something really mean, for the sake of getting what he wanted so badly, but, as though on purpose, as soon as the moment for action came, he always seemed to be too honest to do anything that was too mean. (He was, however, always ready to agree to any petty meanness.) He looked with disgust and loathing on the poverty and downfall of his family.

When his eyes open the dream of the lynching is still there. He does not know if he has slept ten minutes or ten hours, just that the room is dark and the dream is fresh. He wishes for a tape recorder beside the bed so he could speak into the machine before fear distorted the telling. He needed to keep everything blanked from his mind, begin telling the truth into the microphone.

• • •

He is being peeled from the dream. It drops from his consciousness in rotting, musty shreds, the bandages of a mummy unraveled after black centuries of sleep. He is exhausted by the effort. Luminous hands of his watch form an upside down V. Five thirty in the morning. Less than two hours before the first bell. They were before him already, forty-five souls with folded hands, fuzzy headed, dark-eyed, fallen black angels, dropped prematurely into a lake of fire. Sulphur tanned, smelling of soot and gas, ephemeral substance that will not survive the brazen underworld. Oh yes, suffer the children to come. Or wait little tarbabies. Daddy's putting on his white shirt and tie. I will be with you soon as I get respectable. Must brush my teeth. Clean the beer from my breath, the fumes of hashish shake from my brain. Get it together little darlings so I can steal you away to Jesus.

Thomas Wilkerson rose. One foot on the floor, knee on the bed and some anchor stronger than either limb still fouled in the scarlet tangle of dream. He began to ambulate. Across the cold floor barefooted to a sink where he turned on water, dipped his face and tossed handfuls of the wetness against his skin. Cold then hot. Day is the dawning of a roar between the ears. Water continues to run into the chipped sink then splashes into aluminum kettle Wilkerson tilts so that the spout receives the flow. In and out the same hole. Hot water going in, coffee coming out frothing as it rises in the cup heaped with brown powder and white powder.

Wilkerson sleeps in his shorts and undershirt. When he urinates the shorts go down rather than fumble with the slit.

Very yellow it is perhaps the beer or greasy chicken or probably some fatal impurity in the dream smoke he will die a horrible choking death, penis bloated, throat raw, unable to cry out because the yellow bile floods to his throat and there is nothing left inside, just the gritty yellow pulp that once was organs, just the bile slooshing when he walks.

Shorts go up when he is finished, settle, full of the spreading cakes of Thomas Wilkerson, onto the crumpled bed. Someone should clean everything. Shorts, bed clothes, the coffee stained T-shirt, last but not least Wilkerson's own hairy ass. When you are a baby someone comes and lifts your legs. Undiapers you and wipes impurities from the cute, chubby bottom. Then they stop coming. You get ashamed. Your hind end becomes very private, secretive, something to forget about, be avoided, a shameful thing. So no wonder it grows weary, drags, loses its proud curves and declines as Wilkerson declines sourly, flaccidly to drink his coffee sitting on the side of the bed.

Body make its overtures, belches, farts, regrets old pains it must exhume each morning. Body exhales its staleness a thick scent through pursed lips till the room is full to bursting. But the shape created is not round and smooth like a balloon, it is uneven, bulging in places, shadowed, dark cornered, harsh with right angles and sharp inclining planes. Room choked with hissing spiral of his breath, confining him, settling that torpor over his thoughts and movements.

Wilkerson thought of the children, the rooms growing around them, the furry eyes pushing back shadows and finding nothing has changed.

For the children he would raise himself from the bed, undo the pall by snapping on all the lights in his two rooms. He would shit, shower and shave for them. And pull a clean shirt from its cellophane. Clean white breast beneath a suit that needed pressing. Dark suit of course, all his functions merged within that darkness. Whether priest or undertaker or judge or mourner or dead man, the subdued tone appropriate. Wilkerson would pull on his black socks, wedge his way with the aid of a strip of cardboard torn from the backing of his laundered shirt into new black loafers.

He sees little Andrea's hand go up. The other children laughed before she could begin speaking. He knew almost all their names. Handles to pick them up and set them down gently. Why was her harelip so ugly? Why did it trap her? You want to tell them not to laugh but a voice you own chuckles with them, tickles from within, teasingly pulls at the stern mask of your features. Andrea Palmer. The children. Their voices reach him in ripples of crooked singing. He walks up and down narrow aisles listening, a hand he doesn't own patting Andrea on the head. He stares at the pale creases furrowing her skull. Her hair is pulled tightly away from the parts, forming taut mounds spotted with flecks of dandruff, a dull gray Vaseline sheen where it reflects the ceiling lights. Her mother lovingly patting down each strand. Pulling the pigtails tight. Andrea Palmer remembers the busy fingers in her hair. The welcome annoyance of so much attention. She forgets the hanging lip. She raises her hand to answer a question.

Accent lines of bare scalp crisscross atop her head, an elaborate pattern perhaps she has never seen. He wants to touch her. Trace his finger through the grooves.

Wilkerson turned with the pages of his appointment book. Who had decided to represent time in these perfectly congruent squares. A grid of red lines crossing one another at right angles dividing the page into equal compartments, name of the month he had penciled in *March* underlined above the grid, the letters S M T W T F S in succession heading each vertical column, in the corner of each square a bracketed numeral, from 1 to 30. That was March. Predictable, orderly. All Thursdays separated by six days. The last Thursday (31) followed by two blank spaces which meant March had ended but the pattern would persist, other compartments would succeed which differed only because they were arrayed under the heading April, a month which necessarily begins on Friday, the blank space which had no number in its corner on

71

March's page. If you were a good teacher, you planned ahead, accepted the calendar's impeccable vision of the future. You made notations in the squares. Each Monday would bring a test. By Thursdays the papers would be returned to the class. Your promptness and regularity themselves a lesson to the slovenly children. Reward the children who had conditioned themselves to acquiesce to the logic of the squares. Be grateful to those who did not deviate, who arrived on time and did not disrupt the schedule, did not let chaos ramble through their compositions and examinations. Wilkerson drew a heavy line around the vertical column of Wednesdays, outlined five days to form a horizontal crossbar. Rewarded those like himself who had chosen a shape and moulded themselves to it uncompromisingly.

But who had ordained this bland equality of days, months, hours, years. He knew children had to be crushed to believe it. He knew it was a weariness in himself and most men which acknowledged the rightness of the pattern. Somewhere they had lost the urge or the skill to resist. He was beginning to become convinced that self-discipline, maturity, courage, reality, truth were all synonyms for what he now called weakness. Yet didn't he hate his father's life because it seemed accidental, shapeless, best represented not by ruled lines but by a child's aimless drawing all swirls and lumpish climaxes, sprawling giddily, ripping the paper on which it is scribbled.

Were there only two choices? Either cage time in the red lines that marched across the page or like his father in his lost weekends abandon any illusion of control. Littleman believed all men were trapped. No choice existed except to reverse or destroy the particular historical process which at a given time determines the life of individual men. He would see my father and me as equally unredeemable.

Perhaps he is right. I believe in his plan. It may free men for an instant, create a limbo between prisons. But can the instant be extended? Can it support life and a society? I don't think Littleman cares. I don't think my father cared when he felt the need to escape. He could run and that was enough. He blessed the legs and hands that could carry him away. To the high of music, laughter and smoke, the peace of emptying your pockets and sleeping where you fell down.

But while I am full of Littleman's plan for escape, I still resent my father's humble breaking away. I question his right to make one woman suffer yet am prepared for a circus of bloodletting when the plan triggers anarchy. And though I conceive of myself and the plan as a fulcrum turning history, how much further will I have moved it than my father moved it?

But these are not questions to be answered. They are soft laps to lay my head in, to hide from what calls me.

Though the date has been circled many times, he scores the paper again, marking the day of the lynching, defining its square once more in an enveloping ring. A noose he thinks. A wound through to the next sheet. If you lifted June, the day of the plan's beginning would not rise with it but remain a ragged, black wreathed patch on the wrong page of the calendar. Leave fluttering June with a gaping hole in her belly. The day was a thing apart. A hole in time destroying the meaning of the calendar. A mouth drinking the ink from each page. Order, logic, thin red stripes spiraling through the whirlpool, accentuating motion, beginning and ending nowhere like lines on a barber's pole. You cannot reckon time with the squares. They are swallowed too quickly, tumbling end over end, flashing past in a blur like the cars of a train speeding through the windows of the speeding train you are riding.

He turns backward in the book to March. A neatness, order in his jottings. No mention of the plan. Most of the notations concern the children, his pupils. Books for them to read. Presentations on current events he wishes to connect with their history lessons. Reminders to himself of faculty meetings, luncheons. A list in the margin of books read and movies he would harvest in the future. Tanya's name appearing. The references to her as businesslike as all others. His

73

eyes running over the page. No mention of father, mother. Wilkerson was annoyed that the information tediously recorded yielded almost nothing about its author. The most startling characteristic of the writer was his uncanny ability to fit all he had to say within the space allotted by the calendar's framework. Like a well trained child filling in a coloring book he did not let his crayon slip over the thick boundary lines. It was as if some stern parent watched over his shoulder, ready with a stinging ruler to rap the offending hand. Wilkerson had once seen a journal Littleman kept. They were both drunk and Littleman had wanted him to read a poem. The loose leaf notebook passed to him had been opened to the wrong page. Nothing in the jumbled pencil scrawl suggested poetry. Wilkerson turned three leaves before he saw a staff of words centered on the page, slanting like a barbell between two opaque clots of run on prose at the bottom and top of the sheet. Littleman had asked him to read aloud, so laboriously Wilkerson deciphered and intoned. Surprisingly the lyric was regular; two interlocking rhymed stanzas with diction faintly archaic. What was described was the castration of a bull framed ironically by images of soft white hands and maiden tears. He read the poem four times before he approximated the version Littleman wanted him to decode from the chaotic manuscript.

Littleman had said:

—Yes, that's good, that's the way it's supposed to be. Just the way you did it then. Now do it again, please, like that so I can remember.

But the next recitation was no better than the first three. They began to argue, Littleman name calling as he snatched away the notebook. They drank more wine and passed on to the plan.

And though she kiss the black, heaving flank.

Upon the wound lay lily hands . . . These lines were all he could remember. And his disjointed impression of the whole. Quaint. Obscene. Funny. Pathetic. Then the one word. The sure word vivid as the lines he recalled. Transparent. You

74

see through to the man. There is a man writing this poem. Either a sign of amateurishness or of genius. With Little-man's poem an aesthetic judgment not possible or necessary at the time. Just the unavoidable discomfort Wilkerson had felt as he stared through the words at the human shape.

–Today I want to tell you how the leopard lost his spots . . .

He looks at his watch. A half inch crack in the crystal runs diagonally from 12 to 2. He is dizzy. The scarred face of his watch is his face, bruised, lined unaccountably. He is afraid to ask why. To turn time over in his mind.

Still early. A clear March day. Unseasonably warm weather predicted for the rest of the week. Perhaps shirt sleeve warm. The urge to linger outside after dark, to talk and laugh on the street corners, cluster around somebody's front steps and dream lies, tell lies, hear the old stories again. His people. The fathers and mothers of the children he tended five days a week. And where were his children while the night was being whittled into a thousand shapes by the elders' voices. Would they be listening at windows or wide-eyed hunched in the shadowy doorways listening. Were the stories for their ears or was it better that they disappeared into their own darkness, the alleys and vacant lots, at the periphery of poolrooms, sandwich shops, the record store with the loudspeaker outside singing as long into the night as anybody seemed to be listening. When did the children learn to wear night like a badge.

But the children were not alone. Somebody went to them in the alleys and vacant lots. Somebody filled their heads with visions he could not budge when the chidren came to school sleepy-eyed, sated.

Man we killed some good grapes some fine pluck man, we be high as a muthafucka man we be flying behind that stuff we be sniffing and chewing and drinking and poking and man Mary Lou got nice big legs man anybody can get some of that shit.

–Today I want to tell you an African folk tale of how the leopard changed his spots. Lame ass shit. Jive muthafucka.

–We gonna lay at Larry's. His mama be working till six ain't nobody home we gonna get into some nice shit. Yeah man we got some bitches coming.

                         All together, baby
Sunny March day.

                         Albums, baby. You know. I dig albums not that doo wah ditty shit. We gonna git nice behind jazz.
Mansa Musa
Night time.
Fuck it man.

March day. March day. March day. And after this March day another and another. And after those days.

Still early. He tilts his wrist so the scarred crystal does not interfere as he reads the face of his watch. If he hurries he will catch Tanya at Dewey's. She takes her breakfast there every morning. A quiet antiseptic coffee shop. Far enough away from the school so that it is not filled with school faces, but close enough so that a ten minute walk gets you to the front door of the school building. They never talked much over the coffee and rolls, the spatula of scrambled eggs and home fries with which he would begin some days. But when they walked to the school building he felt as close to Tanya as he ever did. Just a few minutes together, but so sane, so private coming as they did before the onslaught of the children, the bells, the classroom walls. They never lingered, never played at lovers kissing in the empty morning streets, but he sensed in her stillness as they clattered together along their special, usually deserted path of back streets that the time they shared was not inconsequential for her. He tried not to worry the mystery, did not question too closely what he believed was special about the brief passage between Dewey's and the school yard.

Though they spoke rarely as they walked, one morning damp and chilly, the broken sidewalks blotted with dark reflecting pools, the sky mottled gray like sheets slept in too many times, he had let his fingers go instinctively to the point of her elbow guiding with the faintest touch her step up a high curb, and still without realizing how far he'd gone he pressed her arm against her side, letting his fingers circle it, pulling her toward him so they bumped awkwardly, swayed forward another two steps before he remembered how she mocked couples clutching in public, her distaste for the sentimental formalities of courtship, and remembering her disdain he squeaked . . .

–I seen Mr. Wilkerson making love to Miss Tanya right out in the middle of the street. . . . Yes, lawd . . . in broad daylight.

He thought she smiled. No stiffness when they had come together. A perceptible yielding. Perhaps she understood the morning as he did.

–It's a miserable day. Did she know he said what he did because those words were the only way of telling her yes the weather is oppressive, what we left and where we're going are unhappy places, but if there is an endless list of things gray and distressing, there is also you, a pair of eyes and ears and legs walking beside me and all the warmth holding you together and so I can speak I can smile at your eyes when I point to the emptiness surrounding us.

–Don't you get the feeling sometimes . . . or rather more than a feeling, a certainty . . . you know you could change everything about your life. He watched her as he spoke.

–You would want to do that. She spoke to the air.

–Many things I would change if I could. But I'm not talking about for better or worse just a knowledge coming, the experience of utter detachment. Like . . . like dice. Dice scooped off the floor and wrapped in somebody's fist.

–I didn't know you were a gambler.

–Dice don't decide, don't know how they'll fall. They are just suspended. Out of the game awhile. If they were seven or two or twelve before it doesn't matter. When they tumble from the fist they . . .

–Somebody picks up the money.

–Sometimes in the morning when just the two of us . . . I lose my bearings. Or maybe I just wish I could lose my bearings. Continue walking.

–Where.

He was going to say somewhere new. He was going to say where doesn't matter. What mattered was her power to lift him in her fist. He had much to say that morning as they approached the iron fence enclosing Baxter Junior High.

But the clamor surrounding the building was a signal for small talk; they maneuvered through the early arrivals, protecting themselves with a wall of earnest, professional conversation.

Voices of children. Swelling traffic noise from the broad street that fronted the school building. Sleepy-eyed sentinels with white Sam Brown belts trudging to their posts at the busy intersections. Mrs. Davis the crossing guard in her heavy clogs and the dark blue cape shrouding her shoulders, a giant bat resting its heavy wings, hooded eyes neither open nor shut as she leans against the light standard.

He had said too much that gray morning. His father believed you could jinx things. Brag them out of existence. You never talked outright about your good luck, you never said directly how much you wanted something to occur. Great need was a crime or a sign of weakness, and his father's law had been admit only what does not incriminate you. Wanting something too much was the surest way of guaranteeing you'd never get it. Be cool. Be cool. Even if it comes don't shout, don't grab. It may blow up in your face. Never turns out to be such a big deal anyway, once it's in your grasp. So never mention the morning. Don't try to pick up the conversation where it ended. You too guard the silence. Just sit in Dewey's red booth and sip your coffee. Walk beside her till you get to the building. Enjoy the complicity without asking if it is complicity, if it's mutual, if when she plunges into the life of the school she feels the transition, if she is aware of how well you work together fooling the others, pretending nothing has happened, nothing has been shared before you are among them, full of business, each getting his set of keys from the board, and striding without a backward glance in opposite directions.

Time to catch Tanya if she stopped at the restaurant. He would have to hurry.

A wave of fatigue and nausea overtook him. His knees buckled. Wilkerson was forced to sit on the edge of the bed. Hunching forward he pressed his fists into his forehead, rubbing his knuckles down against the bony ridges of his cheeks, grinding the flesh around his closed eyes, then allowing his hands to fall limp from his face, his elbows to slide from his knees so his arms dangle full length along his body. His eyes burned. For a second there were short streaks of blue and yellow and white. He was afraid to straighten his body. Afraid his soupy guts would drip from the hole in his belly he held closed by doubling over. The sickness passed. His muscles were deadened, flaccid, but had not disintegrated. His head throbbed but would not explode.

He looked in the mirror. No wounds. No scars. The eternally seedy cheeks, the eyes bloodshot but familiar. Still time to reach her. The subway. The transfer to a bus. The little newspaper vendor who would look past him. Get off a stop early, cross the street. See the window, the red and white stripe of Dewey's sign, the blur of movement within. She will be sitting alone. Not even needing the prop of a newspaper to indicate how absorbed she is in her solitude, how uninterested she is in company. The black waitresses do not like her. Her long fingers and perfect nails. Soft cloud of hair framing her face, a reprimand to the heat and grease with which the others have disguised themselves to serve the white faces coffee and doughnuts. And though she is dressed simply, the rich unobtrusiveness of her shift, her coat, the shoes she wears mock the stylishness of the special purchase each girl has made, the extravagant investment that must be worn long after its elegance is outmoded. She sits minding her business, business which her hands and eyes, her voice as she orders or politely acknowledges, hold aloof from white customers and black staff.

He sees Tanya in the red booth, feels the arms of the turnstyle bump against his thighs as he enters the glass wall.

The metal is cold and he brings his hand to his cheek. He hears the rattle of cups and saucers. Orders shouted at the kitchen. He finds his eyes again in the mirror. Still time. Still time to go to her. He would begin to explain the plan.

Still time.

The water stung his hand. He mixed more of the cold tap. Sink was a bowl. Barely enough border to lay his toothbrush, the razor, set the can of instant lather. Sometimes his father had shaved in the kitchen sink. He would watch from the drainboard where his father perched him. His mother didn't like it when they did that. The way she didn't like it when his father stood beside the icebox to eat rather than sitting down. Father said he could see better in the light that came in over the kitchen sink. He said it was better for shaving than lightbulb light in the windowless bathroom. One day his father brought home a fragment of cracked mirror. Hung it in the kitchen so he wouldn't have to cart out the one from the bathroom. Which had meant going into the bathroom where she was probably bathing somebody or changing a diaper and she would want to know where was he going with the mirror. He'd break it one day carrying it all around the house. Half the time she'd have a baby in her arm and he'd leave the mirror sitting all over the house she'd have to tramp around carrying a heavy baby looking for the mirror, why didn't he leave it in the bathroom why can't he wait till the bathroom's empty, shave where he's supposed to shave why can't he wait in such a damn hurry anyway where's he going so fast no money anyway to go anywhere why can't he just leave it where it is. So he brought one home and hung it by the kitchen window and I would watch him from the drainboard. And the water so hot it would steam, I wanted to put my fingers in he said too hot. I cried and he said go on if you don't believe me. And she heard me squeal when I ran my hand under the faucet. And she screamed at him and I wanted to get down. It was wet under me. I felt it coming through my clothes. My hand didn't hurt but I wanted down so I screamed and they were at one another and I wanted down. Finally she carried me from the kitchen because my feet were bare and glass all over the floor from the mirror she'd torn down.

And it is so easy to remember. His father had a flare with the long razor. Wilkerson winced because straight razor was chill death, nigger throat cut death even in his own hand, raised to shave his own face. He toweled his cheeks. Rinsed his hands and dried them.

He stared at the face of Thomas Wilkerson. Mr. Wilkerson impatiently awaited by forty-five fifth graders in home room 109. He was shabby. Somehow the shadows never scraped from cheeks, chin and above the lip. Never new and shiny. As if the dark contours and hollows had been quickly gone over with a thin, cheap paint. Never really clean or fresh. Not quite but almost a seedy reflection. An old man on a park bench whose indolence in the spring sun seems selfish and desperate. He would not try to catch Tanya this morning.

If you stood on Forty-third Street in the middle of Clark Park, you could catch either trolley. You could see far down the tracks and either go right or left depending on which showed itself first, the 13 at the top of a slight incline, white whale brow first, then slowly descending a curve that revealed its white and green flank, or the 34 a flat, floating cream blur that skimmed above the broken silhouette of parked cars on Baltimore Avenue. Both took Wilkerson below the ground into the same loud tunnel and unreal light. Trolley trapped within the echo of its clumsy sprints, its wheezing, swaying halts. Catacombs of the city. These caverns and the subterranean islands of light madly careening without purpose or destination. These tunnels would be the burying ground of a martyred race. Packed thick, barely leaving room for the screaming hearses, tiers of the dead would peer blackly at those who for the moment were alive.

You blink when you find yourself released. You are relieved because for some reason you were not kept below. March sunshine glories from concrete, steel and glass. You were cramped and now you are dwarfed. Nothing is man sized around you. Speed of the cars is threatening, would crush you if you stepped into the flow. You blink and look down at your new shoes already dusty on the filthy pavement. You are undeceived.

You would whistle, you would about face and walk against the grain of those bodies hustling you forward. But there is no place to go but where you are going. You clutch the transfer in your hand. Put your back against the wall and hope the bus will be on time, the next step toward the children can be taken.

Although it must be over a thousand mornings now, the vendor does not raise his eyes in greeting. He leans against his blue newsstand, aproned, capped as he always is. Runty man with hair on his hand backs, hair you can see curling up his forearms when in the summer he wears a Los Angeles Dodgers T-shirt. It would be so simple to notice the vendor, to speak to him so the next day he would notice you. A thousand mornings and the man has yet to remember or to make a sign of remembrance. And if you bought one of his papers. From out of town so the transaction wouldn't be ordinary. An expensive one and give him a dollar so he would have to make change. Let him keep the nickel, perhaps. Each morning give him a dollar and he hands back the Times and three quarters. In twenty weeks he will have earned a dollar. He will smile and remember. But why all of that. Why can't he see you just because this morning has happened so many times. Up out of the black hole, across the street, standing back against the wall so as not to impede urgent pedestrians, staring at his bearish shoulders and hairy hands, the rituals of shuffling, counting, giving and receiving, the muttering sounds he makes, ghosts of his strong hawking voice that drew customers to his blue box until they didn't have to be reminded, just came and knew he would be there, shuffling, rhythmless dance as he gives and takes muttering.

82

But there is only one of him. One capped and aproned boy/man peddling papers and each day so many wait here where I wait. Obvious why he doesn't remember, why he can't remember. In fact most days the wait is short. I am only unnoticed a short while before the bus comes.

I pledge allegiance to the flag of the United States of America, and to the republic for which it stands, one nation under God, indivisible, with liberty and justice for all.

Forty-five black throats finish. Go their separate ways again, coughing, laughing, talking, sighing, burning, hungry, dry, sore, angry, silent, full of sleep and want, stale with unbrushed teeth, with soured food, with rotten teeth and sore gums.

–Africa is a continent. For a long time it was thought of as the Dark Continent. Civilization looked upon its inhabitants as savages, wild and untamable as the ferocious beasts with whom they shared the impenetrable, jungled land.

Now Mr. Willkerson tell them like it is. Tell them how greed overcame fear and how, after such a momentous push forward of Civilization, overcoming scruples was not difficult at all. Europe and Africa embracing in a Brave New World, peopling two Americas with spangled children. Sing Glory. Sing blessed art thou Fruit of that Loom my orphans.

–We must learn not to shy away from the truth. Africa was dark only in the darkened minds of those who approached her with dark intent. When you come to steal, the past of your victim is of interest only in so far as that past may promote your plundering. But Africa lies swaddled in history and you are part of its past, heirs of its legacy.

Now tell it Wilkerson tell them heirs is anonymous for victims. How you trembled purchasing the luminous dashiki. how its exotic swirl of colors is buried deep beneath your cellophaned white shirts. Tell them how yes the first African you met, black wallflower at an AKA dance, answered politely in English reeking of stiff upper lips and cricket and faggotty blazered, red-cheeked boys, –No my good man, I have never seen a lion, outside of a zoo that is.

Off the smart alecky big lipped bastards for months after

this foray, this sincere attempt to come to terms with my past.

–Benin, Mali. See golden cities my children, see black people in stately, flowing robes glide across the spotless streets, see their poised, quiet shadows rest upon golden walls of sun baked brick. Every man a prince in sandals, striding with effortless grace as some men have been said to walk on water without disturbing its surface, raising not a ripple in the yellow dust.

And though the ghost of a white giggle is restless in your throat, bury it with the full mouthed sound of Mansa Musa, Lumumba, Kasavubu.

–Your history is black, your heritage dark but that does not mean it is negative or nothing at all. Africa awaits you as a full mooned, humming night awaits only your coming to fill it with meaning, with the knowledge of your own being.

–Learning was esteemed. The black scholars of Timbuktu were fabled for their learning and lore. Listen to the black voices from your past, let them raise the veil from the Dark Continent:

Our land is uncommonly rich and fruitful, and produces all kinds of vegetables in great abundance. We have plenty of Indian corn, and vast quantities of cotton and tobacco. Our pine apples grow without culture; they are about the size of the largest sugar-loaf, and finely flavoured. We have also spices of different kinds, particularly pepper; and a variety of delicious fruits which I have never seen in Europe; together with gums of various kinds, and honey in abundance. All our industry is exerted to improve these blessings of nature. Agriculture is our chief employment; and every one, even the children and women, are engaged in it. Thus we are all habituated to labour from our earliest years. Everyone contributes something to the common stock; and, as we are unacquainted with idleness, we have no beggars.

–Olaudah Equiano goes on to describe the physical beauty of his people, their cleanliness, the chastity of the women. Yet Olaudah was kidnapped from this Darkness and made a slave. Only through uncommon perseverance and good fortune did he manage to survive the fatal Civilizing process. His voice in an adopted language speaks for countless brethren whose stories died mute within them. Olaudah's slave name, Gustavus Vassa, a Roman.

Fair weather will continue. Temperature much higher than average for March but the nights deceptively cool. Cover up. Don't forget a coat if you'll be outdoors after dark. Time is . . .

Bell between my temples. Their faces sleepy and impatient.

—Mr. Wilkerson, Walter Brown, he ain't comin. His little brother got hit by a newspaper truck and he's home cause he keep crying.

Giggles sputter from a corner. Foolish to cry. Silly if you cry. You know Walter Brown ain't here cause he found a way to get round coming. You are annoyed, envious. You laugh at staying home to cry.

—Was he seriously injured.

—Nothing wrong with that niggcr. He ran two blocks to tell 'em his brother got knocked down.

Roll call. Time is their names one after another. Either here or not, X or O. And one day, if you could live that long, not one would answer. In fact the room would be empty and the columned book uninterrupted in its droning monotone. What was the little brother's name. Who would note him absent. In what kind of book. What color, what symbol mourned him.

—Andrea Palmer.

Andrea Palmer is Andrea Palmer a leaf shaking in the wind, a face that goes to smoke. Does she still have that sore beneath her lips. Is she already dreaming again or still at home lost in dream.

—She here, Mr. Wilkerson.

She sink lower, lower than that if she could, if she could hide the lip sore beneath the edge of the arm rest, she would sink that far. She is doing her best. Obedient the black arm sticks up, antenna, periscope splitting the horizon, as much of her self she dares risk in an alien element.

85

—Today we are going to talk about Africa. Africa is a continent. Who can tell me what the continents are?

Who can name three?

On the board:

N. America
S. America
Austria
Africa

In it so many times yet when alone I cannot list this room's contents. Just as I cannot pledge allegiance or remember the words to the Star Spangled Banner unless I am in a crowd, threatened by the other voices. Trying to list the things.

The children scatter to lunch. I am alone in the room. It would be easy to remember the lynch dream, bring back the horror and pleasure.

—Are you going to eat? Tanya called from across the corridor. Nothing feminine in her voice, nothing suggesting I am woman and you are man and an invitation to lunch is the smallest part of what I am saying. She was tall and the bright colors she wore seemed brilliant streamers wrapped around a stately column, column topped by spongy cloud of light brown hair. Her features moulded from skin barely beige contradicted the colorful Afro print and hairdo. Green eyes, long, thin nose, lips full but tensely held as if denying the fleshiness they could release. Tanya whip slender and elegant beneath the soft umbrella of hair. She seemed oblivious to the swarming confusion of the lunchtime corridor, picking her way by instinct through the children, unconcerned yet untouched as bodies scudded past, deliberate, never faltering a step till she stood beside Wilkerson.

—More nerve than I have. Wild Indians going to knock you down one day.

—I hardly think so, they know who I am and I know them. No reason for either of us to get in the other's way.

—That's what you always say. But they know me and they know one another and that doesn't stop the pushing and shoving and bumping. She answered him by taking a step in the direction of the lunch room. He forced himself through the oncoming stream of students so that he could walk abreast of her. Things he wanted to say seemed impossible in the clamor. Perhaps because the words were less important than how he wished to say the words, how he wanted his voice to be an instrument rendering through rhythm, pitch and timbre those things he felt which had nothing to do with the meager stock of words he could use in trying to reach her. But subtlety was pointless in the loud current of dark children, free for a few moments from constraint and self-imposed silence, liberated among their own kind with whom they could trumpet and bleat the warm, violent messages of the herd. Wilkerson suppressed the urge to take her slim, perfectly manicured hand, to squeeze warmth from her long fingers which always felt like a bundle of twigs in his fist. He would shout over the other voices, you are beautiful Tanya and we are in love on this island slowly navigating the crowded corridor. You are a palm tree and I am tall enough to stare down into your deep eyes almost hidden beneath the canopy of perfumed fronds. Shout all of that and more to her as they strolled hand in hand to some rendezvous of sunshine through the barred, chained doors at the end of the corridor. But no, we barely exchange a glance as we arrive at the intersection and take the left turning through a steaming kitchen to the teachers' dining room.

–How do you feel about tonight? Or should I first ask if you're still coming? Pipes running the length of the room gurgle and squeak overhead. Each time the yellow door opens a gust of kitchen and cafeteria noise blasts into their conversation. They are alone only a few minutes before others join them.

–Sorry to break in on you love birds. But you got plenty time to get together outside this jungle. Be damned if them kids don't have more space to eat than we do. Stuck in this hot box behind the funky kitchen. I bet if there was white teachers here they'd find someplace else for them to eat. Out behind the kitchen always been good enough for de darkies. And niggers is niggers be they doctor, lawyer, butcherman or sorry assed teachers. Whole thing is nothing but a zoo anyway. Least they ought to provide us with uniforms so we wouldn't have to dirty up the few rags we can afford to buy wearing them in this godforsaken dump. Yeah. Uniforms whips and guns. Ought to pass them out tomorrow. My animals know I got a pistol even if it's not in view. I tell them first day. They better believe it too. The way them fools carry on, you better believe I won't let any of them get up in my face and start wolfing. They carry around everything from hat pins to meat cleavers and I'm having none of that. If one so much as rise up at his desk, I tell them I'm not going to shout or use my fists. I'm going to walk out the door, or run if I have to, but when I come back they'll know I'm for real. Blow one of their crazy heads off. Just like they do to one another every chance they get. A goddamn zoo. And Charlie paying us peanuts for keeping the beasts off the streets, out of his part of town.

The voice continued, but was lost in a cavern at the pit of Wilkerson's belly, a cave where his own voice often settled, curling in the void, swallowed but indigestible, a reeling fog that by inches could fill his whole being with gray sickness. He knew the fury that was building in Tanya. She would not internalize it, not poison her guts but listen hungrily to the speaker's words, fascinated by his performance the way a boa constrictor intently observes the trembling vulnerability of his victims. Tanya savored every one of Edward's words, his bitterness, greed and hate moulting in ragged syllables, piling in heaps around his chair. As if she knew he would be punished and that she would be instrumental in his undoing, she slowly, seeming to discern him marginally if at all, picked at the tuna fish salad and emptied her coffee cup in dainty, poised mouthfuls.

Yes she would come tonight as they had arranged, to meet his parents. Be it for better or worse the girl brought home to Mama. She nodded her assent refusing at the same time to commit herself to more than the mechanical recognition of her barely tilted head, a motion more displacement of eyebrow than nod. As if the whole matter had been previously settled and pointlessly, tastelessly injected by him here among the sordid voices, in the cramped, stale space. But she gave him nothing more to go on. Was her disdain directed toward the others who had settled at the table and their interruption of what should have been an intimate exchange or was she telling him of course she would come to his home since coming to his home could not possibly be construed as anything more than politeness or indulging a child in his ridiculous whim. Home to mother.

• • •

Wilkerson did not realize how far he'd been till the rustling of the newspaper called him back. You read paragraphs then sentences, finally words are the largest unit you can concentrate on, but they too begin to break up, are black shapes flashing in figure ground reversals, counterpoint to whiteness of the paper, blots themselves disintegrating as ink explodes leaving the newspaper blank, a snow bright mountainscape. Your eyes are wind blind and you glide lazily down precipitous slopes, dreaming in the arctic stillness, till in the distance a hiss of glaciers bumping vast flanks, massy clouds of ice whispering thunder as they pulverize mountains in their passage, a rumbling deep in the skier's throat, that sets his veins on fire because the white cliffs are beginning to crumble around him.

Falling to his lap. Wilkerson recalls the last sense he had made of the printed sheets. Paper crackles and sighs as if it is burning. *Thirty-eight Books Written in Prison by Monk. Buddhist monk Venpitagedera Gnanasheeha, released after thirty-eight months in prison, wrote thirty-eight books on Buddhism during his confinement. They included two written in Pali, two in Sanskrit and the rest in Sinhalese, the native tongue of Ceylon.* Gnanasheeha. Chewing the silence of his cell. Digesting it and shitting treatise after treatise hot and funky on the dank floor. Shapes of the guards' faces, ballooning in the corridor's pastel darkness. Your rice, traitor Venpitagedera. May it be laced with elephant urine and may your bowels curdle when they kiss it. The monk chewing wood from the top of his pencil. Writing night and day till the cell is crowded with universes and Gnanasheeha squatting in the darkness smiles with pity at the iron cage outside his world and the trapped creatures within it who stare longingly at the jade river through which he floats.

Wilkerson remembered that he still didn't know the basketball score. Turning the front pages, skimming news, amusements, social notices, he had been anticipating the score, but denying himself the ultimate pleasure until he had done his duty. Perhaps less sense of duty than need to diminish painlessly that superfluous block of time remaining before he could lose himself in the business of getting ready to meet Tanya. Surprisingly a rout. His favorite team, favorite because he could become more involved rooting against them than he could rooting for some other, had been knocked out of the playoffs. Which meant their season was over. Which meant endless, redundant baseball games dragging through till pro football began to gobble prime time again. Sports made it worth owning a color T.V. Not too proud to accept the Empire's circuses. 154 to 120. They hadn't been beaten much worse than that all year. Wilkerson was just as happy not to have seen the game. No joy in seeing his favorites stomped in the manner they so richly deserved. He liked the issue to be in doubt. To be so absorbed in the frenzy of the action that he could actually forget his prejudices. It was best when he didn't know whether he wanted a shot to go in or miss, whether he hoped the referee would call charging or blocking. Then he could feel the anxiety, the thrust of both teams, the tangle of guts and bodies could ensnare him and dribble him up and down the court as if he were some objective seismograph. He was there drinking at the source, at the core of the action as it radiated from deep, underground channels. What pulsated through the players were forces they had no means of reckoning and the best at their best moments simply abandoned themselves to the rhythm.

And this pitching of the earth's innards produced scores. Things you could discover the next day in your newspaper. And was the score a simple minded reduction of all that had happened or did the numbers record a further, truer rhythm? Was the score saying no it never ends because this is how far it is at the moment and obviously since there are so many scores to be tallied the Game goes on.

Season ended. But the playoffs continue until a temporary champion crowned. The King is dead. Long live the King. Banners will hang from the rafters. With dates and scores. But in a back yard or under a street light the King is practicing, or unborn yet first feels the rhythm, the grappling of earth snakes as he is spilled, a spangled arc, a perfect shot swishing through shy fallopian tubes.

Score at the moment was zero to zero. If it could be called a game that he played with Tanya, if in fact what happened between them was tangible enough to register anywhere. When he could be honest with himself, Wilkerson admitted that the sole evidence of any attachment between himself and Tanya was the blank sheet of yearning he worked so hard at filling, but which remained empty, omnivorous as the sea.

He folded the newspaper neatly, re-establishing each section so the pages ran consecutively and placing the sections in order. He had daydreamed and read longer than he should have so now a slight edge of urgency would have to propel him through his final preparations. Happens so often must do it on purpose, not allowing myself to get ready till it's just about too late. Now the tasks take some concentration, some eye for efficiency. I can think about what I'm doing even though each operation is mechanical and mindless. Vaguely excited, challenged to get square peg in round hole. No time for wasted effort, no Yo-Yoing thoughts backward and forward. The fresh shirt from his drawer, the ubiquitous suit brushed then draped on his body. But no. Something different. The tree arches gracefully toward him smiling. Rich with tropical breezes and fruit sweetness the fronds brush his lips. He pulls the dashiki over his head.

Somehow enough. Nothing more to do. Only pick at his hair in front of the mirror. Worn long before long became fashionable and if fluffed out and shaped and seen from an angle that hid the inroads of balding forehead it could be mistaken for an Afro. The shirt was decisive. He could leave now in plenty of time, forgetting his game, his ritual, the score.

● ● ●

—Let me do something to help, Mama.

—You sit still and don't worry me. Nothing to be done. Nothing here to do it with, anyhow. This kitchen as empty as something can be and still be a kitchen. The few dishes is out and pots is on the stove.

—There must be something.

—Sit still I told you. Whatever's done here, I'll do and do my best so's if nobody don't like it that's just too bad.

—Nobody's said a thing about not liking. Everything looks fine.

—What you here for so early, anyway. In that wild shirt telling lies to your mother already.

—It's ten after seven and you told us to come at seven thirty. Are you tired of me? Isn't this still my home?

—As much as anybody else's. You can use it for a whistle stop like the rest. That makes a home I suppose. A place to sleep and eat when you're in the neighborhood.

—No that's not it.

—No, it ain't. You're right. Need a fool tied down to the raggedy boards. No. I'll get it together like I always do. For him or you or the rest when they decide to stop.

—Mama, wait. I'm a man now. I have my own life. I get

busy and don't come as often as I should. But you know . . .

–Nothing. I lived fifty some years and know nothing. Head just as empty as this kitchen. Cut me open all you'd find be a mess of old clothes and dirty dishwater. Everything else I gave up cause I didn't know any better. And if I walked around the corner who'd so much as know my name.

–I'm bringing the most important person in my life to meet you this evening. Doesn't that tell you something?

–I'm doing the best I can. I've laid out the dishes and got this place as close to clean as it gets. I'm waiting to see this lady though I hardly know why you didn't carry her here yourself stead of straggling in first one then the other like strangers if you think so much of her. Could at least walk through the door with her.

–I explained already. This is the way she wants it. She is a very strong, independent woman. That's one of the qualities I like best about her.

–Don't seem natural to me. Strong and independent don't mean she supposed to be traipsing through the streets at night like a man.

–It's a little thing, Mama.

–Did you want it this way? Is you all going to leave at the same time?

–What I want isn't the only thing that counts. You should understand that. A man and woman . . .

–Just stop there. No more "man and woman" talk. I know better than I hope you ever will what counts and who counts and how I don't even bother to ask myself anymore what I want. Do you see your father anywhere in this house? You might say I wanted him to be here. And I knew when I asked him and told him what you wanted and what I wanted that I might as well be asking that sink to turn into an airplane and fly me out of here. This night like all the rest.

–You don't think he'll come.

–Do I think he'll come. To tell the truth I try not to think about things like that at all. Almost two days since I saw him last. He might remember you and your ladyfriend

93

are supposed to be here and he might not. If he does remember, I suppose he'll intend to be here. But I know his intendings don't mean much. When your father is out with his friends they call him Sweetman. Sweetman cause all he drinks is gin. Sit at a bar all night ordering gin. Gin and gin and gin. Mr. Sweetman your daddy.

–Nothing has changed.

–What did you expect? Maybe you're getting like him. Maybe you think something will change if you stay away long enough. Did you think you was coming back to the Ritz? Your mother in an evening gown ordering her maids around. You've just been away that's all. And while you've been gone I've gotten older, tireder and poorer. Your father's still drinking hisself to death fast as he can. He's ashamed to look me in the eye, not so much cause of what he's doing to me. I was never very much to him. He's shamed because he knows I know what he's doing to himself.

–And you can't stop it. He can't stop.

–Maybe you need to go away a while longer. You don't like what I'm telling you or what you see with your own eyes. Leave now before you see and hear too much. Before the lady comes. Both you all come back in ten, fifteen years. This rag of an apartment building will be dust and we'll be dust and you can say what you'd like about your fine family.

–She'll be here any moment. The reason she's coming is to see you. You are all I have and she is all I have and I want to bring you together.

–Sure enough a pitiful world.

–Mama, help me make the best of it. Let me help you.

–Things is ready as they gonna get. I saw your father two mornings ago. Him standing where you are, big nigger half sleep on his feet, a cup of coffee in his hand. God knows where he is now. Just as well he don't turn up tonight.

–He's my father. I want him here.

–You wanted that woman here too, didn't you. Wanted her on your arm as you came through the door into a fine, sweet home. I know plenty else you wanted. And none of it resembling this old, bitter woman and dingy room. Why do you have that bodacious shirt on and hair sprouting all over your head? What do you have to be for her? Who is she to be strong and independent? One thing I was happy about when you all was born. All boys. No little soft, sweet girl I had to lie to and pretty up till some man came along and showed her just whose world it really is. I had boys and was so relieved I didn't have to die three or four more times trying to patch together soft, sweet girls have to walk the world like I walked it. Now here you is, a man, waiting like I'm waiting for somebody to come through the door. Going through changes I've been going through all my life. You, my son. Telling me she's strong and independent. It's pitiful. You looking to do her part in the kitchen. Coming early to sit in the kitchen. Woman talk. Wearing some wild man clothes and hairdo. Just what he got that's worth one evening of waiting. I asked myself that one day. You know what the answer is. And I'm talking about waiting for Mr. Sweetman, your father. The answer is nothing. The answer is he's never given me a thing and never will. What I hate is how I missed my chance to go out and take for myself. I know what you're waiting for. And it ain't never going to come walking through no door to greet you. Whether she comes or Mr. Sweetman himself big as life sauntering into the room. What you're waiting for is what I waited for all these years. Myself to get up and walk out.

—Could I . . .

—No, don't touch me. And don't you dare feel sorry. I'm crying over you just as sure as I'm talking about myself. I'll go on doing the best I can.

—I think I love her.

—I don't understand that. Time and poor and hate and hurt I know something about, but I don't know love.

—She's beautiful. Tall and slim. She has an artist's hands. Her eyes are green with a gray cast. Not dull gray but a special kind of gray light if you can picture that, gray that sparkles through green mist. I've known her a long time. She is intelligent, poised and decent. We teach in the same school. She won scholarships and worked her way through college. Lost her parents when she was very young. Everything she has she's earned for herself. Not an easy life. Passed among relatives, living in institutions when there was no one to take her. Learned to scuffle, fight for what she wanted. We're a lot alike in some ways.

—Except she don't have to take you home to see what's left of those that brought her into the world. She's the lucky one, maybe.

—I didn't have to bring her here.

—She ain't here yet. Smart gal. She arranged it so's she could change her mind at the last minute. You must have scared her away talking about us. What did you tell her? She must have asked. Did you tell her to wear something old, to eat before she came.

—Why are you saying these things. You know they aren't true. Who do you want to hurt? I'm proud of you. And you know you're the best cook in town.

—Sure, sure. Give me a batch of tough greens and all the ends of meat the white man throws away. I'll make a feast. Guts and feet and tails. Scraping, pounding, cleaning, boiling. I can make bones fit to eat. Stretch food for one so it will last a week for three. All my secrets that come from having scraps to work with or having nothing at all. I'm sick of my secrets.

—You know you can cook. You can't keep from smiling when I say it.

—I'm going to slap you boy. Lying to me.

—Then everybody who ever ate your cooking's just as big a lie.

—When do they get it? At funerals or weddings is all. And full of so much booze anything tastes good. "Thank you Sister Wilkerson," "God love you Sister Wilkerson," niggers nodding and crying, eating, drinking, laughing, as long as people got something to feed them and pour down their throats. It's free besides. Course they like it. And you standing there grinning like everything I've been trying to say to you is going to get chewed up and disappear in the first mouthful of chicken and rice.

–And gravy.

–Yes, fool, gravy.

–Crackling.

–Crackling.

–And did you fry the giblets?

–Livers under that saucer keeping warm.

–Remember how we'd fight over who'd get the liver. Putting in claims early on Sunday morning, then starting the day before we'd get in our claims. You got so mad you threw it out one Sunday. Right in the garbage pail and all three of us half grown boys standing around it crying.

–I remember that. And I remember how I felt trying to slice a pie, or divide ice cream or slice meat or count out french fries and eight or ten pairs of eyes froze on my hand waiting for me to slip up a little to the right or left so somebody would get cheated and start to scream. I remember how it felt, sure enough. Trying to make one half of what we needed do for us all.

–But those were good times. We laughed a lot too. We were all together.

–Now you're all gone. The babies and Sweetman who made them. What's her name?

–Tanya.

–It's not a bad name.

–You'll like her. She's strong, Mama. Strong like you always were.

–Strong. That's the biggest lie you've ever told. You get the door. Least I can do is serve what little I put together without burning it. Go on Thomas. She's at the door.

–Thomas. Tom. Tom my school teaching son. Only one to inherit his daddy's brains. I brought her a present. Something I picked up on the route. Good as new. Flowers for your lady. White folks ought to be shamed, the things they throw away for old.

—Why don't you have your key, man.

—Key. My key's right here in my pocket. Key to your heart, sugar.

—Then why you lean on that bell like you don't have good sense.

—Oh, you talking about some door key. Seem to have lost that one. Must be in the truck.

—Or somewhere . . .

—Surely in the truck, old lady. But I'm home ain't I now. To see Tom's princess. If she's fine, don't leave her alone with your daddy. Sing sweetness in her ear.

—You make somebody drunk they get too close to you.

—Woman, you ain't said nothing but nasty to me since I been here. My head hardly in the door and you pickin.

—Nothing came in that door but a drunk man fit for the bed. Don't even have sense enough to shut the door behind you.

—Mama.

—Don't get in our business. Just move out the way so he can stumble past and fall down cross the bed like he always does. Coming in here with some rotten flowers you stole from a garbage can.

—Weren't in a can. In a box. Still had ribbon round it. And nice tissue paper inside. I open that box and they smell fresh like just cut. I say to myself Tom bringing his old lady home so why don't I keep these. Put them on the table in some water to stay fresh. Brighten up things a little. Or just put the whole box ribbon and all in her arms when she come through the door. Let her see we know how to be fancy with the best. So I grabbed them up before anybody saw how nice they was. Little envelope fell out. They was to a woman. You can never tell about women. Something nice as these she just tossed out must have been soon as they came. Bitches is something. Childress talking the other day about one who came to the garage he used to work at. Ain't you going to gimme something she said. I believe anything anybody tell me bout a woman. Thomas, where is this fox got your nose open.

–Should be here any moment. Thought it was her when you rang.

–Now you know you can't keep no fine girl letting her run around at night by herself. Should have picked her up in a taxi. Young man in your position ought to have his own automobile anyway. A big one like I been telling you. Let her know you ain't afraid to spend money. Flowers and taxis and nothing but top shelf.

–That how you keep your women, Sweetman.

–Use my name when you talk to me, woman. I got a name.

–Ain't it Mr. Sweetman. King of the bar stool. Flowers and good whiskey for all his women. That's how you keep me ain't it. Hauling my ass around from one fancy place to the next in a taxicab.

–Shit. You gonna call me out my name and bad mouth me like some common whore. And your son standing right here.

–Get out.

–You ought to be shamed.

–Leave. Go on back to wherever you've been. Don't need you here tonight. No more nights.

–Go on. Talk. Talk. You're gonna be sorry for each mouthful. Sorrier and sorrier but you just keep talking. Let him take it all in.

–Nothing new. Nothing he don't know. He was born and raised in this hell-hole. God knows why he's back tonight or why he'd want to bring a woman he cares anything about here.

–If it's a hell-hole, you set the fires. And stoke em for all you're worth. Screaming at me like you're crazy. Standing over me when I'm sleep cursing me. Throw food at me the way you would at a dog. And laughing when you know you've drove me so far I can't go no further.

–Laughing. Did you say I laughed. I wish I could laugh. Could feel free of this pitiful life for one minute so I could open my mouth and eyes wide and laugh. But I'm past laughing. Crying too.

–You ain't past being knocked down if you don't get out

of my face, fool. I'm going in to put on some clothes. We's having dinner with Thomas and his lady.

—One of us is not going to be here when she comes. I swear to god one of us is not going to be in this kitchen. Now take your choice. I'm staying or you're staying, but not both. You can walk over me or throw me out the window. But I'll fight you till I can't stand up. And if I can't move you, I'll crawl out myself. Now get out. Leave us alone.

—Thomas, you can see how she does it. You can see how she traps me. I could break her in half. And she stands there challenging me, asking me to kill her. Won't let me in my own house. Picks and pulls, tears at me. Trying to do something nice. For you and your woman friend. I bring flowers. I want to get out of these filthy clothes and wash, and pour everybody a drink, and just sit down like people supposed to do. That's all I want. Just to be . . .

—You're drunk. You smell of the streets and the women you've been sleeping in. You can barely stand up, swaying there with that mashed, dirty box in your hands. And you just want to sit down and be like people. Over my dead body. I won't let you insult them or me. Mr. Sweetman sure enough. A rag man. Something barely recognizable for man in my kitchen.

—You ought to thank god I ever come back to this trap. And your terrible mouth. So much hate in a skinny little body. You bitches is something else. You bitches will ride a man to China and if he don't break, stomp him when you get off his back. God damn motherfucking blood sucking wenches ain't no wonder I got nothing never had nothing bled like a stuck pig to keep roof over your heads and food in the children mouths.

—There ain't no children. Only your grown son listening to your mouth. Hearing you threaten to lay your hands on his mother.

—Fuck it. Fuck it. Fuck it. This is my goddamn house and I'll be goddamned if I ain't staying. You or no other bitch gonna move me.

100

–Thomas. The door's open. She's standing there.

–Tanya.

–You trifling bitch look what you done. Decent people won't even come in your house. I ought to knock you down.

–Thomas don't wait. Pay him no mind. Go on away from here. Get her away.

• • •

Wilkerson knew she would not be running down the stairs. Nor would there be tears. He doubted that Tanya would have raised an eyebrow in recognition of the scene she watched from the open doorway. Nothing new for her. No names she hadn't heard before. The threats for all their vicious promise would echo hollowly since she had often witnessed the next step, the laying on of hands, the blood and bone and teeth swelling the words. She would be descending the spattered stairs in graceful, long legged strides, pausing on dark landings to be certain of her bearings, never brushing the dank walls, her fingers resting on the soft, unsteady railing only long enough to assure herself that she didn't need its support, that she had oriented herself in the sighing middle of the staircase. And she would be cat quiet. As if she could will her senses to give no evidence of her passage. She did not exist, warm, tall and elegant within the ramshackle building, just as its stench and darkness and peril could not touch her. She could will that. Could free herself unblemished from his parents screaming. And the squalor shadowing her down the steps to the street.

He could catch her easily. He could call and she would halt in the darkness, listening to his hurrying footsteps. She would slump against him relieved beyond words at the sob of their bodies coming together, melt for the first time. Forever. Throbbing pained heart against throbbing pained heart. Naked together in their need and helplessness. He would confess without saying a word to the crime that had

101

left mother and father trapped at the top of the rotting stairs. She would proffer her guilt, cool balm to his burning. Her stiff sin of denial. Unnail the dark boards in which she had neatly coffined her heart. Everything fallen away except the small, vital heat of their embrace.

He stopped on the second floor landing. Muffled voice of a white man imprisoned in an electric box leaked through the thin door of 2 C. Wilkerson would not send her name booming down the stairwell. If at all he would drop it lightly, a crumpled piece of paper spinning. But not even that. He could not call and he knew he would go no farther. He had not seen the woman outside his parents' apartment. Perhaps it was not Tanya. She hadn't answered when he cried out her name. He had been looking at his father's face when his mother had spoken. *She's standing there.* But he was caught by his father's expression. Father's face for an instant utterly empty, emotion gone, features gone, opaque as eyeglasses glazed by the sun. No face at all. Or every grin, grimace, leer, frown, twist, convulsion the face had ever known suddenly reappearing, present simultaneously in a blur of time collapsed and exploding, his father recapitulated from fetus to reeling Sweetman. Face unlined or the horrible blankness of infinite scars creasing the skin, face is the sum of all contortions forced upon it from the first day. The plane of his father's face a frontier, available this instant in a way it had never been before, something beyond it beckoning, real, accessible if the first step would be negotiated. A wildness and peace, a still center in the hurricane's eye. Your father is a door. You may, if you dare, walk through his face, his life, what he is; what is unimaginable will be revealed.

The smell of death is all that clings to your father's eyes as they return to his face. They had been so far away, in South Carolina, and Washington, D.C., on Okinawa, in Chicago and Pittsburgh, cane sweetness, steel stink, gunsmoke and bulldozers piling the cords of corpse wood. Pungent women, soap, beer, gin, cornbread and sweet potato pie, a black breast soothing its swollen nipple on his lips.

Gone so long the eyes limp back to his father's face and the other features marshal meekly in their places. The face of a drunken, confused man of fifty-five returns. Frontier closes as his lips cluck on a swallowed curse. As death reeking eyes travel to the door *Thomas. The door's open. She's standing there.* And my eyes lose his, unlinking clumsily, giddy, the way I'd feel when he set me on the floor after spinning me in his arms. I hadn't seen Tanya there. I might be chasing anyone in this darkness. I'll run up behind a perfect stranger and she'll scream *murder, rape* and doors will open, people will laugh and throw bottles or she'll kick me in my groin, clawing with long fingernails.

If it had been a stranger at the door, hesitating only to be entertained by the ruckus, then Tanya may still be on her way. If I wait I will meet her. I should have waited outside the building, anyway. Escort her up the stairs at least, even though she'd let me know I had reneged on part of our arrangement for the evening. Meeting here on the second floor would seem co-incidental. An accident which it almost is. Chasing a phantom Tanya I bump into the real one. She might like the irony, the story I could fabricate. So I'll wait here. Make her laugh. Then the lie about dinner. Why we have to change our plans and eat with my family another time. But she will know I'm lying. But I will let her know I know that she knows I am lying. A necessary and half admitted lie. One I am asking her not to believe, but to honor, respect.

I am standing in the guts of a huge machine. Behind each door energy is being generated by the friction of black bodies. I can hear them bumping and rubbing. I hear the low purr, the white voices from another dimension which by subtle magic orchestrate the movement in the rooms. My people are laughing and crying. Radios and television sets giggle at their antics. The building trembles. Through my shoes I can feel molecules unstable, shifting. Something not me leaks through the soles of my new black shoes and becomes part of the doomed structure. The building begins to rain on my shoulders, and the something which is now obviously a crucial part of my being rains down, and black people shredded by futile motions behind their thin doors join the rainfall. I am breathing dust. The engines I hear are grinding flesh and bone. Gray pink powder sticks in my throat. A vast crematorium, slow, plodding, but foolproof. Lights go out one by one in the stairwell. Not sleeping but emptied of cargo, of fuel. Dust of my parents floating past my eyes. Perhaps Tanya's. Perhaps my own.

She's not coming. Or has been here and will never return. Perhaps she could have saved us. A chill to ease the burning.

Urge is to smash the doors. Pull the tongues from the lying machines. Tell them to go, to get out before it's too late. Go. Go, brother. While the front door's still open. While there are still no barricades and sentries, while the Man is content to strangle your dreams, while he is too busy with the yellow men to ring your bodies with steel. One door after another kicked down. Like gunshots echoing. Fourth of July, Bastille Day, Dien Bien Phu, the message loud and clear. Shatter the silver screens, cut the plugs, join me battering down the doors. Ray Charles singing "Unchain My Heart."

Tanya will hear the tumult. Return. Lead with her laser eyes and iron will. Beside me. Mounting to the top floor. Take them in our arms. Away.

He did not want to be seen lurking on the shadowy landing. A door cracked, breathing yellow into the hall. Someone was leaving and voices crowded the front of an apartment, vaguely excited, loud enough and close enough so they passed through the walls. Wilkerson could hear their words clearly. Milton promising to come back later. Bring a taste after he made a little run. Laughter. Wilkerson exploded like a sprinter. Quickly gliding through the slice of light. On his tiptoes until halfway down the last flight of stairs.

Part

2

WILLIE HALL watched the brown body rise, the powerful legs scissor-kick in midair, the explosive force which had launched the player diffuse to graceful control of body and ball as the leap ended in a glide to the basket, the shrug of the net as the basketball fluttered down bouncing onto the court like an echo to the shooter's contact with the asphalt. The player's momentum had carried him beyond the goal and landing in a crouch on the balls of his feet, he spun, barely glancing over his shoulder to record the ripple of the net, the ball's clean drop through it, before he loped back down court to defend the opposite basket.

Besides two teams on the court both sides of the playground were lined with players waiting a turn. Littleman knew the role of this chorus. How their signifying and cheering could whip up the action. How reputations were made and dismantled as the bystanders with the words and noises they made participated in the game. There were no passive spectators. Within the area enclosed by the cyclone fencing everyone's blood was up. Even at a distance Littleman could sense the energy, could feel the rhythm of the game tighten his own chest, accelerate his heartbeat. Littleman thought of gut bucket jazz, of the sound of the ocean as sudden pauses in the game would be marked by a crescendo of angry voices, deep, male voices disputing a foul or an out of bounds. To a stranger the anger would seem violently out of proportion, four pairs of sweat drenched bodies immobile while a wiry, barechested player in red trunks with at least three pairs of sweat socks taped high on his calves, bands of color just below the knotty muscle, has the ball under his arm and is stomping toward the sidelines. A bearded taller figure whose star studded jersey is soaked dark, deep blue in a bib-like yoke beneath his chin mimics the other's walk, stalking behind him bending to his ear to narrate a version of the foul. Both turn flamboyantly on cue and parade to the center of the court where red trunks, unconvinced but wearied by the other's teasing monologue, slams the ball high off the asphalt.

–That's the last fucking thing you're getting. I ain't giving up shit else.

The game resumes. Splat of the ball dribbled, grunts and yells as the players jostle for position under the backboards, work themselves free for shots and passes. An older player, chunky, bearded, head shaven clean bulls his way through the lane for a lay-up. A lean, black boy guarding him springs high, his hand at least a foot above the rim, but all he can do is slap his palm against the metal backboard because the other's shot has already looped around his flailing arm and ricocheted through the goal. The entire standard, orange rim, steel poles, the perforated metal backboard continue to shudder after the action has passed. Littleman liked the way the thick, yellowish man had made his move. No waste of energy. Everything for go, nothing for show. The man was past walking on air, past the rubber legged dunking and pinning shots on the backboard which made the gallery squeal, hoot and shake their heads. But the man knew the game. How to conserve his strength, how to use his bulk to offset the spring of long muscled jumping jacks he contested for rebounds. A kind of fluid inevitability when he drove for the basket. He was going to get his no matter how high the others jumped, no matter what impossible refinements their skills brought into the game.

Sunday morning, barely ten thirty, but the sun was already high and the court crowded. A rainbow of colors, jerseys advertising high schools, churches, hamburger shops, real estate agencies, garages, clubs, colleges, a few emblazoned with pro or semi-pro names, but dominating these was the spectrum of flesh tones from dull ivory to glistening black, the wet muscles highlighted by brilliant sunlight. Littleman wondered how they had survived, the sleek muscles, the strength, the pride, how did it bloom again and again, how were these men so real, so richly full of life. Where did it hide the six days a week they were trapped in the decaying city? How did the vigor, the beauty disguise itself, how did these men slip into the nonentity, the innocuousness demanded of them as they encountered the white world. Black men playing basketball. Less than half of them were high school or college athletes. Most had to be classed as dishwashers and janitors or men who carried mail, men who scuffled to make ends meet for themselves and their families. Yet here they were. Playing this game the way it should be played. Sunday in the playgrounds as far away from this earth as the sanctified people in the storefront churches just down the block, singing and shaking their way to glory.

Willie Hall forgot for a moment why he was here. Relaxed into the game.

The man was coal black and dripping with sweat. He had stolen a pass and streaked away from the others, the ball pushed in front of him in long, exaggerated dribbles so he seemed to be chasing it although his fingertips expertly controlled its speed and direction. He must have heard the footsteps of the pack behind him, but he never looked back. Not a question of eluding his opponents. The breakaway lay-up was his to score. Only a matter of how he would do it, how much imagination he could bring to bear, how much style in the execution, which laws of gravity, momentum, which human limits he would deny. Aside from striped Adidas sneakers and white cut-away shorts, his skin, chiseled by sun and moisture was naked. Lip of the rim hung ten feet from the ground but he propelled his six feet and inches toward it, ball cradled in one wrist and palm, soaring till his fingers atop the ball stretched over the basket and jammed the prize home.

Somebody did the bugaloo. Somebody said *Shit yeah*. Another brought both hands down in a sweeping arc to slap the upturned palms of somebody saying *Do it Darnell*.

Willie Hall knew why he was not jealous. He felt his crippled legs high stepping up an invisible ladder toward the sun. Thrust, parry, thrust. Give one. Get it back. You just had to say ooowhee when a nigger got it all together nice as that.

Littleman heard Wilkerson's voice before he felt the hand on his shoulder.

—Lots of talent out there. It's a damn shame. With a decent break lots of those guys might have been college players or even pros.

—Too good for that. Wilkerson would not know what he meant but Littleman turned from the game saying no more.

—A good day for our talk. I like to walk on days like this.

—Let's walk toward the river then. Down Lombard then back up South. I like the contrast. Primes the anger.

—You mean black and white.

—At least that. Always that but I can be a little more specific in this case about what bothers me. Littleman was moving in his peculiar shuffling gait as he talked, tap and shuffle along the pavement, a pace Wilkerson could match with a casual saunter. Sounds of the game faded. Stillness. Then bells of nearby church steeples. To the left, visible beyond the fenced-in vacant lots which marked newly leveled areas destined for urban renewal, the historic buildings, Independence Hall, the Mint, had been cleaned and restored.

—See all this. Littleman's finger jabbed at the elegant red and white of the monuments, the expensive facades of the town houses lining Lombard.

—Marble, concrete, stone, brick. Money and tradition. Look at this and remember what's over there, just through these walls. Not even a hundred yards away. People are insane. Two hundred years and they haven't learned a goddamn thing. They want to rebuild a lie. Colonial architecture. They want to hide their heads in the sand. Don't they know it didn't work in the eighteenth century and it surely won't now. They want the Enlightenment, the Age of Reason, as if they don't know what those delusions cost, who paid for their leisure and elegance. How many black bodies were cast into the sea to finance what these damn merchants call culture.

–Look around us, Wilkerson. I wish I could teach every black boy on South Street what I see. We can't let them do it again. Order, right reason, the white man just under God at the apex of creation. The buildings foursquare, proportioned, what they call classic because they think they are reproducing the harmony of dead Greeks. Divinely ordained order. History, progress stopping dead because they believe they have all the answers. Fountains and squares and columns, the best of all possible worlds. Sublime order. Everything, everybody in its place. That's what they dream. What they thought they planted beside the water. So they preserve these remnants of the eighteenth century, have an urge to produce an exact replica of every error and misconception. What should a black man feel walking down this street, the Liberty Bell almost close enough to spit on, the fat, ugly boats full of money laying down there in the Delaware. What should he think when he knows about South Street over the other shoulder. South Street giving the lie to every promise, every pretension of the architecture the city is restoring. On South Street you see what really happened. Here is where it began, what they wished might happen, but there is reality, the twisted guts, the filth, the million ways to be crushed. South Street like a sewer to drain off what they don't want over here.

More bells tolling, taking into themselves chunks of the silence and liberating a sound which accented the stillness. Steeples poking above the huddled masses of row houses, an occasional church gray and isolated framed by the emptiness around it. White fencing like that cordoning the demolished city blocks closed the end of the street on which the men walked. Below them a muddy slope spilled down to Front Street, Front the broad, dilapidated perpendicular to Lombard, across which a fringe of low buildings and rusted machinery edged the sluggish river. Nothing moved. They

111

leaned on the fence at least two minutes before a car rattled along the wide, potholed roadway. Littleman spread his fingers on the two by four railing. The river could not reflect the clear blue of the sky. In spite of sunshine the scene before him could be painted with browns and grays. Even the few cars picking their way over gulleys, humps and the railroad tracks that intersected the street were dully nondescript.

–It must have been beautiful country once. Littleman had returned to the pavement and moved toward South Street.

–I mean with all the trees and water. When everything was clean. Like when it was just river and forest and hill and valley and nothing had a name. If we were fighting for some of that, I'd feel better. Sometimes it's damned hard getting excited about winning a piece of this action. Not much left besides the money they made selling the land. I guess that's why so many just want out. A new start somewhere else. But I'm not sure what they'd do. I mean would our people kill the animals and trees and pour cement over Africa. Is power always just a rope nobody can play with too long before they hang themselves. You think about these things, don't you, Wilkerson. I need you because there is this silly ass part of me always wants to sit back and observe, do nothing but talk and think. A part that's past caring about anything.

–I know what you're talking about. Sometimes I think there's nothing to me but the part you're describing. What goes on inside my head, just because it's the head of Thomas Wilkerson becomes more important than anything else. The worse kind of selfishness.

–It's not the selfishness that hangs me up. Who am I. What I am. I'm smart enough to see much more to despise than to fall in love with. I'm not afraid of loving myself. My mind worries me because I can't trust it. It's lazy and preening. And because those things are unacceptable to me, my mind has learned to deceive. Put me in a trick every time. I used to write a lot. Writing cleaned me out. Cleared the bullshit.

112

But it takes too much time. I know what's important to me and writing is an extravagance I can't afford. But I still have to get the words out or they'd spin around and spin around and give my mind no peace.

—I can listen.

—Yes, I know damned well you can listen. You're a gentleman, you can listen till I'm tired of talking.

—And gentlemen are buttholes, right.

—Don't get salty. I was paying you a kind of compliment. What's out here. What kind of world are we in now. We've crossed the barricades. South Street stretches far as you can see. This street means they are killing us, whittling away day by day, a man, a woman, a baby at a time. And most of us just sitting on our asses waiting our turn. If you see this and understand this, doesn't it become obvious that we're all mad. The killers for killing and the victims for letting themselves be killed. That's the total picture. Now to be called a gentleman ain't half bad. I mean a gentleman's a pig, and he's crazy like the others are crazy but at least he hasn't murdered with his own hands, at least he's not dead yet. In an insane world those are not small blessings. You're an ostrich with your yellow ass sticking up in the air but for the moment nobody's after it and maybe you can even believe your head will find something down there in the sand.

—You're beside me walking and talking. What's that make you?

—Makes me sick if you really want to know. Makes me weak and sick. Right now the best I can do, the only way I can walk calmly through the pillage and the dying is to believe I have an answer. To believe that on a specific day, just a few months from now these filthy walls are going to crumble, and we'll be able to stand where we are and see a cleansed plain, this scab of a city peeled back so air can get to the wounded land.

—And then.

—Then I would prefer to be among the dead.

—A martyr.

–No, you're trying to make me sound silly. I wouldn't even want to be a memory because it won't be a time for memories.

–Do you believe anyone would have the strength to start all over if the new day, the emptiness ever really comes.

–Shit. That's the kind of thinking I want to get rid of. I don't need to think about then. Look at what's here. How real it is. Don't you remember what you saw a few minutes ago. Brick and stone and money and marble. All that's still there. You can peek through these ruins and get a glimpse. Let's think about now. About what ails now. Let's make sure this won't be here tomorrow. Then let tomorrow take care of itself.

They were past the wholesale shops, the seven day a week hustlers that congregated at the river end of the street. Through this gauntlet of merchants, then a strip of specialty shops, natural foods, nostalgic junk, arts and crafts galleries catering to the young white people who wore their hair long and the frontier clothes of their ancestors. Bunting stretched over the street and archly lettered signs proclaimed a renaissance. Storefronts were relatively cheap and the whites who felt themselves bohemians, outcasts were attempting to establish an islet of sanity, an oasis which would nurture their life styles here between the businessmen and the troubled black sea. Wilkerson wanted to linger. Stand in front of the displays of painting and photography, handle the trinkets, smell leather, incense, perfumed candles, but Littleman tugged at his sleeve.

–These people are fools. They'll be the first to die. And all this crap they're making, all the bullshit they're talking will go up in smoke. When Hitler and his boys decided to clean up a country, do you know who caught just as much hell as the Jews? Gypsies. The rootless, the transient, the people who had cut their ties and roamed the country trying to mind their own business. These people were automatically criminals. And machine guns were judge, jury and executioner every time the Nazis found a flock. Shit. If black people don't kill these babies their own people will come and root them out. And the smart ones among them must understand. They know they're lambs waiting for the slaughter. Yet they bring their women and children here and whine about love.

–At least they're doing something they want to do. And some are producing beautiful things.

–Look closer. Nothing but crap. Do you think they really want to be down here with the niggers. Do you believe they want to live in these old roach traps and wear raggedy ass clothes and eat shit. Do you think this is what they really want and are happy to be here. Shit. They want what everybody else wants and as soon as most of them get kicked in the ass enough times, as soon as they spend a winter with no heat and stand for days in clinic lines waiting to get the rot cleaned out of their bellies and off their skins, soon as they find out what this nigger street means they'll fold up their tents and slink on back to being white.

–Now we're home. Just a few steps, and, shit, we came the long way, just a few steps and we're on the other side of the moon. Do you believe it, Wilkerson, do you believe we've stood for this shit as long as we have. Jesus fucking Christ. If you listen, you can hear niggers dying around us.

–And you think we can change this.

–Are you still so unconvinced? Why is it so much easier for you to doubt than believe?

–You said you wanted to talk. That's why I got up and met you this morning. Why we're here. So you must think there's more I should know. More convincing to do. I'm not like you. I can't speak to crowds, I have no grandiose plan for the future. I have no desire to lead anyone. Hard enough getting myself together.

–I have to get you ready, baby. Get you ready. But you won't be ready till you believe the plan. All the talk in the world can't get you to believe. I can tire you out, but I can't force you to believe. I knew better than to make the mistake the white man has. He had us weary and exhausted, beat down as far down as down goes, but that didn't mean we had accepted his lies. I'm ready to begin talking to you about details. How we kidnap the cop. How we stage the main event in the streets. For me it's just a matter of putting the pieces together. The plan is whole, real, imminent. I'm concerned with incidentals. With making the parts happen, with making you real.

—You believe we can do it.

—Do you believe what we're seeing this morning? How simple and concrete everything is. Do you see the next step? How vulnerable the lies are that hold this mess together as it stands. Do you realize how we have all the evidence we need to expose the lies, to shatter the arbitrary balance and order. Nothing but an alley between two alien forms of life. The whites are just a few paces away living in a manner which makes a mockery of our suffering. Two people in a fifty thousand dollar town house, eight or ten rooms to stockpile the loot they've acquired. And babies on this street sleeping in drawers, on the floor, in the same bed with their mother and whatever man's come to help her through the night. It's an alley we can cross, we can cross in numbers. Nothing in the world can stop us if we decide the barrier is not there anymore. If we all die at least the lie will die with us. When have we ever risen up as a people, united, resolved ready to die together. Never, never once in our pitiful history. A sane man looking at us from the outside would wonder what is so precious in our miserable lives that we cling to them in spite of hundreds of years of degradation.

—We must strike and strike so desperately that our example is stronger than the lie. We must say No, you cannot define us, you cannot set the limits. No, the flunkies you pay to keep us within bounds are not enough. We must show how the cops are symbolic. How they are too few and how these few can be made to disappear. We will lynch one man but in fact we will be denying a total vision of reality. It's been easy for them too long. Some are almost convinced they understand us, some believe we are transparent, that they can kill a nigger or beat a nigger and scare the rest out

116

of fighting back. Some think they can toss us a few coins and fill our heads with dreams of catfish and watermelon. So many books, so much talk, so many experts and explanations. And they're all right because they're all wrong because what they see is what they have created, what they want to see. The plan begins by sweeping aside what is past. When we lynch the cop we declare our understanding of the past, our scorn for it, our disregard for any consequences that the past has taught us to fear. We also deny any future except one conditioned by new definitions of ourselves as fighters, free, violent men who will determine the nature of the reality in which they exist. Or die in the attempt. There won't be a South or a South Street for these new men. They won't be taught to bow before the symbols of their humiliation. A Liberty Bell, a white hand holding the keys to the kingdom. When did the bell ring. Who did it ring for. I was on a boat while their liberty bells were ringing. All I heard were pipes and whistles calling us on deck to exercise, the rattle of chains when we danced, the life buoys pealing in a foggy harbor three thousand miles from my home. The auctioneer ringing a bell so the buyers could stampede into the pens and look at our dicks and teeth. And I've been listening ever since. To bells and bullshit.

As if Littleman demanded their noise to punctuate his speech the antique bells clanked and gonged, floating over the littered corridor of South Street, hanging like a rainbow of sound into which the black churches sent up their tithe of bell music, tambourines, organ, drum and piano or just the rejoicing voices of the saints in the storefront houses of worship Wilkerson and the crippled man strolled by.

—Wilkerson, the plan's as simple as death. When one man kills it's murder. When a nation kills murder is called war. If we lynch the cop we will be declaring ourselves a nation. Only two responses to our action are possible. They must attack us or back off and either way they must recognize our sovereignty. Since the total community gives its sanction in a lynching, mass retaliation, undifferentiated slaughter of community members is the only suitable punishment and

117

that means in effect a declaration of war, an acknowledgment of the separateness of the community. If a white woman was molested or a slave struck his master and ran away, the South reacted by killing any niggers who happened to be handy. No question of justice, of catching the offender. All black men were responsible and the rules of war meant all were guilty. Now suppose after we lynch the cop they attempt another kind of action. No retaliation at all. The symbolism of our act is too obvious to be ignored. In fact if they don't declare war, they are accepting the rightness, the validity of our rejection of their lies. They are saying yes you are a nation and we accept the truth of your nationhood, your right to establish your own law and justice. Yes, our soldier was an outlaw when he crossed into your territory. Either way our community becomes defined, becomes separate. No half measures will be possible. We are incorporating their understanding of history and power into our plan. We are saying crystally clear in the language they invented: We are your equals. Accept that or go to war. No more pussyfooting. No more slow attrition of our best men. No more battles in which only one side is allowed to fight.

—As simple as death. But you're not ready yet because you're afraid to die. You think of dying as some complicated trip with millions of arrangements to be made before you go. Most people are like you. But I've been alone a long while. I understand how easy it is to disappear absolutely from the face of the earth. You don't owe anyone anything and nobody wants to go with you. You just go. Men, races, trees, bugs, rocks. Here and gone. So we get hung up in this little squabbling between black and white, a fight over land that's going to be worthless very soon. A struggle so goddamn wearying that we forget how arbitrary it is, how irrelevant to larger movements, the flow of history in and out of this moment. We talk around the solitary issue at stake. We avoid putting the whole mess in terms of life or death. They know that, they know we prefer the worst they can do to death. We think they own death because they have bombs and soldiers and cops and rope. Every black man carries a fear of death in his heart, a fear of death at the hands of white men. Each is isolated by his fear of death. It's that terror we must release our people from. But first I must carve it out of you. What is anything worth if you've given up to others the single significant choice, the choice which proves something has value. It's not much but we all have it. The decision to make some arbitrary event or choice worth your life. Can you die for the plan. Can you be prepared at any moment to forfeit your life to the plan. The plan must be worth your death and if necessary a million others. What's at stake is blood, and we must let them know clearly, precisely that we mean business. We must teach them the blunt, blind energy of the plan. But first we must believe. We must radiate belief, glow with it like avenging angels.

Littleman nodded at the men around the ramshackle shoe-shine stand. Six or seven sitting and standing, exiles from another planet huddling close to the wreckage of the elaborate machine which had dropped with them from the heavens. They projected confusion, their eyes and hands moved at the wrong speed, evidence of a subtle deterioration of hidden, vital organs. Sucking on bottles of sweet soda pop, chewing candy bars. Two had climbed onto the platform and occupied the customers' seats. The jaunty angle of the goosenecks on which their feet rested exposed the raggedy soles of their shoes. The men luxuriated under a glossy picture of crisply blue Mediterranean sky and the peaches and cream curves of a naked blonde stretched on white sand, under the shade of a patchwork overhang, under the crumbling brick and gouged windows of a ruined building, under a hazy blue sky through which shafts of sunlight smoked.

• • •

Its cyclops eye bloodshot and spinning, the squad car hovered outside the entrance of Woodrow Wilson Junior High School. Donohue and Harkness listened impatiently to

119

the long string of sputtering static emitted from their two way radio. They glanced stiffly at one another and at the dark watches on thick straps circling their wrists. The windows were up and the air inside oppressive. Air conditioned patrol cars were part of the new law and order bond issue stalled while city hall politicians played both ends against the middle. Sometimes, cruising in this section of the city, Donohue felt he was an astronaut orbiting alone beyond the earth. He felt the astronaut's profound detachment from all things familiar and real, a growing bitterness and fear at being deserted amid the cold immensity of the stars. Only a metal shell between himself and extinction. That his partner sat beside him offered no consolation. In fact Harkness impinged upon his privacy, the necessary, final privacy that would allow a last wallow in tears, farts and blasphemy when Donohue finally knew without a doubt that his mission was unsuccessful, that he would never return.

Though other red cars and personnel carriers, each with its team of special riot commandos were stationed around the school, Donohue could not shake the dreadful sense of isolation intimidating him. He was a defensive safety alone in the hinterlands of the immense stadium bowl, waiting for the streaking ends to attack his position. Where the blue of his uniform creased against vinyl upholstery, cool rivers of sweat drained down his back. And the weight of the gun at his waist. Foreign as the creep of some other man's erection against his thigh. At times he believed he would bring on a hernia if he tried to lift the revolver from its sheathing.

His eyes sought Harkness. He wanted to ask him if he was afraid. But Donohue could only concentrate on the harsh angle of his partner's nose, the bird's profile and thick, black eyebrows. Harkness whose cheeks always looked like they had been sanded shiny after a clumsy razor dug out each whisker. Moonscape. Donohue could not admit fear. His mission was after all beyond fear; he had contracted to operate in a void where humanity with its doubts and fears was the first thing left behind. If he confessed to fear, he would be compromised. All the power that had focused to rocket him into this foreign sphere would be sacrificed to his weakness. He would plummet back toward earth, farther than any man had ever fallen. Cremated in an instant by the same laws of energy and momentum that had been harnessed to place him where he sat, safe for the moment, uncomfortable but secure within the steel capsule.

A voice crackled from headquarters. Waiting was over. The normal pull of gravity was restored. His limbs lost their granite monumentality, slid easily onto the pavement. Boots sent up pleasant shivers through his shins, buoyed him with steady crunching assurance at each stride. *Get the crazy black dwarf off the fucking school steps.*

White helmeted, eyes invisible behind thick sun tinted visors, wearing superfluous gas masks with long wrinkled snouts curling like a nightmare incarnation of the word shouted by the crowd of children, the police moved purposefully, businesslike into formation. A wedge of bodies, indistinguishable one from the other, incredibly obscene in their mirror sameness and identical gaits, the spawn of some amuck geneticist spilling from laboratory vats onto the city street, unreal in the sunlight, threatening in the way ranks of lead soldiers threaten, stiffly alike with their grotesquely painted faces and right legs suspended in the air forever.

They marched, an overgrown wind-up toy, scattering the audience that had ranged itself on the front steps of Wilson Junior High to hear the man who now stood alone, framed between corinthian columns ornamenting the building's ponderous facade. Brown, bearded figure at whose heart point of the wedge seemed aimed, statue rigid, a puny Samson whose arms could not stretch between the false columns, could not bend them inward and topple the temple upon his mechanical tormentors.

The arrow reached him. Its point blunted as the speaker flailed his cane like a scythe about him. Two policemen fell who had underestimated the strength half a man could retain in his stunted body. Speaker striking with fury, waist high, blasting the truncheons back against unarmored blue bellies. Desperate with rage and impotence, ringed by blows, the dwarf crashed his cane down on the cushioned steel helmet of patrolman Donohue, who lay crumpled on the cold stone, wind slapped from his guts by an earlier blow of the cane now splintering harmlessly on his gleaming headpiece.

Those who had detached themselves from the rear rank of the phalanx and had stood with shotguns cocked, some aimed at the brief melee and the others sighted down the steps at the screaming children, rejoined their comrades. Nearly as perfect as it had mounted the steps, the formation descended. If there were wounds or blood, they were not apparent. Only to one on his knees peering into the center of the wedge would a few faltering legs of the centipede be visible, and the dull sparks of metal scraping stone. Sparks from the braces of the little man dragged lifeless from the rally.

• • •

Willie Hall had never been able to explain to himself why he came to the seashore resort. The city was a place where people displayed their bodies, and it was with something less than enjoyment that he exposed his crippled legs to the sun. Night life was plentiful. The bars shoulder to shoulder on a long stretch of Arctic Avenue, then the gleam of Kentucky Avenue with its fanciest Club Harlem and satellite, almost as expensive joints, and finally scattered at the city's edges roadhouses from plush to honky tonk. But bars, restaurants, traveling shows that filled the huge barn of Convention Hall with every sort of hustler and hick imaginable were definitely not what attracted Willie Hall since he could barely afford to drink through a two day weekend in the cheap gin holes that he frequented. Though it was surrounded by architecture that compounded the uglinesses of ostentation, parsimony and greed, though rashers of bodies baking in the sun were a fleshy barricade through which he had to hobble to touch it, perhaps the sea was why he took the bus to Atlantic City the two long weekends a month his job allowed.

Willie Hall strolling on the boardwalk. Metallic wheeze of his armored legs slow shuffle, tap of his cane on the wooden promenade. Scowling above the leonine beard. As if the sun perpetually in his eyes.

Willie Hall drawn to the sea. He prefers night vistas, alone, staring outward into blackness. There is no horizon, no time. From nowhere dull gleam of breakers dancing into being. Steady pounding, a pulse, a giant steel ball slamming into the meat of the sand. Booming and walls crashing around him, city laid waste, crumbling to dust, luminous shivers rising, walking the black depths into which he peers. Willie thinks of his fist smashed into the purple of his palm, the silence of his cell shattered as blow after blow strikes, his arm a piston, rhythmic, tireless, the sea beating the land, his heart beating, the wings of some gloriously colored bird relentlessly ascending, fanning with its beating wings the smouldering city below.

Wrapped in chains the squat shape worked its way from the water toward the boardwalk. Moony night. In the shadows and needle light it could have been a sea creature, swift and sure in its native habitat, but hopelessly unwieldy in the damp sand. A walrus. A snail. All sense of proportion gone where sea and land come together under the moon.

He is grunting or singing tunelessly to himself. Barely audible above the water's roar. Seabeast keening for its lost element. A gospel song dim in recollection. Willie repeated the same few words again and again, varying the lyrics by modulations in the tune, faster and slower, deep or rising, imitation of crude instruments taking up the melody, or the notes passed in steps from dark bass to high wailing of the deep breasted women. To a listener all the richness of Willie's memory would be an embarrassingly inadequate

123

attempt at whistling or singing, but for the man groping from sea to shore, country people in a country church he could revive only with these snatches of words and music, these uneven mumblings of song were all the family, the home, the child's glow of peace and innocence he had ever known.

Willie stopped when he realized he was not alone. After the figure had taken a few more steps he realized it was a woman. Long bare legs, a loose wind blown dress. She continued toward him so steadily he thought she must not have noticed him yet. Night on a deserted beach and she was a woman alone, him a strange man. A wave of resentment was hot in his throat. Perhaps she saw him all too well. Broken man, tethered to braces and cane. Barely as high as her chin. Why should she fear him? Then he wanted to hurt her. Remain concealed in whatever pocket of shadow he stood. Leap out and strike her down with the leaded cane. Pin her body to the sand. A man taking what he wished.

Her voice was husky in the night air. Morning voice stiff in its first venture at words.

—A beautiful night isn't it brother. Of all the fucking things to say Willie thought to himself on this beach in the middle of the night. Of course what else would make more sense. Is there anything at all to say to a little cripple bastard you just happen to meet on a beach nobody supposed to be on anyway after 10:00 P.M. if you can read the signs posted everywhere.

—My name is Angela.

She's trying to make it easy. Legs ain't so skinny up close. Her face in the moonlight modeled in broad planes, like the face of an eroded statue, its painted eyes plucked by the birds, its features superfluous to strong harmony of bones, of contour and volume, firmly suggesting the skull for which flesh is ornament and glaze. She was handsome reduced to these elemental patterns. A strength of line, a fullness in her face. Willie Hall imagined his appearance in the dappling moonlight. Beach was a pocked moon crater. Shallow dunes with scalp locks of coarse grass, the amputated humps of an army of dwarfs just like him. But his shoulders sloped clean, his arms could even be said to ripple from his polo shirts. Her eyes were on him he was sure, but he couldn't see the downward cast he hated so much when women looked at him. Perhaps there, but mercifully obliterated by the night. For the first time since he had begun his night walk he felt the chill which had gradually and now completely absorbed all the heat of day.

–The hawk's flying. Aren't you cold?

–I don't think so. At least I hadn't been aware of the cold until you spoke. I was sitting up there, under the awning where they store rental chairs and umbrellas. It's lower, out of the wind.

–Somebody will shoot you for trying to steal the Man's beach chairs.

–No one can see me from the boardwalk. And nobody ever walks down on the beach this late. If they would, they could pass a foot away and not see me snuggled in one of my cozy lounge chairs. It's a place where I can be sure I'll be left alone. Me and the sea. And I get a kick out of thirking that I'm using those two twenty-five an hour daytime luxuries as long as I wish for free.

–But now I know your secret.

–We're even. I peeked at you when I knew I shouldn't be looking. You stood by the water a long time. And I sensed that you wanted to be alone. Thought you were alone.

Willie Hall smiled to himself. Asked himself was concealing his expression necessary in this half light. He was thinking of all the times he had ended his night staring at the sea by taking a hearty, long winded piss into the waves. He hadn't felt the urge tonight, but wondered what the girl would have thought if she had peeked at that particular finale to the ritual. He wished that he had pulled it out. Shown her from a distance the healthy ramrod of his manhood. A stiff, strong dick. Functioning as well as that of any seven foot basketball player. But the clumsy preparation for such a simple act. What if she had witnessed that.

His three legs carefully balanced in the wet sand so a free arm could liberate his pisser. Fear always in his mind that he would begin to topple, steel and wooden tripod failing him and uncontrollable stream spurting everywhere as his hands go out instinctively to brace his fall. Memory of the days before he turned his rubbery legs into muscle he could sometimes depend upon, when he had to sit like a woman on a pot.

–You watched me.

–It was so strange to see someone here. I've come often and never a soul. I decided I would just get in your way. Risk saying something. Even if you were annoyed. Or walked away.

–Or worse.

–There's worse?

–There are people who kill and maim. Who live to hurt. Werewolves at the full moon. Frankenstein monsters.

–They don't act like you were acting.

–They don't look at the sea.

–Not here and now. The sea calms people at night, doesn't it? I mean if you came full of anger or anything doesn't the water make those feelings much smaller. It shrinks everything.

–If I were looking for loonies I think I might come here first. Madmen have a thing for water and the moon.

–Do you think so?

–I think you are a strange girl.

–Because I like the sea? I get lost when I come here. I mean so much of it rolling in, always rolling in. When I sit in my hideaway, it's like I'm a little baby sleeping only I'm awake and can enjoy every minute of it. That's why it seemed so right to approach you. You were part of the feeling I had. You were something like a dream I could get up and speak to. She was closer. If he extended his arm, he could tap her on the shoulder with his cane. One step forward and he could bring her to her knees with a sudden blow, swoop down and circle her with arms she could not resist. A dream from which she would not awaken.

126

Sea chill. Black water lapping at black land. White bones glowing.

–My name is Willie, Willie Hall. He did not add that everybody back in the city knew him as Littleman. That most if asked could not say what his given name was. He tried to smile, forget the darkness, the sea voices shouting *Littleman, Littleman*.

–Willie. I wouldn't have guessed, Willie, but I like it. It's fine. Any name would be fine. Her voice told him she was smiling, maybe even laughing.

He remembered the whore laughing his name. On one of his first excursions to Atlantic City, when he thought he could take pleasure trips like others took them, he had been drunk, hungry for a woman and found a bar where women could be purchased. One had come to the booth where he sat propped, the illusion of a whole man since his braces trailed off into obscurity below the table. She said yes and they got up to go. Outside when he turned to face her she was laughing. Drunk, uncomprehending, he began to laugh too.

–What's your name little fella? He answered mechanically, his name part of the laughter he thought he was sharing with her.

–Willie, huh. Well you's a game little fella, Willie. You had me fooled in the bar. Thought you some big strapping Papa, and I was hot to get turned on myself. You know a lady likes to enjoy her work sometime. Ha. And I was gettin ready for a good one. Out you hobble cane and all. I wondered why everybody looking at me funny when I sat down. Out you hobble and I nearly dropped my drawers. My smooth talking Papa ain't hardly big as a minute. Kiss my ass I say then I can't hardly keep a straight face walking behind you. Signifying Otis back of the bar chessy cat grinning at me. Game little man. Scrambling outa there like you in a real hurry. Into something, I guess you thought. Well, now we out here, you can forget it. Janice ain't for no freak tricks. Straight fucking all this girl gonna do. That's why I stay away from them white boys.

127

—I'll give you all the fucking you want, sister.

—You ain't gonna scrape my knees with all that metal you got wrapped round your legs. You a freak trick, honey, that's all there is to it.

—How much.

—Ain't no how much to it. Go on up the road. You find somebody up the road do what you want.

—I want you. And I can pay. Extra if you want me to help you forget the inconveniences.

They haggled in the alley. Finally compromised on a figure that left Littleman with only bus fare and loose change. She insisted on half of the amount before she took him to her room. He counted out the bills. Lips mouthing the arithmetic she snatched the payment, stuffed it into her bosom and took a step backward.

—You telling me what a badass cocksman you are. Well, if you so bad, catch my black butt and you can have all the pussy you want. Laughing, she backpedaled two long steps, turned and was gone up the alley in a clatter of high heels. He shouted but whiskey slowed his movements. His mind was spinning, unable to sort any pattern from the swirling merry-go-round of images. The whore's fleeing figure, comical like a duck sprinting, broad assed, skinny ankles, big feet in minnie mouse heels, striding tight legged till she tugged her skirt to the middle of her thighs. The echoing laughter. His cane lazily turning in the air, unaimed, jerking itself from his hand and flying of its own volition, a drum majorette's baton end over end till it banged harmlessly into something metallic, missing the woman's back by six feet, but stopping her laughter long enough for *Cripple freaky motherfucker* to be flung over her shoulder.

Her voice full of smiling. Would this one turn and run? Awkward slow motion in the sand then clattering down the boardwalk. Laughing his name. He was close enough to make her pay.

—Would you like to sit with me a while? Under my private awning? In Mr. Charlie's expensive chairs?

128

Sea roar. A hissing progress up the beach toward the greater sheltered darkness where she led him. He could not tell if she moved so slowly because the loose, heavy sand burdened her woman's steps as much as it did his scuttling or if her pace was a way of holding his hand.

•••

Weekends together in July, then the room they shared during August when Willie quit his job to be with her. At first Angela kept her job selling hamburgers eight hours a night in a drive-in restaurant to supplement the few dollars Willie could salvage from his odd jobs. After her shift was held up twice in ten days, Willie had told her to leave the plastic fishbowl with its glowing dome and crackling neon, its propensity for drawing insects and stocking capped bandits from the sultry darkness. He tried looking for steady work but even in a city where swarms of migrant black laborers became bell hops, porters, dishwashers, bus boys only long enough to amass a stake that could pay the back rent or buy new clothes for the boardwalk and bars, or simply extend their season in the sun away from the oppressive cities of the North and familiar dull poverty of the South, where the brown-eyed, lithe college men played a laughing game of musical chairs with the coolie work available to them, swapping jobs, three men alternating in the same position, hired, fired, retired, rehired, by one employer in one week, even here in this carnival city where open jobs popped up like metal ducks in a shooting gallery, Willie Hall was insulted, lied to, pitied, tittered at, ignored when he presented himself as a candidate for work. At five o'clock after confronting countless faces waiting behind the help wanted signs he returned to the hot room at the top of the stairs on Baltic Avenue. Angela lay on the bed sleeping. Her honey colored skin was damp from the heat.

They had been awake almost the entire night before.

Money was just about gone and Willie knew something had to be done; he would have to force himself to meet the mocking, condescending eyes which would stare at him like he was a beggar extending a tin cup. He had been through such interviews a thousand times, heart pounding, dripping with nervous perspiration. Anger so rampant inside that he could barely control his speaking voice. Almost as if their judgment of him, palpable in their eyes and words, forced him into being the helpless stuttering idiot they conceived. No matter how hard he tried his words sputtered, tumbled, bordering on incoherency because his replies were so distant from what he actually felt, who he was. He swallowed pride, independence, surrendered the image of himself as a man infinitely superior to the red cheeked functionaries at the back doors of kitchens, or gum chewing secretaries with piles of spray starched hair who parroted, barely looking up from glossy magazines, "We'll call as soon as something opens up." The dammed eloquence of his indignation made his lips tremble; his tongue heavy as he replied, straining not to be what his guts told him he must be.

The humiliation of the coming day had already begun as he sat on the bed, back against the wall that served as a headboard, naked in the sweltering heat, the lights out, Angela alternately sitting up beside him or curled, curve of her back and buttocks softly awaiting him to cradle his head. But he could not go to her. Sopping wet. Hot night only partially responsible since Angela's skin was cool to his touch. Rancid boiling of his insides that coated his body with sweat. He anticipated walking the pavements, his body dragging beside him, an obscene animal on a chain he could not let go. Voices full of lies sending him down the next street, up an alley, to a vacant lot ten blocks away. He saw the atmosphere wiggling above the asphalt, the chrome and plastic hotels, rising like diseased exhalations of the surface miasma. Even the broken, old men could wheeze comfortably to themselves when he passed *there but for fortune* . . .

Willie knew the next day, could cite intimate details, quote clipped conversations with lackeys who avoided his eyes. He had been there before, was there now as he sat sleepless in the bed he was transforming into a puddle. Angela must be aware of the stink, the rankled nerve sweat, fetid as a rotting tooth. He was on fire with stink and apprehension. Her back was to him, she appeared to be sleeping, but in the stillness he could discern her quiet sobbing. He stroked her bare shoulder and she answered.

–Another planet. You might as well be on another planet. Willie. Do I have to tell you how much I need you now. Do I have to scream loud enough for another world to hear me.

He buried his damp shaggy beard in the floating coolness of her hair. Brutal sobbing racked her body. For a long while they lay just so, the tears he could not loose from the steel that held him together pouring from her eyes. His heavy arms around her, sliding up and down her body, kneading fistfuls of her substance, stealing the symmetry of her long, straight legs to remould the absurd foreshortening of his own. Finally his fingers shaped to the slope of her back he turns her to face him. In a fluid arc her shoulders rise and she is atop him, a jiggling perpendicular straddling, squeezing him in the powerful thrusts of her hips.

The next day had come again. She had walked with him to the head of the stairs naked under a black raincoat. He descended to meet the dragon, was destroyed and now climbed to the room again.

Exhausted by their night, the coupling that had seemed to go on for hours, the dull day waiting alone, she lay on her belly, honey colored skin slightly damp, black hair piled on top of her head. It angered him that she had not pulled the shades. He saw her exposed to the eyes of another man, the secrets of her body shared with a stranger. Late afternoon sun flayed the room of shadow and illusion. He scanned their nest. Wrinkled, graying sheets on which they had thrashed half the night, another swath of soiled linen draping from the bed's bottom corner to the floor. Both sheets smudged with patches of dull yellow. Two rickety cane chairs, one with its seat gnawed away, a tall wooden end table with newspaper wadded under one leg to keep its wobbling at a minimum, a doorless closet where clothes were tossed, hung, piled on boxes and shoes that littered the floor of the shallow recess. Angela's scratchy record player beside the bed, Thelonius Monk spinning crazily at 78 r.p.m. on the turntable, Rachmaninoff leaning against the dusty baseboard. Tone arm was limp, content in its silent repose. Willie Hall examined minutely the nakedness of the woman he had returned to. In the harsh sunlight her skin lost the gold night glow. Almost no colors at all, a yellowish wash, uneven, splotched with darker regions where the skin was not tautly drawn. The curve of her buttocks that had arched rainbow perfect, fruit lush in his guiding hands was faded to mottled, lumpish immobility. Beckoning darkness of cleft and hollow no more mysterious than the yawning closet with its shaggy disarray.

And yet the stirring in his groin. As if a hand had reached down, grasped the sleeping tone arm and sent music irresistibly swelling through its blunt head. The same urgency of the night before. To mount and be mounted. To spend himself, to root out the terror and fear. Change all those things he knew would never change. But more. Not just change himself. He must annihilate the force that slapped them together, stuck man to woman, Willie Hall to Angela. After a day of futile trudging, of voices and eyes dismissing him, he was dizzy with lack of sleep, hunger, need. But he must rouse her. Fight the day again on different terms. Whip what had whipped him.

He pulls the wounded shade. In stages it rattles down, in stages he collapses, steel and flesh on the bed where she is stirring, turning toward him.

—Nothing, he says.

On one elbow, her eyes still hooded, her whole body yielding, soft as the droop of her breast leaning toward him she echoes

—Nothing.

He knows she will always be there. That some things cannot be changed. He will go down the steps tomorrow morning. Surely she will pad behind him, the black coat draped around her she will go as far as the top of the stairs and he will ask the questions all over again.

• • •

He is going down the steep steps. Mr. Jones is coughing, catarrh thick with melted liver and lungs. Deep snores from Sister Rosamond's room. He wonders if his landlady, the widow Mrs. Carter, is sleeping alone or has the cat-eyed slickster from the first floor tiptoed up to pay his rent. Angela still a warm blur clouding his thoughts. Image of her sleepy eyes caressing his back as he creaks down the stairs merges with the spiritual he hums to himself. Song and woman shredded by exploding whirr, iron jaws masticating heaps of garbage tossed in a truck by brown men in brown aprons. The beast screams, its teeth grating and grinding, as if its roar could arouse the men who move drowsily back and forth, automatons on a conveyor belt, between the clutter of cans and the hungry truck. Too early for the drones to speak civilly to each other, they limit their conversation to brief, violent exchanges with the machine, each container of refuse expelled with vicious force to splatter against the rotating iron teeth.

The gospel song hovered, a refrain whose words were repeated endlessly but whose melody danced through infinite variations. Angela's barefoot tread, her face shadowed, looking down into his. Strong bones, counterpoint to the machine's savage rending, complex fugue of sounds receding, struggling for dominance. Whirr of the truck now reinforced by the workers' voices rose finally an insistent monotone absorbing the last scraps of music.

—Let's get this shit together.

—Let's make this run and split.

133

—Woman don't want me gone all day.

—These be heavy mothafuckas first thing in the morning.

—Heavy and stinking.

—I do believe half these cans stuffed with bodies.

—Cheaper than burying.

—We ought to get the checks undertakers get.

—I read in the paper about undertakers joining a meat packers' and canners' union.

—I'd join a beauty parlor union if it would get me more money.

—Union ain't shit. If you're Black stay back. That's how the unions talk. Always have.

—Two kinds of people. Haves and have-nots. Those that have guns and those unprepared to defend themselves. You can forget unions, Naacps, Kings, Kennedys, meetings and marches.

—Union eat you up just like the Man.

—Out in California they have drive-in funeral parlors. Bodies laid out behind big picture windows. You just drive by and pay your respects. Don't even have to get out of the car. Saves dressing and pulling a long face.

—Don't want my dead ass up in no window. Just don't sound right. When I die my soul is God's and the dust supposed to go back to dust. It's a sin laying up in some window.

—Man, when you're gone, you're gone. They could put you in a jar of pickles and you wouldn't know the difference.

—That be some funky jar.

—Jew pickles funky anyway.

—You know, I bet the Man wouldn't hesitate to use dead niggers any way he could.

—Black buck fertilizer. Makes your garden grow.

—You think that's funny. I know in my heart that if somebody proved to the Man's satisfaction a dead nigger was twice as valuable as a live one, in a year or so they'd give out nigger hunting licenses.

—You're crazy.

—The truth is crazy.

134

—Come on, you all, I want to be out of these rags by noon. I got business to take care of.

—Then get your ass outa the truck. Uniondriverass wannabebigshotnigger.

—Lawd, lawd.

—Guns.

—You better believe I got mine.

—It's a sin.

—But do you know how to use it. And why you must learn to use it. Organization. Nothing will work unless the brothers can get themselves organized. That's the white man's secret. It's not leaders. Kill one president and you have fifty more just like him ready to step into the office. Defeat one at the polls or shoot him at breakfast. You just kill a man. It's the total system keeps us down on the bottom. Offices mean organization. You can't shoot an office. That's what the brothers have to learn. Pool our skills. Organize.

—First it was Liberia, then Garveyites, then the Communists, now you have some other half baked system and prophet going to lead us poor, ignorant black folk to the promised land. I got news baby. I'm neither poor or ignorant. I'm doing all right and my children going to do a lot better than me. The Man knows we're here. And he knows we got something going. I know. Don't bother to Tom me. That's your bag. I know where I'm at. I'm not fool enough to wait for somebody to give me something, I'm going to fight and demand. But within the law. I got a son fighting in Asia to defend the law and my rights within it.

—That's the way it has to be.

—Niggers killing Chinks. And proud of it. If you ain't ready for integration I don't know a Kneegrow who is.

—Heave Hucking Ho

—Biff Bam. I got a whole barrel of rotten gizzards and kidneys.

—It sure nuff do stink.

Going to Kansas City
Kansas City, here I come

Song shattered by song. Lead me. Guide me. Along the Way. Lord, if you lead me. I
I will not stray.
                    Lord.   Let   me
                                 Walk
Each day. Each day. Each day.
Hammer blows pounding, pounding. Skull is an echo chamber. Brain cells cannot feel pain, lack sensation. But pressure builds. Numbing, bone splitting. Eyes sees flashes of red, blue. Gleaming egg on the steps. I try to squash it with the cane.

I am sinking. Down. Sinking.

I am dreaming or hallucinating. Nightmare lethargy. I want to move my finger but the pain is unbearable. I think my hand is stirring, but as it shifts slightly on the white shroud it crumbles from my wrist. I am breaking apart. Each effort to revive control costs excruciating pain. A crippling loss.

But I am already a cripple. The deadness below my groin. If they have tortured my body . . .

Have they . . .

Siren returns. I am tossing on the metal floor. Somebody's booted foot on my belly, keeping me in the center of the aisle, between the rows of blue knees. Sometimes he prods and nudges with his steel toe, sometimes the foot under my ribs shoving hard, almost lifting me from the wagon's bed. Urine smell. Slimy runnels in the uneven surface on which I'm stretched. Another foot explodes in my shoulder, its follow through scraping my face. My beard gives stiffly. Matted, wet. I am rolling, bouncing. The feet shuttle me between them. A game. Wrists being slowly severed, pinned behind my back with a bracelet of razors. I cannot move my arms to brush the thick moisture hanging over my eyes, making me almost blind. I see everything through a burning glaze. Sweat, blood, spit. I shut my eyes. Something dribbles down my cheek. Siren spilling over everything.

Then utter quiet. Bright light. I think I can hear the filaments crackling as they cook. I am naked, bathed in sweat. I see a black face. Kind that plays Ethiopian eunuch in hollywood epics. Cannot read his eyes. They are yellow and bloodshot but tell me nothing. Broad nose, thick lips, almost bald. Stripped to the waist. So perfectly black and enigmatic he is perhaps an angel.

–I ain't got an idea how to get these off. Silence is broken by a scream. After the pain passes I realize the scream is in my throat.

–Nigger still has feeling down there. The lips, thick as if in a perpetual pout have not spoken. I see plainly they are the underflesh inverted, perversely displayed. Slack face unreadable as before. Not a quiver of emotion as the words disintegrate.

–Leave him like he is. That'll do for what we want.

Another ride. Only this time within a metaphysical vehicle. Pain. Of course it was my physical body they assaulted, but the senses have their limits. Much of the time I floated beyond these. Metaphysical because the most difficult times were those in which I could contemplate myself as a helpless object of their whims, myself as someone who would have to bear the damage, the scars of the encounter, once, and if I emerged from the torture.

I awakened in a hospital bed. I had been injured in a fall down the steep steps of Woodrow Wilson Junior High while resisting arrest. I had been fomenting a riot. Had instigated an unlawful assembly. I was technically under arrest although a motion for bail had been made and a bond posted which would release me on my own cognizance once I signed the proper papers. I recalled the other signings. Confessions to a thousand crimes I scrawled my name to on demand. I wondered where they were filed. Who I had maimed, murdered, suborned, kidnapped in their depositions. Among the present relevant charges was assault with a deadly weapon, with intent to kill, a police officer.

Today is Saturday. I was surprised that I had lost track of only seventy-two hours, all of which I purportedly spent

137

in a coma in this very hospital bed. For a moment I almost believed them. Was ready to accept the whole pain dream as hallucination until my body began to throb with the nearly unbearable truth of its bruised nerve endings.

–Quite a tumble you took, Mr. Hall.

I didn't say fuck you, you smiling jackass of a white coated fraud. I didn't say I'm going to get you Mr. Doctor and the rest of the hunky bastards who put you up to the lie of a diagnosis you grin at me. I didn't say that or anything else.

–They sure put a whipping on you, didn't they brother. Saunders stood at the foot of the bed. He moves quietly, assassin's feet thought Littleman who hadn't seen Saunders until he heard him speaking. Mauve Italian knit, white zigzag stitch ornamenting the soft collar. Dark trousers with a light gray pinstripe, snug around the hips, flaring to stylish bell bottoms. Littleman brought the figure into focus. An instinctive process he had to perform consciously since his fall. Belled bottoms and stubby shoes as elegantly italianate as the shirt. Littleman, flat on his back couldn't see below the other's knees yet he was familiar with the appearance the other scrupulously maintained. Not the flashy pimp, hustler weakness for visible richness or the narrow shouldered, bird chested mimicking of Madison Avenue, Ivy League junior executives. Saunders' clothes fit him well. Always suggesting the trim raciness of his physique. Colors distinctive, assertive, but never calling attention to themselves. Littleman felt clothes were the only area in which Saunders demonstrated taste. Though loud and rowdy in his mannerisms, not choosy about what he ate, drank or where, he maintained a consistent fastidiousness about his dress and person. He was proud that he could change his underwear twice a day, that what he wore beneath his clothes reflected the color combinations of his sleek garments.

–The man sure put a hurt on you. Littleman wondered how many times his visitor would say the same thing. Yes, they beat the shit out of me and if I didn't know it you'd sock it to me your voice crowing almost saying little motherfucka I told you so, I tolt you somebody gonna do you in real good. Voice complimenting the cops on a superior manifestation of force, a good professional job to which he is bound to give credit. Saunders in tailored blue and brass and leather for a moment whipping instead of being whipped, letting himself admit yes they have something to teach me yes if I ever get on top I will use the tactics they have so painstakingly labored to impress me with. If the tables are turned I won't forget the simple logic and efficiency of the system your blows have internalized. Saying also chalk one more up for the Man. He's way ahead, a front runner showing his ass but I'm measuring the distance, marshaling my strength for the stretch. Saying many will fall, will absorb the punishment meant for me but I'm still untouched, they haven't gotten to me yet and when they do the hurts are going to be passed out in both directions. Saying to the victim on the bed, chump, brother, martyr, fool. Saying next time, last time, wait.

Littleman had not attempted to stir, grateful that his present position in the bed produced no more than a dull ache. He heard his breathing, rough, nasal, broken like snoring. Swollen face in the hand mirror the nurse had held for him. Eyes hidden in bruised pockets of flesh. Perhaps Saunders thought he was sleeping.

—I guess I'm not as pretty as I usually am. Littleman wanted to smile but hot pincers tugged viciously at his rib cage and the pain reflex contorted his face. Battered mask in the mirror which she held reluctantly, snatching the glass away before he could find the face he knew as his own beneath the lumpy caricature of human features. Would it matter. Could Saunders distinguish smile from wince. Saunders didn't need a welcome smile anyway. He appeared when and where he wanted assuming his presence spoke for itself, asking no more warning or recognition than he gave.

—Pigs usually swing that rubber hose with more circumspection. Don't like to leave marks. *Circumspection.* The word incongruous in Saunders' speech, a loose end like his spotless underwear. Wasn't simply ostentation. Words such as circumspection frequently laced his conversation. Employed always with accuracy, a sense of verbal nuance, but simultaneously mocking the words and himself as he used them. He communicated his awareness of a larger picture, the sense of irony he felt at being trapped in a language whose formal modes excluded him. When he said circumspection he was playing an intricate game, reverse slumming, burying black dogs at night in the white only section of a cemetery.

–You don't understand, Mr. Saunders. Mr. Hall unfortunately tumbled down the front steps of Woodrow Wilson Junior High. I don't know if you're familiar with that institution, it's in the Ghetto, you know, All Black, an Urban Inner City School you know. Well, there must be six, seven hundred steps. Mr. Hall was lucky to arrive at the bottom alive. He of course sustained a knot or two in his resistance of our gallant boys in blue. Though minimum force as always was employed some few pats and taps were necessary to subdue him. A pity he had to trip over one of the fallen officers. But you know he's a cripple and had lost his cane.

–I heard about you, man. Musta been a bitch. Bending your cane on those motherfuckas' heads. Too bad they got them riot hats.

–That's what I needed the last few days. A goddamned helmet.

–Where you been, man. Soon's I heard what happen I called Wilkerson. Rice heard and called me. We called cops, hospital, everywhere we could. Nobody would say shit. Finally got that lame ass lawyer Cecil Braithwaite. He ran his civil rights bullshit down to the police chief. I heard him soft talking this that and the other law to the Man. All the while I knew they was somewhere beating you or you dead already. Finally on the second day they said you was here. On the critical list. No visitors. I figured then they had decided not to kill you. Or at least not this round. I didn't figure you'd look as bad as you do though.

140

–It's bad. But they didn't kill me.

–Wilkerson ought to be here soon. I thought he be here fore now. Cat's in a bad way. His old man, you know the one they call Sweetman. He ain't been acting right. Wilkerson says his mama wants to leave him. Wilkerson been trying to keep them together but he says his old man just won't do right. Out in the street most of the time. Just about come apart when he had to get his daddy out the drunk tank last week. Got Wilkerson shakier than he usually is. I don't know about the dude. I mean Wilkerson's all right as long as things ain't tough but when this deal goes down ain't no room for shucking and shamming.

Easy and impossible to take it all in. Saunders' words, the mauve shirt, the room's shifting and tossing, remember how to open and close the proper valves, pity, hardness, sorrow, cool, feeling yet not feeling so much that sanity is destroyed. He saw Wilkerson's face, his quizzical expression break up into soft planes of vulnerability. Wilkerson seldom spoke of his parents, but he was black, had started poor and made a humble dent in the system, had a profession. What was unsaid in his case could be pieced together from the general phenomenon Littleman had observed. Second generation son with his catch as catch can affluence, sorry for his parents, sorry for himself. Sorry because they gave him everything and nothing. Sorry because he respects qualities in them that transcend the cramped physical poverty of their lives, a poverty he doesn't change because he isn't that far out of the woods himself. Sorry because reverence is a cheap way of quieting his guilt. Wilkerson's scared rabbit nerves, his stiff white shirts. Sweetman. What could Wilkerson give his father, tell him about life. What had Wilkerson learned. Except how to deny in himself the force that had generated him. Perpetually mourning for what. For whom. Black veil, black folds, curtains, sheet, silk, sea rustling, sighing . . .

–Hey.

Room revived. First its astringent odor. Then walls of appalling sea sick green. Nostrils absorb the dominant ether pall, begin to discriminate the subtler smells of sickness gliding in from the ward, the uncontrollable bowels, stale bandages, sour exhalations of cells and nerves collapsing. Blood. His bed swathed in white. Halo of aluminum tubing so a curtain can be closed around him. Brown man in a mauve shirt lighting a cigarette. Smoke curls around his head. Hands suspended in front of him, cupping a match, holding it there forgotten as he stares at the bed. Another curl of smoke twisting from the well of his fingers. Word mouthed with the cigarette still squeezed in his thick lips so that the word too is squeezed, nasally grunted.

–Hey.

Black waves have parted. Saunders is real before him. His gestures and movements have regained their normal speed. No more exaggerated, stop time slow motion weaving. Saunders is a creature of the upper air. Acts like it now. Drags up a chair and straddles it. Calls back over his shoulder.

–Wilco.

Wilkerson with Rice at his side enters from the fuzzy edges of Littleman's field of vision. Blinking, he cameos them clearly, his three friends, colleagues, fellow conspirators.

–Oh my God.

–It's for real Rice, baby. Maybe you better call a cop. Or a doctor.

Ignoring the exchange between Rice and Saunders, Wilkerson moves closer to the head of the bed, looms over the prostrate Littleman.

–You all right?

–What kind of question is that, man. You sound silly as Rice. He's been beat bad. He talks sense a minute then gone. Drifting off like he's a somnambulist or something. I might as well not be here half the time. He ain't dead. That's about all I'd say. Except he looks like death been dragging him through a briar patch.

–I'll survive. I hurt now, but I intend to get up out of this bed. They're not as smart as I thought. If they had real sense,

142

they would have killed me. They shouldn't have gone this far and left something alive. Is my cane here?

–I don't see it. But we'll get it for you. Or a better one.

–Liable to be holding it for evidence. Exhibit A. Dangerous weapon. Headache stick used by one evil, pugnacious nigger trying to break up the police force.

Wilkerson smiles. Not so much in appreciation of Saunders' bantering as from relief. He sees his friend alive, a momentary brightness in Willie's eyes that could be the indication of a smile beneath the distorted features. With difficulty words are formed above the beard.

–Poleece farce.

–Ain't it the truth.

Littleman's outline is taut beneath the sheet, Egyptian in its rigid symmetry, childlike in its inadequacy, feet poking up, leaving one third of the bed, from toes to tightly folded corners, a chill emptiness. Wilkerson winced. His friend forlorn in this strange, outsize bed. A dramatic scaling down, prophet reduced to helpless dependence in an alien atmosphere. Not visiting the land with the black plagues of his vision, but propped up by pillows, ringing bells to summon nurses who feed him, wash him, sit him on a can while he moves his bowels. But Littleman struggled to smile; he punned. *Poleece Farce.*

Where was the grand scheme now? Why had Littleman's words frightened him, why was the hanged cop a bloody reality? Why did he dream about Littleman's words? Wilkerson stared down at the man in the bed. Where were the words now. The threats that had seemed imminent possibilities. The scale. The withering scale. They were challenging something so vast that in one bed of one room among its infinite beds and rooms it could contain the anger, the rage of Willie Hall, not simply contain but swallow. His screaming defiance diminished to the sound of a pin dropped in the ocean.

Wilkerson wanted to weep for Willie. For all the Willies and Sweetmen and shadows like himself dreaming puny dreams, alive at best in some muted fantasy underworld, lying, cheating, even killing to avoid the simple truth. How they dream of dignity, of vengeance, of confronting the immensity that dribbles out their portion, portions which barely fill a box, a can, a paper bag, the cold sheets of a hospital bed.

It was silly. They were all phantoms. Wouldn't it be nice, wouldn't it be right to cradle Willie in his arms? Rock him. Sing to him. Quiet his fears of lightning and thunder, or storms raging and still to rage. Isn't that all there is to do. Whisper comfort. Ignore one's own trembling and confusion. Sleep Willie, everything's going to be all right. The way my father came to me. Be Willie's daddy. Sweetman rocking me to sleep. Maybe drunk, maybe just come from the women who were breaking my mother's heart, maybe not there at all but a memory of that time he did come, pungent, taller than the storm. My arms around the heavy shoulders, laughing together.

Then the horrible reversal. Saunders laughing. The nurses and attendants outraged or snickering. The preposterousness of it all. My father hiding from the storm. And when he's not cowering, dying by inches. Butterfly spurts of drink and lonely women. I see him plainly he has become the child. Within my father's shrunken shadow there are no quiet recesses. Because I see him differently, I try to believe I have changed. I pretend I have outgrown the need for misty dependence. Yes, I look at Littleman and know he is powerless, that his plotting consoled me only because I had a desperate need for consolation. Nothing intrinsically worthwhile in what he had to say. I stand over him. Larger than him, than any vision of my future he can project.

Why am I here? Not out of courtesy to pay my respects. No simple sentimental proddings of friendship for I am sure that Littleman is not a friend. Too much at the root of Littleman that I hate and despise, too much I would not inflict upon anyone other than myself. It was the need. The need to be comforted though there were no comforters. The

144

need to embrace my father, though for years I had accepted and tried to accustom myself to the fact that I no longer had a father. To hear the sweet voice again. To go down in softness and repose.

—Wilco, you trying to stare my man into good health. Move back so he can at least breathe some of this pig fart they call air.

Littleman nodded below him. His heavy head lolling on the pillows, his eyes blinking, pupils bleary when they were exposed.

—We can only stay a minute or so longer. The nurse at the front desk said . . .

—Who gives a fuck what she said. Lying bitch probably got instructions to do everything she can to make Littleman uncomfortable. Short of killing him. If there was that qualification.

—Do you have to yell like that. They'll send someone in to put us out.

—Now that would make this little visit just fine. I wants one of them paddies come to put me out. Saunders wanted his words to carry and the last three, *Put me out* were a challenging crescendo broadcast to all corners of the hospital. To Rice the words were two loud nigger drunks stumbling from a bar.

—Won't you ever learn. And don't you see Littleman is trying to sleep.

—I been here longer than both you and Wilkerson. And me and my man were doing fine before you came. Now if he's sleeping why don't we all just get the hell out of here. And if he ain't, let's say what's on our minds. Not go creeping around like we's in a funeral parlor. Littleman ain't sleep, and he ain't dead either.

—I can hear everything you're saying. But I don't feel like talking. Head throbs even when I move my mouth.

—I wouldn't leave for nothing. How many times we gonna get this little nigger in a room and him with nothing to say, with nothing to beat our ears about. Seems like lately Littleman been talking to me more than my own T.V. And I be steady digging T.V. He done cut into some of my favorite shows.

The room was quiet. Saunders and Rice had both settled on chairs at the foot of the bed. Wilkerson remained standing opposite them. Littleman's eyes continued to blink slowly, masking his attentiveness, but his head was averted to Wilkerson's side of the bed. Across the stiff planes of the sheet Littleman creased with his body the others seemed also to be making a subtle demand.

Wilkerson realized he must speak. That for the moment Littleman had been forced to abdicate his role as leader. Wilkerson understood that the conspiracy up to this point had been only the words of the voice in the bed. That if it were to survive Littleman's temporary demise, he, Wilkerson, was to be the bridge, must take the next step. Clearly his words would commit him and the others in a way they had never been to the fantasies and arguments Littleman initiated. This would be an action. An affirmation that something did exist even when the dreamer was awake.

—We must begin to move quickly. Spring will be over before we know it. Littleman will be ready when the time comes. But we must begin without him.

Someone else was speaking. Not Thomas Wilkerson. Not that aimless, turned in upon itself joke he had learned to despise. Not predictable Thomas with the Midas touch which turned everything to silence. The speaker, this new unfamiliar version of Thomas Wilkerson, so direct, so forceful was a wonder, but a wonder betrayed even as he metamorphosed from the ashes of the old. Tanya's face. The face of his father. His mother's face. The children. They should hear him now. He should be talking to them. Leading them. Perhaps he was. Perhaps the bloody plan would be a step forward for them. Littleman believed it was the only step possible, the necessary action no matter what followed in its train. But such thoughts were too big. They betrayed the speaker. The new man of action could not spiral away into ifs, shoulds, the

146

dizzying possibilities of history, of plans other than the one he had chosen to act out. Action kills. Thought kills. But some kinds of death were preferable to others. Action, thought, both still born. But one gets you out of a room, onto the street, bumps you into other human beings. Tanya. Sweetman. The children.

—Obviously we can't talk here. And the three of us shouldn't meet here again. But those inconveniences needn't deter us. I can draw a blueprint of the plan. Study it as I go, Wilkerson. Make sure you are certain you understand each step. I'll be out of here for the nitty gritty. You better believe it. I need a pencil. Something to write on. We can't wait. We've been through it all a hundred times.

—I know the plan. We will begin.

A stream of images raced through Wilkerson's mind. Readiness. Ripeness. Hamlet throwing off the dark mourning. He heard bugles, drums. Saw a rocket burst from its mooring, the steel chrysalis drop limply away.

Father coming apart. Mother on a cross. Woman in a cool ivory loft. But you move. You speak. The plan is real. Let Littleman sleep. We will take the necessary steps.

• • •

Saunders was looking for Raymond. If he found his brother, a good chance Raymond could lead him to Sissie. Raymond, Mary Lou, Porter, Reba, Jacob, Rowena and his own name, Leonard, though of various fathers his mother arbitrarily registered Saunders as the last name of them all. As far as Saunders knew five of his mother's seven children still lived. He was not sure meeting them accidentally on the street he would recognize their faces. He believed he could capsulize a life history for each one although the accounts would be bare outlines, and the facts probably a bit confused and the stories would not necessarily be attached to the correct name. Prostitute, dead in the war, doing ten to twenty armed robbery, married to a preacher in Detroit, moved west haven't heard from in ten years. Before his mother had died he would listen to her tales. She was long suffering, broken by so many old pains and deprivations, the doctors at the clinic felt it superfluous to name her affliction. She had slipped gradually into incoherent fantasies, reliving her past on at least two distinct levels. She was a pitiable black woman done to death by cruel, lusting men who had forced children upon her and fled back to the darkness from which they had crawled. She was a respectable, church going lady, soul saved, declining into a satisfied old age, proud of the children she had launched successfully onto the seas of life, mourning for the doting father who had tragically died before he could share the peaceful years his hard work and steadfastness had earned.

When she passed, Saunders had been fifteen, somewhere near the bottom middle of the brood as far as he could work out. Only three, Raymond, Mary Lou and he stayed with their mother. He alone had spent time listening to his mother's stories. Perhaps, he later conjectured, her stories had amused him, perhaps since he realized they were the Saunders' sole legacy he had been hoarding them, seeking an advantage over his brother and sister, perhaps he had experienced a momentary victory watching the hard circumstances of his past shredded, destroyed, refashioned according to the whim of a frail, babbling woman old before her time. Any or all of these motives could not explain their long sessions together, his fascination as she unraveled version after version of the family history. Sometimes so fraught with self-pity and despair she keened at him, stopping for long shaking sobs or pausing, eyes fixed on some object in the room, to weep steadily a half hour or more as if she were alone. Once as he watched she had passed from wailing to quiet crying then knelt beside an imaginary bed and mouthed a prayer of thanksgiving to a generous god. Still crying softly she had pantomimed the ritual of shutting down a large house for the night. Turning out lights, locking doors, pulling shades, tiptoeing into rooms where children slept, to cover them and plant kisses on their foreheads, finally returning to the bed, kneeling again, praying again but this time a bitter blaspheming tirade, cursing creation and the cruelty on high which had given her breath and so little else. Saunders had not been able to look away when she, her body heaving, her hands tearing furiously at her hair and clothes, began to undress. If she had bloodied herself, as long as the wounds were inflicted with her own hands, he knew he could not stop her. Would not intrude on what she had earned the right to do.

They had always called him cold. He knew why then. A numbness in his limbs, an icy wind swirling through his chest. Cold and nothing else as she frantically stripped each garment from her body. His mother stretched naked on the floor. Cold. She could have been a strange corpse on a slab rolled out from the morgue's cold storage. Her flesh so arbitrary he could have taken a scalpel, if prodded by his curiosity, and sliced down to the clockwork innards. His mother's body, female because someone had snatched something from the point of her groin and left a hairy emptiness, female because someone had taken two fistfuls of flesh and hurled them with such force against her chest that they had flattened and stuck.

Spraddle legged on the floor. Last act of the family chronicle she endlessly recited to him. Termination and beginning. On her back to receive another lover, to birth another Saunders, to welcome madness and worms. Hunched over her were swarms of bulky shadows she cooed to and called by name. Her bony hips pitching. Her palms and loose backsides slapping on the gritty floor.

Saunders sat rigid in the musty, dull box that was their home. His mother rose unsteadily from the floor, the memories suddenly gone, the complaints of her joints and puckered flesh already a dull buzzing in her temples. He could see the miseries inching back covering her like a chaste robe. Though he had violated her privacy, crept into her dream, she retained the power to restore dignity to herself. Below her clothes was skin, beneath the skin another layer of hurt and memories stretched over her frame, clothes without buttons or zippers, a mottled, camouflage suit. Her suffering excluded him, baffled his seeking.

She gathered her scattered things unhurriedly, eyes bright with a sleepwalker's tranquillity, meeting her son's stare several times, chatting with him all the while in a nonchalant tone of his father's passion for chitterlings and her reluctance to fill the house with their nasty smell when expecting nice people for Sunday dinner.

Saunders walked toward the Red Cap luncheonette. If Raymond wasn't there, no point in seeking further. Logic was simple. If at home his brother would be sick or sleeping, if in a bar, high, if away from the neighborhood, engaged in some hustle that would render him invisible till he returned. The luncheonette was where business had to be transacted. There Raymond would surface, lucid, calm, scheming.

It was easy for Saunders to picture his brother's life. Streets on which he walked treacherously familiar. Faces and storefronts changing but remaining the same. On the corner Klein's had been burnt out and a smoke odor clung to the blackened stones of its foundations. He remembered the crashing of huge plate glass windows, the crunching fragments under his feet as he had stumbled through the glut of broken, overturned and unmovable appliances searching for something to fill his arms. Only a few summers back. Klein's, the liquor store, a few other insignificant scabs had been peeled away. But all that seemed a thousand years ago, children breaking their favorite toys in spite. Scabs torn away while the cancer continued its ravages deep inside the body. Nothing had changed. Saunders knew the life, believed he could submerge himself again, move as efficiently as lethally as he once had.

Something about his memories was nostalgic. The rhythm which had moved him, his instinctive responses like an insect or flower to the subtle play of light and energy. He didn't

150

have to think to move; life had been a series of appearances and disappearances, of being someone or no one, and it all happened simply because he was Lenny Saunders and couldn't be anything else. The streets, the bars, the faces. Saunders was revisiting himself. But he had grabbed at one of those unpredictable hooks that occasionally disturb the sanctity of the medium. From the bland, blue-eyed sky a job in the post office, the alien chemistry of a half forgotten caution *Make something of yourself* causing him to seize the opportunity, cling to the hook as if it were salvation. Rise and go away. Perhaps to make room for his brother back here on the street. He didn't know why he worked in the post office or why Raymond had become a mirror image, thief and hustler, of his own days on the street. Saunders was certain neither one of them had a choice. The deal went down. Skinny white fingers, manicured, sandpapered at the tips, laid out the cards and if you were a joker you joked, a king you reigned, a spade you couldn't scrub away the blackness of your ass.

Sometimes the sameness was sweet, was good to come back to, a woman always there, soft legged when you needed her. He could go down in it again. His reflexes would come back. He could learn the new names of the faces. Forget going to the Man eight hours a day, forget time clocks, supervisors, the post office routine learned in two days then endlessly repeated. He could respond again to subtle tugs of the environment, fixing him, spangling him, a bright piece of glass in the kaleidoscope swirl. He could be Raymond. Offer Raymond in exchange one hundred fifty dollars a week, a decent apartment on the quiet periphery of the neighborhood. Good clothes.

But he was not here for trades. No sweet bait for Raymond. Just. *Where is Sissie?*

And Raymond answered:

—No good bitch still fucking for that paddy cop.

All Saunders needed to know. He did not waste an instant studying the ghost his brother had become. The thin body, unhealthy skin, gaunt eyes were beginning to shiver into focus, the ghost was almost his brother, something about the way it carried its shoulders, the right one higher than the left like a shield it would talk safely behind, but when he had heard what he came for, Saunders was quickly far away, gone as suddenly as a stone smacking the still surface of a lake, disappearing as it explodes the perfect reflections held in the water, rippling shadow of Raymond blurring outward into larger and larger concentric circles till the circles themselves dissolved.

Sissie could be used. Yes. And should he feel remorse because she would be killed and mutilated? His brother's woman led like a cow to the slaughterhouse? No more remorse than she felt abandoning Raymond for a surer, more competent protector. No more remorse than Raymond would have felt if he had known he was dooming Sissie and her pimp cop when he spoke to his brother. In Raymond's voice had been the bitterness of betrayal, the frustration of one who has had the final insult delivered after an eternity of injury. Anger and hatred so deep that he was ripe for killing, but the delicate balance had not been tipped, murder was in his blood, but not the specific death that would avenge him. He could not kill Sissie and the white cop without losing his own life. Raymond preferred living, keeping the shell intact no matter how rotten the insides had become. In some form the flesh must survive and its bare maintenance seemed Raymond's sole concern. Saunders knew his brother's capacity for emotional death was limitless. Raymond had been ripe, sure handed, laughing. He had said, *Brother, I'm getting it together. I'm going to walk tall through this shit and when I get out my shoes still be shiny*. Watching his ragged descent was like seeing a drunken man dragged by his heels down a steep flight of stairs, the skull cracking as it bumps from landing to landing. Always further to fall. Life guaranteed that. Perhaps not a bad bargain. If you feel you've hit bottom, you're wrong. His brother would continue to survive and the seeming bottom on which he was now floundering wouldn't seem so bad anymore.

Perhaps Littleman wanted to show the bottom could be reached. After the white cop was lynched, the old lies could not be believed any more than the corpse could strut its beat. Lynching the cop said we can fall no further, we give you license to kill us, but we are going down no further. Things have come to this. We have chosen and here swaying in the breeze is our decision. You will die or we will die but we will not submit.

Perhaps that was what Littleman meant. But this was no time to try and figure it all out. Sissie could be used to get the cop. By taking certain steps she had lost all power over her life. She was dead already, a puppet in the hands of those whose whims controlled her, a doll who could perform certain lifelike tricks, simulate when the proper strings were pulled, *love, passion, desire.* Now he would steal the strings, and after she had wiggled her necessary dance, he would snip them.

•••

The rain came from far away. Light but steady he felt its weight accumulating in the creases of his raincoat. Glancing skyward, his gaze was cut off abruptly by the blackness which seemed clamped like a lid a few feet above the tops of the highest buildings. The rain assured him privacy. He had parked two blocks from his destination. In spite of the rain he enjoyed the thought of filtering through the usually crowded streets silent and alone. At intersections the light posts were hooded with dim cones of yellow through which slants of rain blinked. Other than the rain's patter, the occasional hiss of cars along the streets, there was quiet, the yellow hush of the street lamps pervading the neighborhood.

Moving by instinct, surer than any memories could have been, Saunders negotiated the narrow streets where ten years before he had hunted other human beings, preying on them with the unquestioning regularity and rectitude of a bank clerk arriving promptly each morning for work. He realized he hunted still. He must stalk the whore who had supported his brother. Study the habits of his quarry, decide when, how and where she could best be struck down. He knew it would be easy. She was already dead, part of the submarine world which floated the city, but that with its tall buildings, grinning signs, its frantic hurry of business the city denied. Sissie would be vulnerable a thousand times a day. Ten Sissies would have to die, cut down in some mad ripper's crusade before the newspapers would react, the police conduct a rigorous investigation. Saunders had recently read a story about Jack the Ripper and now, strangely, here he was in his English mackinaw shrouded in rainy fog, gliding along deserted streets to a rendezvous with a prostitute whose violent death he was planning. Saunders had promised himself that he would read more about the Ripper. The notion of Jack reforming his society through murder had surprised him. In movies the murderer was always a beast, a dark villain the plot trapped and executed. Perhaps the reality of murder was never that simple. At first the idea of killing someone already a pitiable victim had been distasteful. Then Littleman showed him how Sissie's life had been stolen, how she could not forfeit what she no longer owned. Since she functioned as a puppet in the oppressor's system, taking her life would be a minor act of sabotage. He hadn't pushed Littleman to answer the next question. Wouldn't all sufferers who submitted, who allowed themselves to be used rather than striking back at the users, wouldn't all of them be guilty, eligible for slaughter, his sick mother if she were still alive, one of the most guilty since she had endured to the breaking point and past.

Rain collapsed about him, gathering in the broken pavement, sleeking the street where cars wheezed past, staining his eggshell coat with darker patches. From far away. Rain had always seemed out of place here. He remembered himself as a child watching it bead the rusty fire escape, gather in pools at the mouths of clogged drains, drench the back of an apartment house visible through the kitchen window. The outside of the next building had matched the one in which he lived, thick shouldered twins lurching on one another for support, derelict, diseased, frescoes of soot and pigeon shit decorating the flaking brick, old men breathing rank poison into one another's faces. He had watched. Struck by the foreignness of water dripping from the sky. Fascinated that the rain came at all to this world of black faces and crumbling buildings. Rain not an intrusion. Rather a simple mistake. Something that belonged to white people, which had erred in its course and dropped reluctantly in the wrong place. Like the white voices and faces on radio and television, the brittle faced teachers who raced away when the dismissal bell rang.

In the darkness, rain and solitude his thoughts were a nagging companion. He had a job to do, and that for the moment was the answer to any uncertainty imposed by his imaginings. Too many questions made men cripples like Wilkerson. Littleman's runty legs could not make him the cripple Wilkerson was. Yet something new seemed to move Wilkerson. Perhaps Wilkerson finally understood what it was all about now. Maybe he would have a glimmer of determination Saunders had not detected before. Maybe he would start acting like a man. At most Wilco could be stubborn in an argument, even get angrily self-righteous if he thought his opinion was being ignored. But that was when they talked. Something lacking in the man. If their words had suddenly become things and what had been said had to be backed up with action, Saunders guessed Wilkerson could not be depended upon to follow through. To do as he said, to not back down were instincts like the others remaining strong from Saunders' years in the street. He suspected part of his distrust of the teacher might have something to do with Wilkerson's education, the manner in which his trained speech and thoughts subtly erected a wall around him. But Saunders could dismiss this thought quickly when he counted the many ways there were of being smart and how the flaw in Wilkerson prevented the man's intelligence from concentrating its force in all but a few narrow areas. Wilkerson was often not

155

much more than a fact man. He had information. Could spurt answers before the contestants in the T.V. quiz shows. A good machine could do that. Maybe more than facts comprised Wilkerson now.

But Saunders would not mistrust him less for any vein of iron which surfaced in Wilkerson's voice or will. The flaw ran deeper. Back at least to the days when a fair skin and a soft voice meant goodies from the kitchen rather than hot fields all day and gruel when the sun went down. The whiteness in Wilkerson's complexion and features that yellow niggers like him wore so proudly in their mongrel faces, would always earn them crumbs from the Master's table. In Wilkerson's pale face Saunders was confronted with the image of the raping white devil astride black women.

Saunders asked himself how little of the enemy remaining was enough to taint. When the deal went down, when it was kill and be killed would Wilkerson make a clean break, could he shed white man's ways, white man's blood. Saunders scorned white blood. Throat cut, slopping the gutter red, he would rather die than have the sickness from a white man's veins enter his black body. He recalled Big Red, Malcolm Little, pouring the burning lye into his hair, how reading that scene had caused him to plummet backward, relive his own experiments with evil smelling brews cooking his good black man's hair. His cool when, rag tied around his gleaming stew of grease and dead hair, he went forth preening, to rob and beat the kinky topped brown people around him.

If Raymond were right, she lived in the second row house from the corner. It couldn't be the houses on either side of the one his brother had designated since they were sign-posted and boarded shut. At least every other house in the row had been condemned. Where no boards slanted across the windows, chunks of glass were rooted, jagged and uneven like crudely carved teeth in the mouth of a pumpkin. Nearly all the dwellings seemed deserted. Down the block dim rectangles here and there cracking the obscurity. Coldly glowing, glass like fresh snow banked on the thresholds, glass

156

crunching under Saunders' feet as he moved close enough to the second house to peer through a low window into the dark street floor. The window moulding smelled of damp, rotting wood. A sludge of weary paint and filth glazed Saunders' hands where they pressed against the window frame. He called into the gloom. The front window of this house was boarded like its neighbors, only more subtly from the inside, a sheet of uniform darkness, thick cardboard or wood painted black, backed the cracked fragment of glass which ended a quarter of the way up the frame. He drew his hand back quickly, wiping his fingertips on the wet bricks. Glass was loose. A good shout could bring it crashing down at his feet.

He stepped back, mounted the first step, called again. On the second step still hearing no answer he stretched to his toes peering through a vacant slot where once a vent had graced the top of the door. He heard footsteps, then saw an unstable glow of light moving toward him. It was flame rather than electricity, solid, tearshaped like a match but burning too strongly for a match. It responded to drafts inside the house, twisting as it drew closer.

—Who's that. A woman's voice from the bottom of a well.

—Leonard Saunders.

—What you want. Voice husky, challenging. A tough assed tone that would make killing her easy since it said she knew the danger surrounding her and had prepared defenses, defenses she was cocksure of.

—I'm Raymond's brother. He gave me something for you. Easy to scheme and lie at her.

—Don't want nothing of his. And I ain't got a thing for him, coming or going. You get on away from here. They spoke through the closed door. Saunders could see the wavering light play through the vent. He pictured the woman inside. She would be holding a candle in one hand, the other hand would be on her ample hip which was jutted toward him pugnaciously. She would be pouting, angry at the intrusion, at the strange voice from the night calling out names that never had, or no longer existed for her. He sensed her woman's parts, lips, breasts, thighs denying their softness and roundness, promising instead with eyes that cut at him through the locked door that she was a rock, a cast iron figurine set down to forbid his entrance. He sensed her weight wedged against the door. If necessary at another time he knew he could crumple the old wood with one swift blow of foot or shoulder. But not now. He filed the information, recording also the desolation of the adjacent houses, the unlikelihood of interruption from anyone who lived on the block, the imperturbable stillness that would swallow the sudden splintering of a door, the one or two screams Sissie might trumpet before she could be quieted.

—Raymond gave me something for Lisa. *Yeah, the bitch live over behind South Street with her bastard she call Lisa.* He hoped the timing was right, that the unexpected name confused her, allowed a part of him to insinuate itself through a crack in the wooden barrier. Her daughter's name a key.

—He gave me some money for Lisa. He heard metallic clicking on the other side of the door, a deep wheezing sigh, a string of muttered epithets in which his brother was damned copiously, the whole business of locks, keys, doors and chains cursed. Could have been the sounds of a robot undressing, Sissie lugubriously stripping away the tin and wire that secured her body, and Saunders half expected the door to open upon a massy ebony nude, lewdly posed to recompense him for the payment he carried in his pocket.

In the flickering candle light a scrawny silhouette split the partially opened door frame. He saw a cadaver's face, saffron skin gouged out by black shadows, eyes and mouth empty pits.

—Give it to me. The voice demanding, fearless as it had been through the door, issuing incongruously from a small figure facing a stranger in a dark doorway.

—Mama.

—Damnit Jewel, can't you keep that child quiet a minute.

A little girl's cry for her mother had come from somewhere, but as he strained his eyes to sort out shapes in the darkness Saunders could see nothing. The room could have been full of people, things substantial as she was, or else the woman at the door could be conversing with squeaking phantoms. Saunders could not see beyond the ghoulish icon and dancing flame below it. But his foot was in the cracked door. He had to go farther.

—He said to give it to Lisa. Nobody else. He wanted to match the terseness of her words. Give no room for qualification or doubt. If she barred his way curtly demanding, he would make her come to him, drop a cold take it or leave it in her lap and wait for her whore's greed to respond.

The child's cry again, sudden, breathlessly desperate as if its mouth had been wrenched from a stifling hand. Light cascaded from an outflung door, a yellow wind cleansing the room. Saunders could see a tiny figure outlined against the blur. After hesitating an instant, it rushed into the room. The blind charge of the child carrying it past the candle into Saunders. He recoiled from the hard bump of bones against his legs, the frantic groping at his trousers. He heard a panicked whine, the rustle of another collision and could see as the dim halo of the candle lowered, stick arms grasping stick legs, a plaited head burrowing into the scantiness of the woman's short dress.

—Jewel, you ain't good for nothing. The inner door slammed shut but the woman with the candle continued to yell over her shoulder stooping simultaneously to gather the child into her arms.

—Lisa. Lee lee, baby. I'm right here. Mama's going nowhere. Hush now, Lisa. Open the goddamn door you simple woman.

Seemingly forgotten, Saunders fell in behind mother and daughter. If the three women noticed him when he entered the second room, no gesture or word betrayed the fact. He felt invisible. He was one more piece of battered furniture standing beside the door.

Kerosene lamps lit the crowded inner room. Two cots, a table, three chairs of bent chrome tubing each with plastic covered pastel seat and backrest. Not one was intact. They had been bent, sliced, gored, oozed their stuffing like neglected rag dolls. A curtain drawn across the entrance partially screened a smaller room opposite the doorway where Saunders stood. In this alcove Saunders could make out another cot and what seemed to be the shattered bottom of a toilet. A sink, its exposed pipes irregularly snipped away, gaping holes in the plaster above and below it, dangled limply in the far corner to his right. Atop the sink's scarred drainboard sat the rusty base of an alcohol burning stove. Around the room numerous excavations similar to those framing the sink had been dug from the plaster and floors. Somewhere in the shadows water pinged methodically into a pan or bucket. The house had obviously been ransacked, everything of value carted away, even to the iron pipes which would at best bring pennies in a junkyard. The burner on the drainboard, the kerosene lamps, the gutted sink implied that all utilities had been shut off, that like its neighbors this shell had been condemned.

Though physically dissimilar the three women seemed somehow related, as different as crawling and wings but issuing from the same shrouded chrysalis. The girl who had run into Saunders' legs sat subdued, melting into the loose springs of a cot. Though the iron bed was low, only the toes of her sneakers dangled as far as the floor. She wore elastic banded slacks, red, filthy, rolled several times at her ankles, and a short sleeved candy striped cotton shirt whose bands of color around her torso emphasized the frailty of a rib case he could encircle with his hands. Large eyes, hair tightly braided into a profusion of pigtails, delicate brown hands cupping her chin, one thumb slipped furtively between her lips. Her body seemed shrunken so that it occupied the smallest space possible, but her eyes did not reflect her timid posture, they were wide open, preying, independent of the room, of the quiet face lodging them. If they expressed anything it was cool neutrality saying everything will be absorbed, nothing revealed. Saunders knew the girl had been crying minutes before, that she had flung herself desperately, headlong into the darkness and had been frightened by a strange man's hard, unyielding legs. In the room she had watched mutely as he had watched the bitter, violent screeching, her mother's hands shoot out to shove the older woman skittering against a chair. But the slack mouthed serenity of the features as she sucked on her thumb and the hungry blackness of the eyes were unchanged, articulated only a bottomless capacity for more. Saunders thought of the African fetishes with their unflinching eyes of tin or bits of shiny stone, their potbellied wooden bodies nearly invisible beneath nail studded skin.

The woman called Jewel, plainly the oldest, though of an indeterminate, beyond fifty age, all distended bosom and belly balanced on bony, razor sharp ankles that protruded incongruously from the wide girth of her long housedress, had turned her broad back to the others, screening one of the kerosene lamps, adjusting its flame so a humped sail of light billowed on the wall she faced.

—You gonna go too far one time. You gonna go too far, she muttered into her corner. Her shoulders were trembling and her words broken by a wheeze.

—You ain't so goddamned high and mighty. The woman stuttered when she spoke. Saunders could not tell if she always did or if her rage twisted her tongue.

—I ain't such an old fool as you think laying your nasty hands on me. Saunders guessed at what she was saying. Her clucks, slurs, the asthmatic sighs made her speech opaque as a child's. She was a witness he hadn't counted on. A possible complication. Two deaths uneconomical in the logic of the plan. Was she the child's nurse, a relative, cousin, aunt, mother to Sissie? Her eyes glowered as she suddenly turned, dismissing him at the same time as a thing familiar and predictable worth no more than passing contempt. Saunders thought she had eyes like a pigeon. Bird eyes and bird legs old bitch cocking her head so it aimed at what she wanted to see.

When she spoke to Sissie again she was whining. Like the child she drew herself in, shrinking to a soft, quivering ball inside the shapeless dress:

—I ain't staying here if you don't treat me no better.

—And go where? Where some worn out thing like you gonna find it good as you have it now? Sitting on your ass all day calling yourself taking care of Lisa. Him slipping money to you on the side so's you can stuff your fat mouth while you're spying on me. Don't think I don't know. You tale carrying, loose tongued old witch. You tell him every breath I take. She's gonna tell him about you, too, Mister. So give Lisa what you brung and git out. I don't want to give her lies nothing to feed on.

She was short, trim. Nothing like the fleshy idol Saunders had imagined. A hint of her daughter's eyes, large, round, disguising their hunger not with the other's neutrality, but with a constant, surface animation, the fire and ice of her moods playing across her eyes so they were never still long enough for him to gauge their depths. Her hair was cropped brutally short. In slacks she might give the appearance of an adolescent boy, but in the brief dress she wore Saunders admired the completely feminine texture and grace of her legs. He measured and classified her with the word petite. Deceptively inconsequential at first glance, revealing soft curves, perfect proportions if your gaze lingered. Saunders could imagine her, a wig of flowing, luxurious hair crowning her model's figure. She would look as soft as the pampered red-bone girls his new post office job and status made him eligible to court and fondle. Yet he had heard her mouth, seen the springy strength of her arms manhandle Jewel.

She probably looked best in the dim light of bars where she picked up her tricks. In the morning waking up beside her in a strange room the charm would be lost, gone with the shadows, the lazy glide of a high. She would have been a mistake, there would be an urge to hurt her. Feeling her perfect body twisting in your arms would have teased out a

162

private itch, made you believe you could find something you had given up as lost forever. In the morning, what had begged you to cradle it in the strength of your hands, would be cheatingly undersized, your hands would want to throttle.

In the weak light of the oil lamps she could have been anyone young and pretty. Women Saunders had known slipped noiselessly into her face. Only the lonely smack of the dripping ceiling confirmed the room's presence, the now of the three women whose lives had been consecrated to the plan.

–Lisa, that man has something for you. He says it's from your daddy.

–Is she Raymond's child?

–Nobody else's. Though I guess he don't do much bragging on it. Not even to his brother, if you is his brother. He don't lift a finger to help her get along. If he sent something by you, it's the first penny he's give her. Easier for the nigger if he believes she ain't his. But he damn well knows she is.

Saunders searches the girl's face for a trace of Raymond, of himself, for whatever links the Saunders' scattered seed, dumb to one another though they are. She looks more distant than before. He wishes the girl would speak. The proof of her right shoulder raised like a shield. Sissie could be lying. Trying to wring an extra nickel's sympathy for her bastard. How many times had Sissie sold the child to her lovers?

–Sit up straight. And git your thumb out your mouth. Mister, if you got something to give, give it and go on your way. Of all the women in the room the prostitute's face bore the closest resemblance to his brother. She had the female counterparts of his clean, even features, fast welterweight's physique. And his brother's hooded eyes were once like hers, liquid, full of heat.

–She ain't gonna get up and come begging to you. We don't need nothing he can give us that bad. You tell him I don't need nothing from him and I'm just letting her take this cause it came in her name. So he don't need to be creeping around here to hear her say thanks. Or me.

The room stank. The longer he stayed the more its squalor

oppressed him. Stinking pipes, stinking plaster, woman stink, wood stink, the rain methodically filling a cup with water, the cup patient as it overflows, the brackish contents crawling over the unswept floors. The child, perhaps his niece, patient like the cup, receiving the words, the stink till she is filled to bursting. Just a matter of time. The derelict shell of a house. The girl's skinny body scooped out, looted, abandoned, fit only for desperate transients. For trespassers. He started toward her, fumbling in his pocket, fingering the clipped bills. He didn't care what he pulled out. A ten the biggest he had. No matter what his hand extracted he would give. He would return his hand to the pocket only to draw more. For a moment he thought of shoving everything into her outstretched hand. Couldn't be much more than a hundred dollars. He had bet five times that on one roll of the dice.

He saw the wrinkled money slowly consumed by flames, the cop's wet thumb riffling the notes. No sense in throwing good money after bad. He couldn't buy the girl away from this house. If that much money existed, he had no idea where in the world it might be.

He paused before her. He saw Lisa was shivering, had a snotty nose that probably never stopped running in the damp, chill room. A sorry assed, wasted little black gal. Not the first he had seen. Already she knew the trick of looking past him, through him, just as he had taught his eyes to see and forget in the same instant.

—Here, baby. Sounded too much like what he'd say to her mother, his joint placated, smiling as he dressed beside the flimsy bed. Not an urge to save the child, but an impulse to free himself, pay and be gone. His sudden generosity a sham. As his fingers flipped through the bills he knew there had never been a chance that he would come away with empty pockets. Good money after bad. He could not fight a lion with a stick. Crazy Littleman taking on the whole police force with his cane. When the time came Saunders would be at a desk, pressing buttons, watching miniature mushroom explosions on a video screen as red squad cars disintegrated.

164

–Raymond sent this honey. You use it to get something nice for yourself.

–I just might wipe my ass with it and send it back to her pitiful daddy.

Lisa avoided brushing his hand when she took the money, then held it at arm's length, an insect plucked from some intimate place of her body. She crushed it in her fist, the extended arm petrified, unable to release what she had trapped, to acknowledge what it was, where it came from, the heat and dampness sliding through her closed fingers.

More to do, more to learn, but he wanted out. They would take care of business. If the old crone in the way, she would die too. And the child. Lisa. Swallowed by the bed. Her outstretched arm still rigid, waiting for someone to snatch away the strange paper from her grasp.

–Raymond said he's sorry and he'll try to send her what he can from time to time. A foot in the door. A way to enter when the plan sent him on an errand.

Sissie. Jewel. Lisa. Wipe all the silly bitches off the face of the earth. Walls were pressing in on him. Had to get out. He could feel them ignoring him again. A man out of the night. Business done he was gone forever. That's the way it was with nigger wenches. The stink. The chill. Too familiar to Saunders. The bare routine of their lives resuming behind the door as it slams in his face. Muffled voices already squabbling as he picks his way through the black front room.

• • •

They are watching me all the time. More than before they seem to be controlling my life. But what do they see? What do they touch with their knives and needles and rubber gloves?

The plan proceeds while I lie here. To their eyes I am helpless. Once the fuse is lit nothing remains but the waiting. I am content to wait in bed. I wonder what will reach me first. Gunfire, explosions. Door bursting open and who will enter. Hearing it begin will be enough. Whether I am carried out a hero or a corpse.

I awakened dreaming of Angela. Strange how the need for luxury never completely leaves us. The condemned man rankled because the vegetables in his last meal are cold. A symptom of unquenchable vanity. My need to recall the interlude with Angela. To possess her in a dream even though my mind recognizes the absurdity of an Angela where I am now and with what I have to do. Angela is part of that summer. I needed her body to feel like a man. I knew something was missing and she appeared to be a piece that would fit. I am able to recall moments when we were liberated by an illusion of wholeness. My dreams are still confused by those accidents. Dreaming, I treat the luxury as something earned, something that should persist. I forget how useless Angela would be in this stinking hospital. How hopelessly she would be entangled with the plan. In my dreaming I am like a man who would slit a flower's throat, tuck its bloom in his lapel, then weep when it withered.

They watch me but I will reveal nothing. They might as well be observing a catatonic idiot, waiting for him to break into sociable conversation. As far as they can see I have no concourse with the outside world. No telephone, no T.V. or radio. No other patient in the room. I will have no more visitors. Send nor receive letters. The movements of my body communicate nothing to them. I have reduced my motion, even the blinking of my eyes, to a minimum. I co-operate with them to the extent of swallowing the food and medicine they bring, nodding at the doctors' inquiries, facilitating as best I can the rituals of pissing, shitting, having my body washed. Beyond that I have systematically concealed from them any indication that I am still beset by the collection of vanities they associate with humanity. Of affection toward them, toward myself, toward any other individual or group of human beings I wish to seem as innocent as a dead man.

I write at night. During the day I soak the pages in a basin.

The water gains a bluish cast as the words dissolve. I dump the sodden unreadable remnants into a waste basket before I go to sleep each afternoon. The writing is a conscious attempt to retain my sanity as I lie here imprisoned. My dreams such as the one of Angela are an unconscious safety valve, but I believe they too can be brought under control. So much of my life that was formerly haphazard I have subjected to the dictates of my will. What I am, all I wish to be is a finely honed mechanism functioning within the plan. The only parts of me, of what I am or do, which I would not willingly release, are those indispensable to the plan. Thus I relinquish easily the pleasures of a body, an identity, my scribbling.

Appropriate that my papers will not be read. No longer difficult to destroy them, to watch the words leak into the water or blend with the yellow pee when I amuse myself by shredding them into the urinal. I wonder if one of the drones has the job of searching my garbage. If one has to dry the pee stained bits of paper and try to piece them together. A scholar whose duty is to know everything about me. Oblivion for my words appropriate because my people have always written their history with their mouths.

Just before I awakened I was listening to Angela and she was telling me why she hadn't met me as she had promised. I passed under the archway of City Hall. I sat on a low stone wall in the open courtyard at least an hour before the appointed time. In ten minutes I was despondent because she hadn't been driven as I was to come early. I counted the clumsy turrets, read the bronze plaque beside the West arcade. Finally four o'clock, the appointed time. Then five numb rings of the tower bell separated from one another by eternities in which I held my breath, disbelieving as long as I could the inevitability of the next gong. I made a circuit of the four broad walkways North, South, East and West that emptied into the courtyard. I felt completely unsure of myself. Invented ingenious mistakes that I might have committed. Entertained the possibility of any error, tortured myself for one stupidity after another rather than admit the most likely circumstances. Was she dead? Had I forgotten the hour, the day, the year? It had been over fourteen months since I'd seen her. We both had laughed at the idea of a rendezvous in the middle of the city at the castle of the bureaucrats. We joked that we might not recognize one another in a crowd, with our clothes on. At five thirty it seemed feasible that I might have seen her and not remembered her face. I tried to recall all the young women I had seen that afternoon. I felt a surge of sympathy for Angela, regretted how deeply I had injured her when our eyes met and I had turned casually away to search other faces in the throng. I reasoned that since I had been an hour early she could be two hours late. Perhaps she was testing, teasing. Watching me from a window high in the tower. The rush hour crowds thinned out. Pedestrian traffic through the arches diminished to a few footfalls echoing on the brick and stone. An old man tied down the canvas flap on his cart and wheeled his load of unsold pretzels wearily, stoop shouldered through the sun dazzled needle's eye opening onto Market Street. He was probably going to the row of penny arcades where sailors and prostitutes congregated. With Angela beside me I could have smiled at the women and their shiny purses, the young men whacking away with miniature twenty-twos or jamming the knobs of the shuddering pinball machines. Alone I would not go close to their corner. A slow, burning rage, the only cover I could draw over my loneliness, would make me grab one of the rifles, rip it from its mooring and fire into the passersby. She was not coming. I took hours to form that sentence. Say it to myself. The next sentence came instantaneously. I will never see her again. But seemed just as final, just as true.

In the dream she was explaining why she had not come.
—I don't think love's possible anymore . . . love . . . not in this world. It demands the best of us. And we're not used to doing our best. The best is never asked of us. At school, when I work, when I talk to my friends or family the same deadening half-ass effort is always enough. Nobody really

wants more. They're frightened by it. Don't go too far, don't try too much, go part of the way and we'll bridge the difference by smiles, clever talk, build a world which makes a virtue of our mediocrity.

–In you there was an intensity which spit upon the world I had known. You had an anger, Willie, a rage that drove you, held your world together without lies and compromise. I felt your anger from the first moment. It was rigorous, total, it began to clear my head. Make certain things possible again. And when I felt you giving something to me that was not hate, but just as pure, just as consuming, I began to hear and see things again. A new world opening.

–I had been hiding for a long time. You don't know my middle name, do you. Rowena. Angela Rowena Taylor. My initials if you please spelling in capital letters A.R.T. An endowment. A legacy from the good Dr. Taylor my father and Marie Eleanor Taylor née Hudgins, my impeccable school teaching mother. I could play the classics at ten. I was invited to parties in the best homes. Even little white kids came to the Taylor house to celebrate my birthdays. If I was not exactly a prodigy on the piano, I was a prodigy of politeness and punctuality. My oiled braids so long I could sit on them. I could read, talk, sing and spell better than anyone in our integrated class. I learned to cheat early. Learned a clean starched dress and shiny hair was what my teachers responded to when they read my compositions. I stayed top middle outstanding all the way through, maintaining with countless shortcuts and deceptions a bright, polished Angela for the world to measure and admire. Of course I despised this heroine. And though I still don't have a very good idea of who or what I am, I could keep the perfect Angela miles apart from anything that seemed to touch me. And I was touched by books and music, people who carried themselves in a certain way, a special way which proclaimed this is all of me, everything I am held apart from the world, no lie, no split to deceive others or myself.

–My parents were proud. I won a scholarship. At the prestigious school they were ingenious enough to name in every sentence they formed concerning me I met Teddy, Teddy the poet, Teddy the mad white boy who could put into words all the anxiety, the fear, the uglinesses I felt in myself. I was dumb. I thought I was different, unique, and here by the grace of the gods was one more exile, a rare one like myself. Teddy ate me up. He broke apart the bones and cleaned the silly meat off them with his yellow teeth. And always his little pinky elegantly greaseless, pointed at the ceiling. He was ugly beyond my fondest dreams of myself. After they cut his leavings out of my belly I stumbled around for almost a year feeling sorry for myself, loving anybody who'd pity me. I thought I had spun free from the Taylors. I worked. Went back to school at night. I liked the feeling of independence, of being one Angela. I'd go along for a month or so fairly content with myself, working, studying, close to a few good friends. Then the whole show would abruptly go to pieces. Shattered by something different each time, but each time utterly demolished. I'd want to die. Job, books, people. Nothing mattered but the overwhelming sense of failure. The certainty that I had betrayed myself. The Angela I had buried, had denied for so long, still eluded me. In the moments of depression there seemed no doubt that she was gone forever. The only decent, honest thing to do was not mourn, not try to forget, but die, destroy the shell, the mockery. I hid. Sick and alone. Waiting for strength to return to the routine I had established. After a while the difficulty of returning was too great. I couldn't go through the explanations, the lies it took to get back into people's good graces. I finally cut myself off. Lived like a kind of ghost waiting for the fits of suffering to come. At least during the suffering I was real. My life was substantial enough to be painful, to be a burden I wanted to remove. When I was a ghost, when I believed people could look through me as I looked through them, I consoled myself with the thought that next time the utter desolation came, I would not be a coward. I would recall the emptiness, the frustration and rid myself of them once and for all.

–I haunted the beach so an instrument would be close at hand when the time came. When I saw you that first night, I thought you might be a suicide. I wanted to watch it happen. I saw your braces and cane. Took those for a motive. I wouldn't have tried to help you. I was too excited, I knew a door was opening. I would follow you. I would be changed. Then you came up from the water.

–When we said good-bye I really believed I would see you soon again. That a year could not possibly make a difference. I would return to school, feel better about myself and bring someone back to you who might someday match your strength, your intensity. I thought I could make it. Be someone for you.

–Now you know I couldn't come. Without you close I failed. I see Teddy again. He came back six months ago from New York. A novel he wrote there will soon be published. I can be the Angela he understands. I have grown up to despise myself at least as much as Teddy despises me. You didn't offer me an easy way. You did not tell me what I had to be for you. I would have floundered. I would have come apart. I was frightened because I saw the best thing in you was relentless, demanding. In many ways it is a sick, evil thing, but it is the best of you. I could not come back to you and wait for it to expose me, for it to grind me into bits. I am more afraid of dying than anything else, and the best thing in you is death.

She spoke this last waxen, rigid, dissolved to a hovering mask. The uncertainty, the vertigo of the lost rendezvous returned to me. Who had been speaking in my dream? Had I heard simply what I wanted to hear, stuffed conveniently into the form and voice of Angela for effect? A theatrical production staged for my benefit?

Had I invented a life for Angela? The story seemed too authentic, too independent of me. Something real somewhere and mystically transmitted. Or simply a letter I had both repressed and committed to memory. If I doubted the dream, why not doubt the total memory of Angela, accept the interlude as fiction, a prop, an anchor created by a lonely man? What proof were those hours of waiting beneath City Hall? What proof was Angela's face divided among a hundred women at whom I stared? Rather than accept the fact of her non-existence I cling to her through strands of remorse and bitterness. Now I conjure another vision, fashion one more visitation so I may continue to believe. I am almost tempted to accede to a miracle. Angela telepathic, filtering her voice through molecules of air and matter so it reaches me, undimmed, full of truth in this antiseptic closet.

Perhaps Angela is all the poetry left in me. For what it's worth. Not much at the moment. A sonnet won't lift me from the bed. No metaphor will hold the bed pan or change the shitty tailed gowns. If there is orderliness, precision, cleanliness, rhythm in the world, they are most visible in an action, a plan such as I have conceived. Formulating a rite totally consistent with the logic of history, yet harnessing the blind rush of events, opening a momentary wedge so a new myth can shoulder its way into the process.

The gods of fire, of wine, of blood are not co-incidental. They are the faint impressions of mortal men blown up a million times. History is a consuming, crackling fire and time is a vast bland screen and all that men can understand or believe is the play of shadows, the outlines of men or nations caught for an instant before they drop into the flame and ascend in shapeless smoke endlessly climbing the screen. Most men read the smoke, most men pass so easily to oblivion they are the smoke. But some are free. Are gods because they print themselves against the screen. Then the smoke readers, the smoke itself cannot ignore them, will never quite be the same again.

To free the Black God I will drop the hanged cop into the fire. The contorted silhouette will flash darkly on the screen. There will be no turning back, no hiding in the shivering smoke. The lynched white cop will not only be an ineradicable element in the future, but it will seem as if he and his lynchers have always existed, patiently waiting to be perceived, a mystery to be worshipped.

172

To tear such a hole in history. To assist at the birth of a God. These are worth any sacrifice. I would lie here a millennium, if my organs continue to function, calm as a sail waiting for wind.

A black boy cleans my room. He is gangly and tight lipped. A vacant look in his eyes, which seem fixed six inches beyond his wide brogans. The animal taciturnity and sullenness white people associate with laziness and stupidity. They cannot conceive of the discipline, the self-denial such a mask demands. It is that discipline I seek to divert from self-effacement, from obsolete survival techniques. This boy could play a part in the plan. Could serve as a link between me and the others outside. He has learned to wear his brown skin like an impenetrable veil of ignorance. He moves freely here in the gut works of the enemy and no one trembles when he walks by. He is treated as a drone whose imagination could not possibly go beyond the routine prescribed for him. Like the three boys in Atlantic City who held one job simultaneously, alternating each day in the tasks of sweeping and washing and carrying out garbage, called by the same name, paid with one check, their trinity opaque as father son and holy ghost.

But the Man is wily. This boy may be a plant. A good loyal darky praying for tales to carry. Or he may be a scared one. Hopelessly unmanned already by his dependence. As frightened of me as he is of the haunts and bogey men he learned to dread in the tales his mammy whispered to him.

I will not make the first move. I have leisure to study him. Gauge his usefulness.

—Do you smoke.
—Uh, huh.
—I've never seen you smoking.
—Ain't supposed to smoke in here.
—Why not?
—That's what they told me.

—And you didn't ask why.

—Don't matter to me that much. I go on up to where nobody bothers me. There plenty places to smoke.

—But you don't smoke here.

—I don't want no trouble.

—Who would see you?

—Nurse maybe and the supervisor comes round some time.

—What would they do if they caught you smoking?

—Something . . . I guess.

—Do you think you'd lose your job?

—I don't know. People always coming and going.

—What you're saying is the job ain't shit. Right?

—I suppose . . . in a manner of speaking that's what I might be talking about.

—Then why do you give a damn about the rules?

—I don't want trouble.

—Trouble's what you got already with their piece of ass job and rules.

—It's better than nothing. Lots of people got more trouble than me.

—Like me.

—Maybe. I know who you are. I was at Wilson when you trying to make your speech.

—You look too old for Wilson.

—I don't do too good in school. They keep me back but next year I be too old they got to pass me. Don't matter anyway. I be tired from work. I don't hardly go to school now and I ain't planning to stay much longer. Don't make sense when I could be out working full time.

—You're working now and you can't even light a cigarette when you want it.

—Least I can buy me a pack now and then . . . and help out my mother.

—There's a pack in my drawer you can have. I don't think it's even open.

—You don't want 'em.

—I stopped smoking.

174

–Doctor make you.

–No. I make my own rules. I look in worse shape than I am. You know what I mean.

–These your cigarettes.

–Yes. But wait a minute. You can have them all but first I want you to light one. Smoke it here.

–I ain't supposed to.

–This is my room. I make the rules. I want you to understand that. You can have the pack but you must smoke one here, now.

–What if I don't want no smoke now?

–Are you afraid? If you are, I think you should ask yourself what it is that's scaring you. You'll see matches in the same drawer.

–I got my own.

At least once a day during his shift he comes in here and smokes. We both look forward to it though I'm sure for very different reasons. From a distance I enjoy the faintly stale, rough aroma of the tobacco. The first few times he was stiff, perhaps felt bullied. Now he takes deep drags, seems infinitely relaxed as he exhales through his nose and lips. His mannerisms with a cigarette remind me superficially of Saunders. Yet the boy is not taut enough or abrasive enough to be a Saunders. He doesn't have the assassin's skin which fits too tightly over the bones, the unsettling efficiency of gesture, the face crowded by extra shadows that appear to move independent of any light source.

He talks more freely. I am almost positive he can be trusted. Be of use. His name is Anthony. That's what I call him though he says the sound of *Anthony* is strange. He is Tony everywhere but here. And school. A Miss Collins with whom he is infatuated. A white teacher of social studies. She calls him Anthony, displays posters of black heroes on her classroom wall. The class listens to recordings of Paul Robeson, of Malcolm X speaking, they read Richard Wright and Eldridge Cleaver. She has drawn him in. Many days the only class he attends is hers. Of course he can't really read the books, but he listens, watches her as with a shining face she reads her favorite passages. He hears the cream skimmed off the top, sweet, heady in her young, white woman's voice. He is taught five and dime moral lessons. A mortician's version of the bloodily martyred artists is displayed for him, all powder, paint and rigid smiles that reek of formaldehyde. What grasp does he have of history? Of the larger context that destroyed the black men whose words and music are now being exploited by their destroyers?

I tell him stories. The full biographies of the men with whom Miss Collins claims such intimacy. Occasionally he understands. Sees them. Sees her. But the dumb black boy is in love. He returns.

Yesterday I played a game. While he in his painful style rattled on, huffing and puffing on one of the cigarettes I make available, I reached up to the cord dangling beside my headboard and pushed the emergency button. For some reason, perhaps because I signal so infrequently, a pink baby elephant uncomfortably trussed in white nylon immediately responded. The nurse was inside the curtain pulled across my door staring at Anthony some moments before he was aware of her bulging presence. He was deep into a tale about a classmate raped by a teacher in the girls' room, when the nurse shouted at him.

–What do you think you're doing. Put that out this instant. As she stood in the doorway, fat, flushed, breathing heavily, I wished it had been Miss Collins. This nurse was too easy. Ugly already.

–Don't put it out, Anthony.

–Out this instant or I'll have the supervisor in here. You . . . you don't interfere. I don't have to take smartness from your kind. Didn't you hear me say out. She screeched the last command, her voice no longer feigning any sort of control or rational authority. Her words bubbled and boiled as absolute in their stridency as the power she believed supporting them.

—Why must he put it out? I am the only tenant. He has my permission. No one's afraid just because you raise your voice. Call the supervisor. Bring him in here. The boy was lighting the cigarette for me.

He was slow. Confused. I had to say *Thank you, Anthony, for the cigarette,* extend my arm before he stepped over and handed it to me.

—He lights my cigarettes all the time. I have difficulty doing it myself.

—You . . . you people stick together don't you.

—Black birds of a feather. Is that what you mean?

A slow but irresistible wind pushed her from the room by inches. She knew she was going, knew she had no choice, but stubbornly planted her heavy feet, squared her broad shoulders and fought as best she could, spitting threats, face saving phrases of rule, regulation and privilege, rote-learned from her manual.

When she was gone and the curtain sighed back across the entrance, it was like some thick, viscous fluid had been drained from the room. I didn't mention her, asked him to go on with his story. I wanted him to see how she was an absolute irrelevancy, a hulking glacier unable to comprehend the end of the ice age as it slides into the sea. Though she had departed without determining my reason for ringing, he knew I had summoned her and almost belligerently asked me why.

—To demonstrate something about their rules. To show you what I said earlier is true. This is my room and I set the rules. I did not recite for him the most obvious lesson: they are trapped just as circumstantially as we are by the rules they have chosen. I knew he had enjoyed the nurse's discomfort, her absurd floundering. In the space of a few seconds he had seen how ruthlessly lines must be drawn. After seeming to betray him I had treated him to a show of his own force, the power we could wield together. How utterly we could exclude her, dramatize her foolishness. At some level he must have laughed. If for the moment he understood nothing else but the liberating power of that laughter, my little game had been exquisitely managed. I could deal with his mistrust later. I could sermonize on the parable another day. His muteness was not a sign of stupidity, it was the organism's compensation for an inner life tumultuously astir.

I think I can use him. An unexpected boon. I had reconciled myself to being excommunicated. After the unforeseen circumstances of the rally and my *fall* and this imprisoning bed, I had no choice but to resign myself to passive participation in the plan. I had conceived it, launched it, but would have to entrust its implementation to the others. Doubts pound at me of course, but the scheme is much larger than any individual involved. That's its grandeur, what insures the inevitability of success. History has provided a raging sea, a flimsy dam, the corrupt village within hearing distance of the waters but refusing to acknowledge its peril. I have seen the total picture, examined in detail each element without losing the sense of the basically simple configuration. I know the dam will not hold. Its solidarity is a myth as transparent as the myth which describes the water as low and placid on the other side of the wall. I want to inundate the city with a dream of drowning. I want to flood the gutters with the sticks and mud depended upon for salvation. The vision of the end may be simultaneous with the end, but that is not my affair. I have divined the means by which the vision can appear. It is ironic that I need no more than a few hands to help, someone to lug a bucket of water, another to tote a sack of wood and garbage. Flat on my back I can direct the charade.

The boy, without disturbing the logic of the plan, may provide me with a window on the proceedings.

The metaphor is almost too obvious. This boy as a messenger, as youth entrusted with the secrets of the plan. Our link with the generations to come. He will not understand the words, not realize they contain the possibility of death and resurrection.

Careful above all. My vanity must not be allowed to jeopardize the undertaking. I have steeled myself against its promptings. If Angela walked through the curtain and said we may have the best moment of our time together extended for an eternity if you leave with me, I know I could refuse her. I must weigh my motive carefully in this case. Are there practical advantages in communicating by courier with Wilkerson? Is Wilkerson's conviction deep enough? Is Saunders cold enough? Rice stupid enough? Had the endless rehearsals of the event in our talk established the plan for them as clearly and purely as it sits in my imagination?

The last time we were all together I drew a diagram. Step by step from the kidnapping to the lynching and disposal of the body. I couldn't have forgotten anything. Wilkerson nodded assent, said he saw no problems, understood everything. Yet we were inhibited. They are always watching me. I wouldn't be surprised if the room were bugged, if some lackey who has earned the honor of spying on me isn't dozing right now in front of a closed circuit scanner beamed on me. The possibility of surveillance is enough to make the strictest cautions necessary. Except for Wilkerson's one visit when everything is in readiness, the others cannot return here. We did not talk of the plan on the single occasion they thoughtlessly arrived together. The drawing had to suffice. And Wilkerson's reaction to it was limited to what would pass as casual conversation.

Though the plan reduced itself with mathematical precision to a series of incidents which I numbered and circled, though the beads would be strung together by the immutable logic of history, and though the events were no more or less than anticipations of the rhythm of history prematurely externalized, the plan retains a minor, co-incidental dependence on the conspirators. Timing is most important. I'm sure I am the only one whose sense of the timing involved is faultless. In this bed I have become the plan. I have emptied myself of

179

everything but what is necessary to the plan. My pulse is its pulse. I have been content to lie here blind, deaf and dumb to the only reality which concerns me. The boy could restore my senses.

The first task is to be sure of him. I will have him carry a message that is his death warrant if he gives the slightest cause for suspicion. Tell Wilkerson to have Saunders shadow him, watch for a sign that he intends to betray us.

Meanwhile, more preparation of him I can do. I have often regretted all of my fellow conspirators were as old as or older than myself. But I had to work with the available material. We are not quite ancient. Rice, the eldest by two years, is just thirty-six. We are, however, at least a lifetime away from the college kids and the children mimicking them. Our extra life consists of disillusionment, the string of failures and deceits that disqualify us for a better world if by some miracle a better world began tomorrow. The others can wear their hair and clothes differently, sing, shout, call one another brother and believe themselves identical with the new wave, part of a new world, containing and contained by it. We have lost any vision beyond a wavering faith in something better than the misery we have lived through. We are certainly not any part of a vision of something better. We are not even vessels of transition. The men I picked to carry through the plan can gauge change only by its distance from the wreck they have made of their lives. Change must destroy them. They can't call anybody brother without inviting them into a room contaminated with the plague. I am appalled by Anthony's ignorance, but once as we discussed some trivial matter, he shouted at me, as peremptorily, as uncompromisingly as I had ever heard him speak. He said it's always better to tell a person the truth. Never, never is telling them a lie better for them than telling them the truth. I raised the obvious objections. Offered concrete examples which I thought proved the ambiguity inherent in the word *truth*. The virtual impossibility of differentiating truth from falsehood in many complex situations. How truth could be a superfluous

180

value, outweighed by other considerations. He dismissed my arguments summarily. Said he had been lied to all his life, and if he could change any one thing about his life, it would be to remove the web of lies told to him for his own good.

I was astonished by his innocence. How it furnished him with a clarity all my cogitation and cunning had not achieved. Parts of Anthony had flourished in the ooze. If light had not penetrated to illuminate him, neither did it tarnish or corrode. The torpor of his barely realized life was often repugnant to me. I had struggled long ago to exorcise from myself the demons of sloth, fear and self-denial I saw rampant in him. Yet he sat teaching me, flung open doors that made me shrink from the sudden light they exposed. I had killed an Anthony in me, rejected his weaknesses and strength. Though in many ways I had been Anthony, his life now was unimaginable. I could only react with sudden flashes of awe and despair.

Anthony. Suppose a great leader, a black man like you, discovered a way to turn this country inside out. Suppose he knew how to free black people once and for all from their oppressors. He could do this but first he'd have to lie. Offer his people all the things most think they want, cars, clothes, big houses, promise them possessions in order to rally support, to prepare the way for the liberation. Would you tell him not to lie? Would you tell him to allow the suffering of black people to continue because hearing lies from him would be worse than the beating, stealing and killing they are subjected to every day? Would you say freedom is not worth that lie on your lips?

He pondered, his face vacant of any sign he had understood or even heard my question. When he answered it was blandly, as if he had no idea his life was staked on the question.

—If I be working hard for a car and when I do everything I was supposed to do somebody give me something that ain't a car I'd be pretty mad.

—Even if somebody gave you freedom instead?

181

—That's why people lie. So they can give you what they want to give you and not what you want. They lie to keep you from taking.

—You don't understand freedom.

—Maybe not. I don't know much about anything. I ain't hardly supposed to.

—You're right. There are blinders over your eyes. But whose fault is that?

—Whose fault don't seem to matter. I just know I got to get along with what I have. I'll make it. Lies ain't helping.

—You said you heard me speaking at Wilson. Do you know why I was there? Why they were scared? Did you see the army they called out to silence one man? They were frightened of my voice, no matter what I had to say. The barest chance that you might listen or any of the others listen, even to a pack of lies is a threat to the Man. The Man controls everything you see and hear. To play the kinds of games he does with your mind his power over you must be absolute. An outside voice, a desperate act, so barefaced and brutal they won't be able to cover up its significance. These are the only ways of penetrating the veil. For a while the impact of Watts burning or revolutionaries kidnapping and ransoming a judge are raw, crude sources of energy. They are answers in progress to the questions you have been afraid to raise. They make you angry and ashamed because you realize someone else is paying your dues, doing your dying. For an hour or a day or a week you are changed. Your vision of history is concrete, unobstructed. You understand the white man's power, its intimidation and threat. Then most of us are only too grateful to have the veil restored. The radio television and newspapers begin their juggling act. Words are invented. A cast of cartoon characters appears with their roles clumsily stenciled on their sweatshirts. They are grossly inhuman, and slide neatly into place, Humility, Virtue, Innocence, Evil, the same old refugees from a morality play shuffling through the same tired situations. We have seen it before and we assent wearily. What we thought was new, daring, perhaps even liberating, is after all cowboys, Indians and the inevitable blue coated, blue-eyed cavalry speeding to the rescue.

—It's that simple and you hear me but you'd still prefer a car to freedom. Don't shake your head. I know better than you do what you're thinking. They've put it all there for you to think. You are the history they have manufactured. Tony. Anthony. Exhibit A. A monument to their success. Do you have any notion of what you really are? How many carbon copies of you walk the streets of this great nation? You all spit and scream and fuck in the same way. You duplicate your teeming, cramped hives across the country. The resemblance is disgusting. The unanimity. They have a wind-up key stuck in your ass so far it tickles your brain. Your nose is wide open and I can see the key twisting. I see you now and I know where you'll be tomorrow. You're that safe, predictable. They have you on a tight schedule. The stages are clearly marked and you'll go through each with a blindness and enthusiasm. You'll think they are you. Till one day you'll reach the last stage and perhaps a glimmer of how you've been cheated. Of what a clumsy, repetitious trap they've made black manhood and how eagerly, foolishly you've performed your paces. Do you think it's a co-incidence? Do you believe there could be such undeviating failure and frustration without a program? Of course exceptions exist. There must be exceptions. But almost to a man the energies of those successes are made accessory to the white man's control or superfluous to black people's freedom. With the Man's million eyes and ears, the images of *now* they bombard us with, they have forced us to lose a sense of before and after, mistake their programmed version of our present lives for history, inevitability. Only a violent reversal will do. The fabric they have strung together must be torn apart. One sudden rent and every thread will unravel. The smallest and largest lies will go at once. After the chaos, if nothing is comprehensible at least nothing will remain of what once was thought to be solid, real, forever. That is freedom. Metaphysical revolt.

—If you prefer I will call it an automobile. A house in

Scarsdale. A Brooks Brothers suit. I will call it Black. I will call it Pan African Unity. I will call it God. Scream revolution. Armageddon. I will metamorphose it to the comeliest dream you have ever dreamt. Kill you with it if I have to.

I realized I had lost him. For three or four minutes I had been shouting at no one in particular. I was rankled by this burst of vanity and ego. Ranting to please myself with the sound of my words. The boy could have been insulted as well as confused. All my patient preparation of him would be wasted.

I attempted a smile. He wouldn't look at me. I felt my own skin lifting. I saw what he must see. A battered half man flat on his back, chained to a bed, screaming freedom. The irony oppressed me. He could not remain in awe, puzzled by such a creature. I couldn't allow him to dismiss me as loud and powerless, a clown to laugh at with his friends when he left the hospital. I thought of disclosing the plan, of offering him a role. I began to hint of dark, portentous events. I reassumed the part of master, seer. I drank in his attention, it rose so palpably to his eyes, his lips relaxing from sullenness.

Then I stopped. Just short of disgust. I had been wooing him. Not for the plan—I was on the verge of betraying it for any paltry gesture of affection from him—but because of a vain, selfish urge for comfort, for luxury. But of course the plan was everything. And if I was the plan as I had conjured myself into believing, what prompted the urge? Where had I hidden it from myself during these weeks of abstention and self-denial?

I would have been overjoyed at that moment if the inklings of a plot I had revealed to him were transformed to poison coursing through his system. Nothing less than watching him shrivel to a lifeless heap would compensate for the injury he had forced me to inflict on myself. I knew then my mind was infinitely treacherous. I could deny or convince myself of anything. In my desolation, a prisoner of their violence, their bed, I could attach myself as hungrily to this hard-legged, thick-headed black boy as I once had to Angela.

184

Saunders would have to kill him. My life, the lives of the conspirators, the plan itself could not be dependent on the boy's ignorance. How much had I actually divulged. I could dispatch him now if necessary. The razor blade under my pillow. Draw him close to light a cigarette for me. Make him bend till his pimply throat is in reach.

—Do you understand what I mean? How a few men with the proper insight and unflinching resolve might change things. They wouldn't necessarily have to be great or unusual men. People like you or me I'm talking about. If some co-incidence put them in the right place at the right time and they acted with all the determination the situation demanded . . .

—No, we must talk about history first . . . before you could understand. . . . You . . . must understand the rules in order to break them . . . if you understand fully . . . there will be no rules but the ones you make as you act . . .

—Supervisor told me not to be hanging around here. I been here long enough to be done cleaning.

—Then you better go . . . we can talk tomorrow.

Whatever advantage he had gained, I could win back. The plan was safe. He could only go as far as I explicitly led him. He could piece nothing together from the generalities, the suggestion that my world does not end an inch beyond my fingertips, nor is it bound by the curtain and three walls that contain my eyes. I had not chanced the plan in the game I played with him. I had merely been fortified by the plan's power. Felt its strength well up within me, refusing to be belittled by what the boy with his untutored eyes thought he saw. Pride moved me to entrap him again. Pride flowing from my knowledge of the plan. I had toyed with his life and possibly my own, but the plan had never been in jeopardy.

If all has gone according to schedule, and there is no reason to doubt it has, Wilkerson should come here in two weeks. By now Saunders should know the best way to ambush the girl. Her lover will be annoyed the first day she is

185

missing. The second day he will be angry and on the third start searching for her. We will assist him in his hunt. He will find his whore and his doom together. We will hold him until it is time for him to make his grand entry on the platform. He will be drugged to minimize his fear, any chance of untidy panic. The rumors will have circulated. Her mutilated body will have been discovered, described. He will personify the guilt of a million jailers and executioners. The sharp crack of his neck breaking will be a thunderclap above the mob. His body will convulse with explosions of piss, shit and bile at the moment of truth, all the rottenness inside the man suddenly decorating the blue uniform.

Perhaps the sack of flour should wait till then. One last mockery of the man's image of himself, one more coat of white dusted over the foulness.

Then . . . then. The horror. The outrage. Everyone knowing the truth. A heave and explosion as the dam splinters, the earth recoils from the first onslaught of mountainous waves.

I dreamed I was lying on a rock. The rock was on a narrow point of land jutting into the middle of a lake. Twilight. A full moon preserving the color of the sky. Only a few of the brightest starts were visible against the pale turquoise. One pinpoint of light directly over my face as I lay with my back pressed into the stony contours seemed to be moving. I thought it might be a satellite, or a plane whose altitude negated its screaming engines. The darting shadows on the sandy strip of land, the constant rush of water across the rock strewn tip of the point and slapping rhythmically along one smooth black edge, the nervous rustling of trees sometimes in concert but also one tree at a time quivering alone in the grip of a giant, invisible fist, something about this ceaseless animation that extended even to the sky where scudding clouds made a star seem to move, placed me outside of time. I thought I could listen forever to the water, watch for eternity the changing shapes of the clouds rushing overhead or the fire and blood streaked setting of the sun blazing molten through the purple clouds piled on the horizon.

But everything stopped. I felt a birth. A god donning skin. I believe a man must be conceived twice. To exist, a man must first be imagined by other men. The mind of at least one human being must become a breeding ground, must nurture some possibility of itself in the quiet of spirit and will until the thing it could never be has a throbbing potential life. The spiritual incubus will then float immune to time and space in a vast blackness whose dimensions are only suggested by the phrase: there is nothing it does not contain.

Soon, since time is superfluous and a second or a millennium are both soon, the incubus will unite with a human form. This is the second accidental birth. A sputtering urge to rebel that seemed lost in the flesh of a slave tossed overboard to lighten a Spanish galleon in a stormy sea will be reborn wire taut and indestructible in the soul of an infant whose first home is 125th Street, a drawer in a vermin infested bureau. As there is no fixed interval between the two conceptions, neither is there continuity of nation, race, sex. I sometimes feel that animals, plants, even a rock with its slow thoughts that need millions of years to form exude a spiritual exhalation that is realized in man shape. After a certain type of man is imagined he may be reproduced endlessly, all variation co-incidental details of the flesh. A god is created when the will and spirit of the many focus repeatedly on a lack, an emptiness each senses in himself. The collective energies are projected with such force that the god achieves an existence whether or not a co-incidence with flesh has occurred. The imminent messiah remains incomplete, however, until he has been a man. A man for a day or a lifetime, a man long enough to converse with some storyteller who can spread the news abroad.

Though the many create the possibility of a god, one man must dream a human guise the god can assume. Stretched on the slanting rock I know I watched the Black God pass to manhood.

I was aware of the transition first as an absolute stillness, then a flood of patience, an unquestioning certitude. All that seemed to move around me—water, light, wind—must come to rest. Motion was imperfection, was form seeking form, continuous dissatisfaction. I don't know how long everything stopped, but it did. Not peace, not rest, not quiet, or stillness, or oblivion, nothing I could anticipate. Just a stop, a space between. Not an abrupt cessation or a hurried pause. Just everything stopping, kissed to sleep by the God's touch. He was not there. Then He was there. All I could comprehend of the transition was that it filled the space between not there and there. Filled it so completely that nothing else existed. Water, moon, stars, heartbeat. When I began to breathe again and the rhythms of the finger of land crashed around me once more I knew I had assisted at the birth of a God. I could see the earth as fatally afflicted, see its dance of forms as a futile attempt at curing its disease. Though I could visualize my own existence as one of an infinite number of mirrors reflecting the earth's fitful struggle, I could be composed, in fact accept my own mortality as blandly as I did that of the stone I rested upon. The God was father and son to me simultaneously, revealing gently, compassionately, the way only flesh can, that I had been born and would die, that these arbitrary limits were as far as the flesh could go, but his coming, clothed in flesh, was a guarantee that these limits were fitting, ordained, that the parenthesis which contained me was not entirely opaque at either extremity.

The dream ended without a revelation of the God's precise human shape. My contentment was spoiled by a worrisome curiosity. I wanted to be able to recognize him if I passed him on the street. Despite all that had been revealed, I resented what had been withheld. I wanted to see the face, the body, the vulgarized form of his mystery. Perhaps Anthony or one of the conspirators, a face teasingly close and unreadable. Perhaps some tall, straight, brown-eyed handsome man who would stride from the crowd, roaring like a lion as he feeds upon the body of the lynched cop. Perhaps a baby sleeping on its black mother's breast while the woman quietly weeps. Whatever, wherever, whoever, I can no longer doubt the spirit has been released and received, a new man born.

I cannot trust the boy. Perhaps I should say I cannot trust myself with him. At some crucial point I might ask too much of him, put into his hands words which could destroy us all. I will wait for Wilkerson. I can subdue my curiosity for ten days. If some drastic modification of the plan is necessary, Wilkerson will certainly consult me. The boy tells me it's getting hot outdoors. School will soon be dismissed. Old people will be squatting on their stoops, women hanging from their windows, young boys gathered around the newest, sleekest car on the block basking in its elegance, daydreaming, telling lies in which they function with the machine's speed and brute force. In spite of the oppressive city scape framing the scene, I see a street momentarily pastoral. Something in the old people's faces, the skinny children idly abandoning themselves to motion, to crying, to any stick or bit of junk they find on the littered curbs, the vacant lots where one rotted tooth has been razed from between its monotonously decaying neighbors. I hear the music I always hear on such a block. The houses leak the same heady perfume of manured fields. I sense discontinuity, inappropriateness. A mass of people have been displaced. The stumbling rows of houses cannot contain them. They spill onto the streets and the streets cannot hold them, the people keep slipping away. Rivers are in their eyes. They disappear behind luxuriant trees. Run across wide, grassy fields. Superfluous clothing falls away. Their arms and legs are sculpted by a wind that never aired these streets.

But a sense of another life, another world asserting itself in the midst of the fallen city dims in each generation. Only rarely does the teeming life glimmer across the surface of the things I see as I walk down our streets. Perhaps I dream it to the surface. Need to forget what rots and stinks and dies around me.

I see a man walking down the block weeping. He stops at

each grouping on the front steps or sidewalks. He makes the vacant eyes meet his. He stares until the only sound between his face and another is his hand reaching out to touch. Silence a wake behind him. The old walls dissolving soundlessly to dust. The people joining hands. I visualize him at times moving in this manner. In certain moods I prefer that to my image of him bronzed, bare chested outside the city gates, his trumpet raised, and ten thousand trumpets echoing his first note. The walls tumbling. Smoke, fire, thundering apocalypse. The blind given sight. The lame walking. The rich man guillotined by a razor shuddering down to close the needle's eye.

My strength is slowly returning. I do my exercises faithfully, flexing my muscles, holding them tense for sixty second intervals. Beneath the sheets a silent, unobservable recovery. With help I believe I can walk. I grabbed the boy's arm as he swept under my bed. He couldn't free himself. He laughed because I was smiling. He treated it as a game but I knew my sudden show of force surprised, even frightened him. They all believe I am helpless. Perhaps the boy knows where they keep my braces and a cane. Is he ready to recover them for me? He might call it stealing. I must tell him a story about Frederick Douglass. Explain how it's impossible for a slave to steal from his master.

Anthony described a ward on the seventh floor. It had been a refuge for him. A place where he could smoke undisturbed since the inmates of a particular section on that floor couldn't have cared less if Anthony was lighting a cigarette or putting a match to a fuse which could blow him and the ward to bits. They call it the Sanitarium. It contains the madmen. The staff has incorporated a phrase into their jargon. *You'll be sleeping on the seventh.* It's a humorous catch-all used to characterize anyone whose speech or actions don't conform to the rigidly observed hospital routine. According to the boy most of the staff considered me a good bet to be sleeping on the seventh. A few thought I was not there only because I was too dangerous, too criminally crazy for their benign loony bin and that I would be transported, as soon as I healed sufficiently, to a padded cell in the state institution. I was sure the rumor had been purposely started. Such a reputation would serve as a moat around my prison rock. The authorities are clever. They are determined to exile me, isolate me from any aid I might receive from my people. They don't miss a trick.

I was encouraged because this piece of scuttlebutt came from the boy. He was truly beginning to serve as a pair of eyes and ears for me. If I thought they would not be replaced, I would ask him to locate and dismantle the camera and microphones that make this room like a fishbowl.

It seems the nurses on the seventh floor are very liberal. One of the few places the boy felt he could relax and talk. Most of the patients are harmlessly insane, immured in psychoses that blessedly protect them from this world. They are as docile as plants and their inner turmoil if it exists is opaque to the nurses as they water, change the soil and move their charges in and out of the sunlight. The others receive heavy sedation. Doses so large that many never move from their beds. The nurses like to show off their prize patients, have them perform. Since Anthony is available and has a big smile he often serves as an audience. There was one old black man who on command would spit shine your shoes with his tongue. A girl of thirteen who had been raped and brutalized by a street gang sang sweet lullabys to a non-existent baby she rocked in her arms. Anthony would smoke and quietly listen to the gossiping nurses if the patients were all resting. The seventh floor had been his favorite spot before I came.

Through him I gained a familiarity with the hospital. I knew which part of the floor I was on, had a fairly detailed map of my surroundings which I could depend upon if the occasion for speed and stealth arose. He knew nothing more of the plan, but he understood that my situation was precarious. I let him connect my speech at Wilson with threats to my life I anticipated. I embroidered upon the fragment of speech he had heard. He admitted he hadn't gone to listen. The rally simply had freed him from the monotonous routine of his life. A rally brought bodies together. I wrote the outline of the speech I had planned for that day on a paper towel. He promised to study it, repeat the guiding ideas to me the next day. No satisfaction came when he faithfully parroted my words. I demanded more, tried to draw him out.

—I ain't ready for this.

—You mean you don't understand.

—I'm tired. It took me a long time to say those words you put down. And I still got a lot of work after I leave here.

I saw him sitting in Miss Collins' class. Listless, bored. A student to be diverted to the vocational track. Incurious. Inherently lazy. A dull thing who would never learn the correct answers.

—Are you stupid, Anthony? Who has convinced you of your stupidity? I thought he shrank from my question. Visibly cringed as he took the butt from his lips and let it drip from his fingers into the pool of dust and trash he had swept into the center of the room. He stood motionless, the broom a third leg rooting him to the floor. I half expected a hole to open beside him, a gurgling drain that would suck his body and the dust together into the cloacal darkness reigning beneath the foundations of the hospital.

—I'm tired. If I didn't stay tired, I'd be crazy.

—Maybe crazy is preferable to hiding. If the others are right, I'll be sleeping on the seventh to keep you company.

—Company don't do much good up there.

—What I wrote down frightened you, didn't it? You understood the message perfectly well, what it asked of you. What it would make of you. But you recited the words with no more feeling than you'd give the ABC's. You pretended to be ignorant of what you were saying. You were protecting yourself.

—Like I said. I got lots to do. And I'm sleepy already. You don't do nothing but lay here in the bed. Plenty time to just think and write anything comes in your head. Plenty time to do nothing but worry and tease me. I'm gone on about my own business now and you tend to yours. I do what you ask me, but what you ask ain't really what you want. You always want more. You always asking for one thing when you want another. You just want me in the habit of doing what you say.

–You're forgetting why I'm here.

–Cause they whipped your head at Wilson.

–At Wilson. Wilson. Wilson, Woodrow, twenty-eighth president. Racist fucking bastard wanting to found a League of Nations. Goddamnit. Yes, at Wilson Junior High. Some lily white League it would have been. Perpetuating his name. Perpetuating the tight assed little Miss Collins who mangles your dreams. Yes that's where you saw me. A crippled bastard they broke into even smaller pieces. At White Woodrow Wilson. White Woodrow Wilson Junior High filled with black bodies and black sweat. The stones ooze white pus. Do you know white is the sign of death, of extreme putrefaction? The orientals have known that for thousands of years. And every day you are driven like cattle into the rotten white barn. They whipped my head at Wilson. And my balls and my back and my hands and parts I didn't even know I had, they whipped me at Wilson and didn't stop for days. So long I lost track of time they got me good at Wilson, whipped me enough to last for the rest of my life. Why? Do you know why? Because I came looking for you. For you who came looking for some fat ass to rub up against. You who hides on the edge of the crowd, not listening, not caring who is whipped or why. You who would watch and cheer whatever spectacle was provided. At Woodrow Wilson I got a head beating and you think that makes me a fool. That you're safe because you keep your distance, hang around the edges. You with that silly broom when you ought to have a rifle, be killing yourself or killing them. You weren't reciting a nursery rhyme a few minutes ago. You had in your hands a recipe for liberation or death. One or the other. Doesn't matter which comes first. But one or the other is coming and

I tried to tell you that. But they whipped my head and dragged me away. And you sulked home with your tail between your crusty legs. Cowering like you cower from any words which don't put you to sleep.

I must have been shouting because a nurse and an orderly rushed into the room. From the corner of my eye I saw Anthony disappear, a black slinking shadow the others would take no notice of. I knew they would come to my bed. They would flood my guts with some tranquilizing poison. As it crept through my system I would become calm as a daisy. I considered the razor blade I had tucked away. Each day I concealed it in a different spot. Always instantly accessible, it could be in my hand before they had time to react. I thought of the nurse's pudgy arm slashed from elbow to wrist. The syringe dropped from numb fingers. Skin nerveless puckering back from the wound, a red path through her flesh, my wand striking, like Moses plowing a furrow in the white sea, my people marching down the bloody highway.

Instead I let them drown me. After the needle's bite everything was extremely funny. Shudders of laughter, a velvet undertow dragging me down.

Part

3

RICE heard it first on his favorite radio station, the one with all talk shows and news so you could stay informed. He heard it just after the announcer gave credit and a twenty-five dollar bonus to the lucky informant who called in a story worthy of a flash bulletin. You got a fanfare, twenty-five dollars and your name on the radio just because you were lucky enough to be on hand when something happened and had a dime you could drop in the box to call the station before anybody else did. Rice envied the lucky bystander. Jealousy made him pout because during his entire lifetime he had never been witness to anything newsworthy. Certainly nothing worth a flash bulletin. Once he had come upon a man squashed on the pavement. But a crowd had already begun to gather and somebody officious had covered the head of the suicide. He expected no more men to plummet out of the sky and fall at his feet. The only thing he knew that other people might want to know he couldn't tell because it was a secret. He would never be interviewed. Never get a check or a plaque delivered to his door.

After describing the twelve alarm warehouse fire and honoring his informant the announcer had detailed a murder. He said the victim was Wilbur Childress and the suspect being held Orin Wilkerson of 6540 Simon Street.

Rice was indignant. The old man had no right. Just when they were on the verge of trying to make things better, he had to go out and act a nigger. Cut somebody to death. And his son about to become a hero. Rice was angry. Could they allow Wilkerson to continue as one of them? Bad enough with loud Saunders. Rice doubted for the thousandth time his own wisdom in joining the conspiracy. He had never been enthusiastic about the plan or the role it allotted to him.

There never seemed time or occasion for him to have his say. Rice could plainly see how the others were using him. He resented Littleman for his bullying and co-ercion. But as long as they all thought of him simply as a tool Rice felt in control of the situation. He could, in fact, stay a step ahead of the others, even Littleman, because they underestimated him. With Wilkerson compromised by his father's crime, Rice felt himself clearly as the number two man, just behind Littleman. Saunders had always been out of the picture. A thug for the strong arm duties, replaceable as soon as his usefulness ran out. Now when the revolution came, the son of a convicted murderer could not be placed before the people as a leader. Rice knew Littleman would want to remain behind the scenes. And since Littleman thought of him as spineless and weak, someone easily manipulated, he, Rice, would be the logical person to head whatever provisional government the revolutionaries instituted. Littleman would believe he had a patsy, a puppet who would respond mindlessly to his whims. Well, Littleman was not the only one who could plan.

Twenty-five minutes later the bulletin was repeated. A report from the scene of the fire, and in its wake the murder item. Rice caught every word this time. No mistake. Wilkerson's daddy had killed a man. Drunk and fighting in some vacant lot. Though Rice condemned him and all the lost creatures like him, he couldn't help feeling pity for Wilkerson's father. Like a child, really. Grown men with families, out in the street acting like children. Wilkerson would be crushed. It was a damned shame. A black man like Wilkerson trying his best to make good, to be somebody and he has to worry about his own kind pulling him down as much as he has to worry about the white man. Niggers are backbiters and spoilers. Ones at the bottom have no better sense than to try to keep everybody down. . . . You just have to cut them no count niggers loose and go on about your business. What his mama said, and a million times he had seen how right her advice had been.

But he was stuck with the others in the plan. Even though Rice believed he would turn it all to his benefit, that he would come out on top, he hated how the plan exposed him to the ugliness of the other conspirators. Saunders' boisterousness, Littleman's devious cunning and now the cloud of murder hanging over all their heads because of Wilkerson's father. A smart man shouldn't let himself get too connected. And the plan was all about connections.

Well, he would call Wilkerson and tell him about it. Wilkerson would still be at school. They'd call him to the office. Rice would make his voice urgent, let them know it was an emergency. He would be the first to tell Wilkerson even though no check or plaque was forthcoming.

• • •

Wilkerson watched the dish cloth twist in his mother's hands. Her knuckles whitened, the rag was an infected organ she had dragged from her body. The children's faces had been displaced by his mother's face. But she grew younger, vulnerable, more like the children while he talked. Wilkerson had left the school building moments after the call from Rice. He had checked with the police to verify Rice's announcement, then had rushed to his mother so she might hear the news first from him. He didn't understand her eyes. Suddenly young and innocent and untouched. Where were all the years, all the weight she had been carrying. He didn't see his father in her eyes or even himself. Wilkerson hated the drone of his voice, but could find no better way to say what had to be said. Before he had finished he was certain she knew more than he could tell her. She knew and she didn't know. He must stop altogether or wedge himself brutally into her consciousness.

Wilkerson realized he was in the wrong place. She had been telling him to go, to leave her and find his father. She appreciated his coming, his love, but she would be all right, she would work out a way of understanding. But her husband, his father . . .

Go get him. Go get him, Thomas, and bring him home.

199

Down the steps. A million times down the rotting steps of his parents' building. So many times, he had forgotten the pee stench, the crumbling wood, the softness suddenly underfoot that could send you spinning into other worlds. But you descend knight errant tippy tip down the steps and into the streets you've forgotten too. And the caves beneath the street. Bold hieroglyphs spray painted on the subway walls. Puddles. A blood red trickle leaking from under the platform into the murky bed of the silver rails. Muck and cigarettes. Obscenities five foot tall decorating the crumbling plaster walls of the station. You wait for the roof to cave in. The rumble of trains to be swallowed by the groan of shifting earth.

Then at the courthouse you had to wait in line again. Like you did for groceries or tickets to a ball game. His father was just a few yards away locked in one of the cells. Wilkerson glanced around the small, square waiting room. Green walls freshly painted, but already pencil scrawled, inset benches lining three sides, women and children in watery pastel colors. Cowed by the dead green walls that were window bare, coldly glowing. The women fretted over children absent and those who shuttled from lap to lap. Conversation was subdued, marked by sighs and long pauses, by the sudden departure of animation from the women's eyes.

Wiggling her narrow hips toward one end of a bench and scooping a sprawling pile of infant's bottles, diapers and miniature clothing toward her lap, a young black woman made room for a newcomer. It could have been his mother who brushed by him as he stood just inside the door. Same age, same size, a brown suit like his mother would wear here, the familiar scent as she made her way past him to the bench, adjusting her skirt around her knees, sighing as she sat. Her will expiring, a perceptible afflatus stately rising, Wilkerson believed he could see it reach the ceiling and blot itself to soot. Picking nervously at her brown outfit, but firmly in possession of her corner of the bench, she was stiff in the semi-circle of women, her eyes fixed on a child crawling across the gray green concrete floor.

200

A voice squeaky and singsong like the voices of his students softly chanted a nursery rhyme.

This is the church
This is the steeple
Open the doors
Out come the people

He watched a dark skinned girl build the church, then the steeple with her long, bony fingers. When the gates opened her ten fingers, each tipped by an oval of pearl, galloped into the ribs of the boy standing pressed between her knees. He giggled and squirmed as she tickled him under the chin and ran her hands down his body. He was laughing aloud though his pudgy face was still streaked with the tears of a moment before. His mother played the finger game again. Church, steeple, the explosion of scurrying people. Perhaps it would be that easy. Open the door and his people come laughing through. Free. Free. Free at last. Scrambling through the outflung gates.

Twenty-five feet away the cages began. Barely room for shoulders and hips in the passageway between the waiting room and the barred steel door. When your name finally was called you pass through the first steel door. On the other side a guard calls your name again and lifts one layer of your skin with his eyes. The guard holds an oversize key ring. He sifts through cast iron keys that clank dully against one another like cow bells. Oiled steel hinges, sliding bolts and latches, keys jammed home but you are barely fifteen feet from where you started. The floor is stone. The guard mumbles, and though you do not turn to meet his eyes again, you hear a number. In a dream you repeat the number five, you say it to the guard who has already turned and left, slamming the steel maze shut behind you.

Moment of panic. Wilkerson realizes the deception worked upon him. He had been tricked into this dungeon, locked in, and now the grinning guard was throwing away the keys. No way out. Never see sunlight again. Never another human

201

face. Guilt stinking through his pores. Of course they knew about the plan. Of course his role in the conspiracy had been discovered long ago. Rice was an informer. He had tricked Wilkerson into coming here. Meekly led to the slaughter. Laughter rattling the bars. One of the cops patting Rice on the back, buying the traitor a drink. Wilkerson's helplessness made him shudder. Not a thing he could do, they could beat, maim, torture. He saw Littleman's bloated face, the eyes closed by lumps of bruised flesh. He saw himself, a toothless madman giggling in the hooded corners of his cell.

Wilkerson forced himself to stop trembling before he stepped to number five. Free men and men in cages, men separated by arbitrary inches. He must face his father across the incalculable space. Perhaps it would be easy. His father would come forward, bow to his audience, grin as his cell is unlocked, as the farce ends. Guards stripping off their paper uniforms. Childress, the victim, wiping ketchup from his shirt, the cardboard bars of the jail set no longer menacing as house lights go up.

—Thomas

—How are you, Daddy

His father's heavy eyelids drooped once, but quickly popped up again. Then his gaze steady, deep and naked, greasy-eyed like a dog.

—It'll take some time but I'll be all right. I don't need a lawyer or putting your mother through a trial. You save the money and trouble and worry of it all. I'll just go to the judge and tell him I did it. I just want to say I took his life and here's mine, take it and be done.

—You know it doesn't work that way. We're doing everything we can. You should have called us so we could have started sooner. I talked to a bondsman just before they said I could see you. He thinks he can work out something we can afford. You ought to be home tomorrow.

—Where is your mother?

—She'd be here if she could. But the rules allow only one visitor a week. And I wanted to let you know what had happened so far. What I could manage about a lawyer and bail. Mama said she wouldn't be able to remember anything once she saw you. She knew she'd just break down and make things worse so we thought it best for me to come. I know you're upset and worried. And I know how anxious you are to get out of here. I wanted to relieve you in any small way I could. If things don't work out tomorrow, maybe they'll let Mama come in. Your hearing is tomorrow at noon. We'll both be there in the courtroom.

–No that's not necessary. I appreciate all you all doing. But I don't want to see her here. I don't want her in this place.

You slowly recall what you came for. A man is framed in the viewing window. Behind his head a sheet of striped ticking sways. It is a curtain he had pushed through to begin his performance.

–Daddy, I don't know what to say. Wilkerson had sorted through countless definitions, had many words for what his father had become. But no satisfaction came in saying: *drunk, philanderer.* In saying the worst, trapping with a word all that was formless and unmanageable about the man who had entered his mother and left him there to live. In a cell now. Murderer staring back at you through the thick glass partition.

–Nothing to say, but I was hoping you'd come. I was worried about you. Hadn't seen you since that night at the house. Orin Wilkerson bowed when he spoke to reach the metal circle that allowed words to pass between visitors and prisoners. Bare patches show his scalp. As if a fist had rubbed hair away. Forehead still smooth, sun rich brown Wilkerson had always envied, coppery brown that had been fumbled by the genes, transmuted to pallid tan in the son's complexion. Father's cheeks needed a shave. Thomas Wilkerson clambered onto a chair, chubby legs dangling precarious for an instant but worming his supple body till he stood upright, bare toes curling on the wooden seat, hands grasping the chair back, eyes riveted on the mirror image, on the soapy luxuriance of his father's chin, the gleaming razor and its lisp through white foam. Cheeks did not have the tautness of the brow anymore. Age was the eyes, nose and mouth growing smaller in the face, losing their dominance to encroaching folds of flesh. His father had a way of shifting his lower jaw so it jutted to one side. When he had the migraine headaches, you could almost hear his teeth grinding, hear the pressure building inside his skull, pain which he fought silently, grudgingly, tightening his crooked jaw.

Twitch in the pebbled cheek. Excess flesh betraying him. Cheeks could not exercise as the hands did, could not grasp the cans and hurl garbage into the rumbling trucks. Hands could die with their toughness intact, ropy veins binding them. His father's dark hands. Mother loving hands. A man nearly twice his age who could probably lift twice as much. If he challenged him, fought him wrist to wrist the way he fought Littleman, the calloused fingers would bear him down. A child for them.

—Daddy what happened.

—I wish I knew. God knows I wish I knew. The grate through which he spoke distorted his voice, made it quaver, fade, a long distance telephone call from a foot away. Wilkerson bent, resting his elbows on a well rubbed shelf below the window like offering his ear for a kiss in order to make out the words. He had never heard his father's voice shake. Perhaps on the other side the visitor's voice sounded just as uncontrolled, perhaps the speaking grill was meant to cheat the speakers, to reinforce the distance and isolation of the prisoner's world.

—I try to put it together, but it don't make sense. Just sit here with a terrible ache. I try to figure out what happened and nothing comes. Like I ain't had no life outside this jail.

—He came at me with the knife. Childress was drunk. He came at me with a knife. My back was up against a wall. I couldn't run away. And he had stopped playing. He was coming at me for real. Nothing I could do but grab for my own knife. So fast I didn't even have time to think. Got the knife in my hand and had to open it with my teeth. He was so close I shoved at him with the knife in my hand.

–I tripped trying to get out of his way. We were in that lot on Collins Avenue, the one near the show. We had hustled through the route. Barely twelve o'clock. Radcliff had his car parked there and we were carrying a can of gas to get it started. Me and Childress and Radcliff. I bought the gas and Radcliff was supposed to pay me but Childress screaming Radcliff better give him the money because I owed him. And Thomas, I swear to God I didn't owe him nothing, but he got mad. I told him Radcliff was giving money to nobody but me and Radcliff said I was right since I bought the gas and I didn't have anything that day anyway, hardly enough to get me a taste of something after work but Childress he just keeps shouting and getting madder. First he tells Radcliff he's gonna take his money from him, then he's on me talking about money or cutting me so I get tired. You know how he is. Childress always jumping bad, talking about who he's gonna cut. And him hardly big as a minute. But that bad mouth of his I told him to go on back to the truck before I broke his arm. He went running and when he came back had his knife open. I backed up. He's pulled it before and waved it around so I hardly paid attention, but he kept coming. I could see something in his eyes I never seen before. And he wouldn't say anything make sense. I kept trying to talk to him. Backing up and saying wait a minute, man, wait this is your man I remember trying to get him to say something but he was staring wild right in my eyes and circling with that knife. I knew he meant business. Too late, he was too close. I tried to run but tripped over a log. I was down when I got it out remember opening it with my teeth and pushing myself up and him on top of me I shoved with it in my hand and fell on him.

–He said I'm cut bad. I was up and my knife on the ground somewhere. But he didn't move. Just said that one thing *cut bad* slumped over on the ground. Radcliff told me he had been hollering the whole time at both Childress and me and hollering to get the others to come and stop it. I hadn't heard a thing. Radcliff had his arms around me I think when I was standing over Childress. He didn't need to do that. I wasn't mad at Childress. He didn't need to hold me. I thought I was cut. I was wet and sick feeling. I saw the broken glass, the garbage spread all over that vacant lot and the sky getting dark. And then it all just goes to pieces. I know we put him in the car to drive to the hospital. We took him and I was in the back seat with Childress holding his head.

—If I could just understand a little bit better. I keep seeing Mamie Childress and the kids. What they must be thinking. He was my friend. My best friend. I don't know how many times I've been in their house, eating their food, drinking their liquor. I could always talk to Mamie. Say some things I couldn't even say to your mother. And she used to talk about Childress. Tell for an hour what a wrong, no good nigger he was then cry for fifteen minutes cause she loved him so much. Now he's gone. She got kids hardly more than babies. Why did the little nigger have to get so mad about those pennies. Happened so fast and now he's dead. I was trying to get away. Shoving out at him. Don't matter what they do to me. You know his head was on my lap while we were driving to the hospital.

—White faces when we got to the emergency ward. *A stretcher, we need a stretcher.* And one answered wait a minute mister we decide what's needed. One looked at Childress. There wasn't much blood. While we were riding his head seemed to get heavier and heavier.

—They eased him out when the stretcher finally came. I was afraid to let him go; then I thought they didn't want to take him. They had to talk first. Him dying and they wanted a story.

—I was sick. I vomited beside the car. It was on my jacket and when I had to talk to them I could see what they were seeing, an ignorant razor fighting nigger, stinking of sour wine.

206

—When the questions were finished I sat and watched a clock while Childress died. Didn't take long. I was staring at the face of the clock but I couldn't tell you where the hands were pointing. I just heard somebody say dead. Radcliff had been trying get Mamie on the phone but stopped and came over to me when he heard Childress was gone. He looked at me and I knew he was saying man, you got to call now. But I had no voice. If Childress was dead I wanted to follow him. Just stare at the clock a while longer. The minute hand jerked from black spot to black spot.

—We carried a dead, nothing nigger in that hospital. They opened his shirt and saw a hole in his black chest. The juice run out let's throw this one away. Dead they said. Him and the other playing nothing nigger games. Stab for a nickel, stab for a quarter. The nigger juice runs out. And he got heavier instead of lighter. Snoring like you did when you had asthma. I thought of rocking a baby. In the car with the horn blaring I thought maybe there was man still in me. Maybe the whole situation was one I could handle. I thought about our children and his children. I started crying when I thought of you all looking at us, two grown men, two ghosts in the back seat of a car. Nothing to say to your eyes. Nothing to say to him. Just his head lolling, getting heavier. I wanted to hide in him. I wanted all that was still alive in me to fall off my shoulders and give him back his life. I wanted to be dying in his arms, but all I could do was cry like a baby. And cry because I was crying because I was so pitiful in your eyes and their eyes and had nothing and he had nothing but I was so pitiful because I took his, stole his little bit from him and it was so little so silly in my arms. Where could he be going. Why did I have to be left behind to speak for both of us.

You are standing in a narrow corridor. Your father has stopped speaking. A jerkiness to his words and movements. You cannot see down past the third button on his lime green shirt. You think the shirt is one you received from an anonymous colleague in a grab bag Christmas party at the school. It was too big and you seem to recall disliking the color and giving it to your father. And how grateful he was. You look down the narrow passage, barely open parenthesis between concrete and steel and you see other people carrying on conversations with invisible partners. Studying their faces you can make up stories about the prisoner on the other side of the wall. Faces of the women from the waiting room. Mostly young. Almost all black.

Corridor is loud with voices, reeks of indignation and regret. You stand among them doing your little dance of gestures and words truncated by the partition. All you came for within reach. If your fingers could press through steel.

—I been steady fucking up. I knew but I just kept it up. Now this . . .

Both know he must go on, but the words fade, will not penetrate the glass wall, they return, deflected to the source, silenced within the green shirt.

The lack of privacy becomes obscene. The men content themselves with a simple exchange of information. People are shouting all around them. Wilkerson saw himself listening through a crack in the bricks of another man's house. He could slide along the row of windows, peer into each frame, hear at random the lonelinesses of the trapped men. Would it be to him they were talking. Did it matter who spoke or who listened. Didn't they all talk only to themselves. His stomach tightened. For a moment he was on the other side in a cell standing before a yellow, opaque square. Madness of all the visitors' voices an incoherent jumble tittering through a hole no bigger than a pinprick. On the walls were painted gross caricatures of human mouths and ears, lewd graffiti mocking the prisoner while he sowed his anguish through the one way glass.

—I only talked to the lawyer a few minutes but he sounded encouraging. He'll see you in the morning before the hearing. He said not to worry. He said . . .

Wilkerson could not tell from the eyes whether his father listened or not, if the busy words had reached him or lay in broken pieces littering the concrete floor. He heard rattles and clanks, then footsteps, heavy, methodical, time, death,

the executioner, black theatrical footfalls pompously fore-
shadowing the end of the interview. The sound seemed to
pause, enter and resound within his father's thick walled cell.
Nothing more to say. Just stand in the corridor and wait for
the stones to stop shuddering, his father's voice to climb from
the stillness.

• • •

How is he, is he all right. His mother half whispered the
words. Although her voice was barely audible above the
groan of static haunting their connection, Wilkerson talked
till the end of his dime, pressing the greasy earpiece tight
against his cheek, afraid to ask his mother to speak louder,
more clearly because he knew he would be asking too much,
that her words, feeble as they were, could disintegrate any
moment if a straw upset the precarious balance between
speaking and sobbing. Wilkerson recalled coal black Rev-
erend Watkins swaying above the makeshift pulpit. When
you tells the Lord's truth it fill up our mouth and the back
of your throat and telling it hard as a woman birthing a ten
pound child of God. Wilkerson promised he would go to her
as soon as he could. He lied, said he didn't have another
dime. Speaking was like handling the clothing of someone
newly, abruptly dead. He had to weigh each word, let it run
through his fingers, touch it as he resolved a rationale for dis-
carding or keeping each obsolete possession.

–I'll see you soon, Mama. His last words swallowed by the
metallic burping of the machine, lost in the yawn of emptiness ending the connection.

Drinks in an anonymous downtown bar. The subway surface car rattling underground then emerging into the sirupy
light of early dusk. His stop was a few blocks beyond the
tunnel, aboveground beside the park. Wilkerson couldn't return to his apartment; he picked a bench and sat down to
wait for night.

Darkness settling was a plug opened to drain life from

the park. Wilkerson detached himself from the bench and shuffled to a playground in the center of the park. Usually teeming with kids when he passed during the day, now the outlines of sliding board and monkey bars, unbroken by the tumbling forms of children, were skeletal in the fading light. Wilkerson stepped over a low stone wall surrounding the play area. Tanbark inside the compound was soft under his feet. He stroked the metal pipes of the jungle jim. Perhaps made by the same people who made the steel of his father's cell. Wilkerson remembered climbing up a similar contraption, the forbidden kiss, lips pressed against the smooth, money tasting chill of the steel, he always had stolen when his mother looked away.

The sky was light enough to frame the twisting leaves if he stared up through the tops of the trees. In spite of the heat he was almost shivering and the shaking leaves seemed to be part of his skin, black, brittle, hoarsely rustling fifty feet above his head. Someone was pounding on a congo drum. Wilkerson had watched two people: graceful silhouettes, a black man, trim and tall, a white woman in a mottled red and yellow tunic shuttle between the thick tree trunks. They had seemed to move closer together as they walked, finally merging perhaps and swallowed in the same mouthful by the darkness. The drummer wasn't good. The instrument would die on him. Refuse to move another inch beneath his fingers. But he attacked it again and again, half in, half out of a wedge of light suspended from a pole farther down the walk from the bench he occupied. Before the couple disappeared they had stopped beside the drummer and the tall figure had hit the drum a few licks. Obviously he had known what he was doing. Drum quickstepped to the rhythm he had chosen. Sweet and insistent. Music made the sultry night warmer. The man had lost himself in the drum only long enough to make the owner self-conscious, to say you got a long way to go, baby, to catch me and I got a fine bitch besides and here you sit beating your meat like a fool on this drum head.

Easy for Wilkerson to identify with the clumsy apprentice still knocking himself out in fits and starts of shallow rhythm. He watched the frenzy of the drummer's hands, how the light blurred their movement. Dull axe blades hacking at a log. Apart from the drummer the park was empty as far as Wilkerson could see. No dog walkers. No baby strollers. No Frisbees. No thump of basketballs on the asphalt. No yells from the hollow where interminable games of softball or touch football kept the ground slick and brown. Just the two of them. Drummer in the semi-darkness of the bench, Wilkerson surrounded by the low, sinuous stone wall of the kiddies' playground, resting his back against the monkey bars.

Two days before, a community fair had been held in the park and from where he sat he could see trash piled high on the curb. A man, a woman and a child were picking rags from the debris. Wilkerson was too far away to tell what they decided to keep and what they tossed back on the heap, but the woman had accumulated a sizeable stack of rags which she kept draped over one arm as she bent to sort with her free hand.

They were sifting through the rags of the rags of two days before. Good citizens had raked the carnival's remains to the edge of a sidewalk bordering the park. Somebody had tossed the unsaleable second hand clothing on top of the mound of trash. When her arm got too full the woman would pass her load to a man Wilkerson took to be her husband, standing in the shadows. She was wearing shorts and a sleeveless sweater so nearly the entire length of her arms and legs was naked. Her body would be silhouetted in the glare of on-coming traffic when she stretched her arms above her head to assess a garment in the cold glow of a street lamp. She was slim waisted between the fullness of breasts and hips and as she rummaged efficiently through the leavings, Wilkerson's hands went numb compressing the nothing squeezed between them.

Rags flapping when she held them aloft. Wilkerson

211

thought of proud sails being tested in the wind. The child stopping his forays into the junk to inspect as she inspected, deadly serious, discriminating, knowing what she wanted.

Lights had come on in all the buildings circling the park and they made the few square blocks of grass and trees a world apart, an island of deeper shadows and uncertain footing best avoided until the sun rose again. The booze haze from late afternoon drinks had worn off. Wilkerson felt his senses quicken, night sounds distilled and amplified by the open spaces around him. He could not name the sounds, the trolley did not hiss or glide or shiver or rattle or clank. But the sound found his ears and shimmered in his chest and he heard it fully, richly, had that shock of recognition and discovery he experienced when matching just the right word to the thing he needed to understand. Another trolley car at the opposite end of the street revealed itself to him as metal striking metal, not the banging of the clumsy steel car against the steel rails, but cymbals slightly muted, brought together once on time, precisely pitched, then slowly opening to release the singing lines of force trapped between them. The sound was visible to Wilkerson as it crossed the park, rippling the pool of darkness in which he sat. As the shimmer spread Wilkerson resisted its subtle tug, the death by drowning it suggested so pleasantly.

In the city, there was always a reservoir of noise faintly roaring in the distance. Even in the middle of the night in the empty park Wilkerson had heard the noise of the city's rough breathing as constant as ocean crashing on the sand. The roar could never be silenced. A siren's whine or the surge of a jet would emerge from the gray rumble and dominate while it passed, but such explosions were as close to silence as the city ever came.

As suddenly as it had descended, the clarity passed. Trucks, cars, planes, sirens, trolleys, the wind, the drum, the leaves, his own breathing were again a frustrating muddle. He was alone in the park and nothing made sense. Not the wall, or the bones of the playground equipment or the fumes of alcohol belched up from his empty stomach.

212

The man hunched over the drum was insane. Not a dedicated apprentice but someone who would always mangle the drum, warp it into his image. Only a madman could allow himself to thump out again and again the same fractured pattern. The man stuttered on the drum, he could not finish a phrase. He would stop and begin again, stop and begin again. He would whip his hands to bloody stumps rapping out the beginning of a measure they could never resolve.

But was the drummer mad because he didn't fear for his hands, his sanity, his life, was he insane because the reality in which he felt himself rooted granted him a serenity beyond anything Wilkerson could imagine? Was insanity torment or when you stopped tormenting yourself about those things you couldn't change?

Wilkerson couldn't ask the drummer how it felt to be insane any more than he could have asked his father how it felt to kill a man. Yet he needed to know. He needed to understand.

The bondsman had promised he would swing a deal. Have his father out by the next day. Tomorrow Wilkerson could speak to his father without the bars intervening. But would they be any closer tomorrow? Could he ask what he needed to know?

He needed to know about Sissie, the woman he was plotting to kill. And all the other deaths. Was killing Sissie unavoidable? Had she forfeited her life? Had Childress forfeited his? And the Sweetman? Was everything an accident? The madman an accident, the white people, the cop? What was the limit of accident? How could you form a plan in a world where all that mattered was accidental, a blind jumble of blind forces?

Who was Sissie? What accidents had made her the plan's first victim?

Steel bars, stone wall, the synthetic floor of the play area yielding under his weight. Wilkerson stood. He was startled by the sudden reversal of scale. The space he occupied had been built for beings half his size. From the ground the shapes had loomed over him larger than life, but now he saw

213

once more how easy it would be to step over the enclosure.

He must have answers. He must seek out the girl.

The urge was on him and he couldn't do a thing about it. If she were going to die, he had to be sure. He must speak to Sissie, he must be sure. And he decided the only time to do it was now when the urge was on him. Tomorrow the first step would be taken. Tomorrow would be too late.

He walked a long time not even considering what route he should take just going generally in the direction he knew would ultimately lead to the dying quarter of the city in which Sissie lived. Walking into darkness no longer fresh. Around him the hot lights of the city swarming against the night. How far would it have to be? One step at a time when you thought about it, steps that you could weigh and count if you had nothing else on your mind, if the urge wasn't so strong that it made you a walking machine and you covered ground clackedy clack shuffle clack on the pavement. And you were getting there without even knowing it. Wilkerson was on a bridge. Below him slash of brown river, above a sky that seemed low and reachable if only the bridge were a little higher, rose a bit more steeply from its concrete moorings at either end of the void. Traffic rattled by, exploding the metal plates of the bridge's surface. Iron and soot and coming apart at the seams. He got as close to the tubular railing as he dared, gazing at lights and dirt and low slung warehouses crowding the banks of the river. If you still noticed, it stank terribly. Engines coughing, smokestacks belching, the bad breath of the filthy river seeping up to surround him. He didn't see any other pedestrians. It would be a good time for the clumsy structure to collapse. Minimal loss of life, a spectacular unseen splash in the dull waters.

On a corner three Negroes waited for a bus. Wilkerson joined them and mounted the high step when they did, found the necessary, exact change and seated himself beside one of the women who had been waiting where he waited. Her face was broad, lemonishly oriental and as he edged closer to her to make sure his left buttock did not mash the man's

214

thigh or the paper sack resting on the man's khaki work pants, he could smell powder or perfume or both escaping from the damp, covered parts of her body. The scent was familiar. The woman in brown at the jail. Perhaps all women used what his mother used. The thought of his mother's small, feminine vanities made him smile. He never conceived of her as simply a woman, so when she bought a new hat or coaxed her hair into the latest fashion or dabbed behind her ears with perfume, the point of these intimacies was lost on him. He would laugh the way he would laugh at a little girl in a grownup's dress and high heels, stolen lipstick painting a bright red tulip that bloomed over half her face. It went even further. As a child he was always looking at females, up dresses, through windows and keyholes, accumulating every secret he could. He couldn't see enough of women's hidden, mysterious places. The impossibly soft, indolent breasts, the bush where all the lines of their bodies rushed together and disappeared behind a patch of darkness. He would hide and wait and scheme and hunger endlessly, yet he always looked away if he thought his mother might carelessly expose some part of her private body to him.

Across the aisle, in the double rank of seats toward the back of the bus, a transistor radio was trying to draw music through the metal hull of the bus. Wilkerson could see only black people on the bus, and gazing out a window he thought his way through the yellow tinged reflection of himself and the other passengers to view the cliched scenario of South Street rolling past. He remembered the fear Littleman had spoken of. How could you allow yourself to see the decay and dying without either killing white people or going mad? Above the rotting, steel boned seats he could see Afros floating, the soft teased hair of his people. The radio was held by a young man in a purple shirt. With its ballooning sleeves, the plunging V of its neck, the delicate pattern of brocade alternating with transparent gauze, the shirt would have been seen as outrageously feminine just a few years before. Wilkerson knew he would not wear it even now, but the boy with

215

the radio was oblivious to compromising overtones, his frilly shirt, his music encroaching on the wheezy silence of the bus's interior were all part of the mood he shared with the huge-eyed girl sitting beside him.

I want to take you higher, higher

Then an oldie but goodie. Time past recovered by the disc jockey as he leafs through his collection of records and retrieves a year, a month, a day, a mood and you hear it coming back just as if it had never been lost, never gone forever. And Wilkerson remembered himself before the mirror, arranging the mandarin collar of his shirt, squeezing a pimple, anxious to be away from his house and family, but dreading the darkness into which he must slip noiselessly, coolly, sliding on in and like some wisp of black warm smoke wrap himself around the soft legs and slow drag and grind and never know and care less whose softness you've trapped on your stiff, straight leg, just thrusting it out and hoping somebody wants to mount it and slip and slide up and down and grind and slow drag cleaved together in the shadowed basement. But always a light in one corner. And sometimes too much light everywhere. These were the nice parties and nice people looking at you and people sitting down and talking and knowing one another so you just can't glide in on the still of the night and disappear in a corner with somebody's soft yearning. Shit no. Too many lights and light, nice people. You find the potato chip bowl and hover over it. Get your hands greasy and your mouth greasy and you can feel the pimples swelling and bursting in the hothouse light. Stuffing your face but the chips won't last forever. You get down to the crumbs and the grease at the bottom of the bowl and you are licking salt from your fingertips because that's all that's left and the faces are watching you and you get uglier and uglier. In the Still of the Night. The Five Satins doing it for you. Mellow oldie. Dusty disc. Blast from the past. And the dee jay's voice is calling everyone brother and sister.

The back doors sigh open and the couple eases on out. Purple shirt sticking to black back, her towering Afro round

216

and full as the sun, their music soft stepping through the double doors of the bus with them.

Wilkerson leaned his forehead against the glass porthole, twisting in his seat to pick out the number of the cross street at which a red light had halted the bus. The man and his lunch bag had gotten off two stops before so Wilkerson had scooted down to the edge of the bench he now shared with the woman. He wondered if the people in the streets noticed his face pressed against the window. While he was still in the bus he was part of another world. A fish in a lighted aquarium passing through. He felt a sudden discomfort. His body was remembering those parties, the painful flaying of his skin, the nightmares of nakedness in a public place, the dream of being on stage, of being an actor who had completely forgotten his lines. He felt nauseated, his stomach fluttered, his heart seemed to crawl into his throat. Yellow light. Smell of grease. The bus's stuttering progress through the snarl of traffic. Would have been faster to walk, but he was weak. He was utterly alone and his body was failing him. There was a bowl at the bottom of his guts and inside it churned the burnt edges of potato chips, thick, sour grease. The street sign outside told him he must escape. Must remove himself from the yellow belly of the lumbering bus. Get out. Find Sissie.

The silver poles that defined the aisle were cool and tight as he trusted his weight to them. His fingers would grip, then he would lurch ahead to the next one, the heavy feebleness below his chest dragged forward by the momentum of each push. For a split second, inching his way through the bus on legs foreign to him, he was Willie Hall, the little man. Wilkerson blinked the recognition away, but could not control the vertigo as he came spinning back to himself, as his muscles trembled, negotiating the light years between another's identity and his own.

The bus pulled away from the curb without him. Except for the dusty, hot fart of exhaust it squeezed off at him, the vehicle looked innocent enough trundling into the darkness, its shape disintegrating, its red lights and yellow light lost in the splash of illumination at a busy intersection farther down the block.

—*You've found the girl, then.*

—*I've found her.*

—*And you think we can . . . we can get to her.*

—*Just like Littleman said. We can get to her. She lives with an old woman and a little girl, Lisa. In one of those abandoned houses on a little street back of South. If the whole damn street wasn't there one morning nobody would give a fuck. Only one who will notice Sissie missing is the cop, her pimp. He'll know soon enough and come looking. Protect his investment.*

—*He'll come to her house.*

—*Close enough for us to get him.*

—*Does she have to die. Can't we hold her until it's over. I mean we can just accuse him. Nothing else would be different.*

—*Everything would be different. We can't change the plan. The whore's as good as dead and you mize well get used to the idea of a little bloodshed. A good chance plenty blood be flowing. After we lynch the cop, I believe they're going to come down on us hard. Hard on man, woman and child. Everything that moves. Not the usual light shit, not head busting and a couple niggers shot resisting arrest, but down harder than they've ever come. It'll be a shooting gallery. And niggers won't be the ones setting the fires. And you worried about keeping one whore alive.*

—*Not really, Saunders. If you pushed me I'd have to admit I'm concerned about myself. My own sanity.*

—*Shit man, ain't you tired going through this same routine. You can talk a thing to death. We're past talking. We're moving. . . .*

Saunders had continued speaking. He outlined the details of the plan, rehearsing once more what had been said a hundred times. Everything did fit, the perfectly wrought components of a deadly steel trap. Littleman was a genius. The

plan was absurdly simple, but faultless. A lynching in black-
face. Though Saunders had been speaking, the words were
Littleman's. Littleman the poet. It would always be his plan.
Wilkerson had listened to Saunders without interruption,
vaguely aware of comfort in hearing the words spoken. Per-
haps it was the familiarity of the words, the memory of Little-
man's voice taking possession of the words though Saunders
was speaking. Or, Wilkerson admitted, the words were safe.
He could react to the design, the texture, the idea of the plan
and ignore the reality of bloodshed, of kidnap, murder and
all hell breaking loose when the words became things.

The sidewalk was crowded and Wilkerson was forced to
pay more attention to the night people materializing around
him. June just beginning but the weather had already turned
hot and muggy. Weather perfect for the plan. People were
in the street because they had nowhere else to go. Someone
had begun stacking tiers of bricks, walling in the black people beneath a yellow dome that was airtight and superheated
like an oven.

In his hospital bed, masked by the inscrutable beard and
permanent furrows in his forehead, Littleman would be
smiling. He had willed nature into the conspiracy. Three days
of heat and humidity goading the black people. Shortening
tempers. Forcing the inhabitants of the tightly packed row
houses reeling onto the sidewalks seeking any kind of relief
or explosion. In their frustration they would strike out at one
another. Hadn't Sweetman, his own father, killed?

A few hours and everything would begin. First the woman,
then the cop lured into an ambush. Rumors would be easy
to spread. The Black Dispatch would have news of the murder the day before the cop was exposed. The rally. The rope.
A few more hours and it would all be set in motion. The
plan unfurling, inevitable as a flag's stiffness in the high wind.

But the people passed by him as they always had. Each
sunken in some alien universe, speaking another language,
thinking words and forms indecipherable to him. Did they
know how soon all of this would be changing? How suddenly

and brutally they would all be thrown together? And they would either survive or die together. And even if some survived, Saunders was right, many, many would perish. Martyrs. Victims. Impossible to determine. Did it matter either way. Certainly not to them. Suppose I stopped one. Got him to listen to me. Explained that I was staking his life on a desperate gamble. What could I tell him he had to gain? Who could I say gave me the right to use him as a forfeit? Consider the look on his face. The shock. A perfect stranger coming out of the night saying I am your brother. I may need your life to save our people. He'd think I was crazy and laugh or smack me down.

Wilkerson tried to picture the street cordoned off. Barricades, rubble, floodlights, the smell of burning buildings, gunsmoke, charred flesh. He heard sirens and helicopters, the rumble of tanks. Where would he be? What would it mean?

And what would it be like if the new day came. He was asking people to be prepared to die. What was he offering to them? Wilkerson knew the question was fair, he had to have an answer. Even if it was an answer he wouldn't give the others, he needed one himself. He saw the puzzled, disappointed faces of whites who had dutifully appeared to support various causes: they asked the question too. Painfully, apprehensively because when they asked it, they acknowledged the chasm separating them from the blacks whose struggle they had come in good faith to join. *What do you people want?*

Wilkerson forced two words from the confusion in his mind. *Peace. Dignity.* But these words made the question rhetorical. They say I want what you want. They demanded that the questioner hold a mirror up to his own life, that he see clearly for an instant the only answer to such a question is everything. Everything. And I want it with the same hunger and ruthlessness you see in yourself.

Wilkerson wanted to shout. It was as if suddenly, for the first time, crystal clear, for the first time, he heard the voices inside the black men around him, the voices identical with

220

the one inside himself he had been listening to so long. Insistent whisper troubling each black skull. *I want more. I want more.* More love, more food, more space, more world. More of everything. In this need they were his brothers and sisters. He was as close to them as he would ever be. He didn't feel they were demanding anything from him. Nobody could give you peace or dignity. Those sensations came from knowing you had in your hands some way to quiet at times the constant clamoring for more. If this power wasn't in your hands, the voice could destroy you, drive you howling mad, run you in circles like a dog chasing his tail.

Where did the power come from? Wilkerson seldom felt it in himself. He had tried with Tanya and tried with the children but the friction of bodies rubbing together or minds rubbing only produced more longing. Instead of being quieted the voice screamed at him. More. More.

Nobody could give you peace or dignity but other men could create conditions which made either quality a luxury inconsistent with survival. When white men held the mirror up to themselves, they were frightened by what they saw. Desolation, need, emptiness. They couldn't face the image of themselves crying for more. So they said, that's not me. I'm not that way. Normal people aren't like that. They said only someone not white, not free, not a man could be so filled with yearning. Black people are the hungry ones, the lusting ones, the half man I thought for a moment was me. And it all fits. Blacks are a species apart. A dangerous species since contact with them may contaminate whites. So the rule is niggers may survive, but if they ask for more, they are criminals. Because the more they want is everything. And wanting everything is chaos.

Pavement was wobbly under his feet. Wilkerson's eyes were downcast, testing the broken terrain before each step. You had to spend so much time on little things. Down here nothing could be depended upon. Phones, sidewalks, furnaces, the meat or eggs you bought at the corner store.

If you spent enough time at the piddling, bullshit tasks,

you could survive. But you were drained of every resource. You had to deny at every turn the voices within you saying life is not this, life is not this constant hassle and haggling over how much of the shit end of the stick you get.

Did he teach this to the children? Did he teach them anything? When he asked them questions or assigned tasks, did he keep in mind how little his proficiency in such routines had served him? Was he goading them, making sure in the little time of their lives spent with him they never lost sight of the everything? Or was he in league with the devil, stealing the most human thing about the children? Crushing the voice which cried for more?

He had reached the street. Just two houses from the corner, if Saunders had been accurate, was where the women lived. The entire block seemed shrouded. Parked cars straddled the curb, blocking half the sidewalk to allow through traffic to pass down the narrow street. Steeply sloping sidewalks, the tilted cars, broken, displaced slabs of stone fronting each doorway. Boards and sheets of tin slapped across window holes in the brick walls, the way the walls themselves seemed to lean heavily toward the pavement, made the street resemble a picture of a cluttered corridor in an immense gray castle, a drawing whose perspective had been rendered imperfectly.

These streets hidden away, draped in gray like crumbling furniture in a deserted house. They were what it was all about. No one was supposed to be living here. No one could live here. But Saunders had said the women would be in one of the houses and Wilkerson believed him. Not only the women, but other black people would be haunting these ruins. And around the corner were shells as desolate as these still teeming with life. Black life consigned to the underbelly of the city. The way it had always been. Would be forever if Littleman was right. The last first and the first last. Only violent reversal could change things. *Grab these fucking rags of buildings and crush them in your fists. Hurl the poison dust into the eyes of your enemies. Blind them, let them taste the shit you are supposed to thrive on. Then scream. Scream like a million trumpets till every grain of sand and stone in every brick in every wall flies apart. Scream on till you forget how to weep and cry and wail the blues. Remember. Remember the war cries of the Arabs. How at night the windows in the European quarter of Algiers rattled as battle screams winged in from the Casbah and the desert.*

Littleman had the words. The images. He would say what had to be said while the cop dangled at the end of the rope. Wilkerson would not have the words. In the moment of truth they would need Littleman. Littleman's breath blue in the flame. The fire spirit hot and rising. The walls tumbling down.

Something moved on the steps in front of the third house. Deep shadows cleaved by the flicker of a match. Wilkerson could make out a little girl sitting on the second stone step of the stoop. One by one she was striking matches and tossing them into the gloom. Little girl in a striped polo shirt, bare legs dangling off the side of the steps. Light. Darkness. Light. Darkness. Her image blinking on and off as if lit by a flashing neon sign. A sudden flare as the paper container fired by the last match kindled at the end of the girl's outstretched arm. In the stillness Wilkerson had heard each match dragged along the match book cover. Now he could hear the girl talking to herself. She spoke in storybook phrases, imitating the sugary tones of an adult reading to a child. Wilkerson could not follow any particular tale. The fragments of mannered sentences, the speeches of animals and elves made no sense because he could not see the pages of the imaginary picture book the child's mind was turning.

> *Once upon a time*
> *The goose drank wine*
> *The monkey chewed tobacco on the street car line*
> *The monkey broke, the street car choke*
> *They all went all to heaven on a billy goat.*

Wilkerson recognized the rhyme. Now the girl's fantasy was touching his. She wasn't reciting what she had read in a glossy fairy tale book. Somebody had sung to her about monkeys and wine and billy goats going to heaven on trolley cars just as the Sweetman had once bounced him to the silly music of the same verses. Open the gates and out come the people.

On this hot night in this dead street she remembered that someone had loved her and sung to her. And Wilkerson remembered. He wanted to put her on his knee and tell her how sweet the singing was. Tell her how sweet and then say baby you sing so nicely but let me sing it again and you listen to how it goes, and how the *street car* broke and the *monkey* choked and they *all* went to heaven. He had never taught anyone a song. He was self-conscious of his own voice so he had never tried to get his pupils to sing. His father could sing. Not just the rhymes and riddles and the nasty toasts about monkeys and Shine he taught his sons before they knew the meaning of the words, but he could sing anything, his voice would tower over the congregation and the choir and lead them richly on. And his mother singing gently, melodiously along with gospel music coming from the radio. All of that within him somewhere. Wilkerson knew it couldn't all be lost. Shouldn't be lost. He would sing to the children. They would sing together.

The girl on the steps had stopped her chanting. But the stillness had also gone. Her face was aimed directly at Wilkerson, denying his privacy as abruptly as he had shattered hers. Guttural clamor of the city filled the space between the corner where he stood and the steps on which she sat. Wilkerson had not come to the street to take the girl on his lap, he was there to kill her mother and even kill the girl if she threatened the plan. He was a stranger lurking under a broken street lamp. He wanted to call out the girl's name. Say *Lisa don't be afraid.* It had to be Lisa, it had to be the house. *Lisa don't be afraid. I mean you no harm.*

He heard desks scraping. Chairs pushed aside, the shrieks and cries of forty-five children scrambling headlong all at once to get out of the door he had just entered. Fear widened their eyes as a million firecrackers exploded at once.

Run, Lisa, run. The night had mottled his hands with

blood. He turned away from the girl's stare, hurrying toward the glitter of South Street.

● ● ●

Did she love this man. Did she care at all what happened to him. If he lived or died. Tanya faced Thomas Wilkerson across the narrow space of her living room. In the subdued light he was almost handsome or at least something about his face was different enough to make him easy to remember among the thousand faces encountered each day. She noticed how his eyes clung to the shape of his face. Eyes were silly and smouldering at once. Darting around the room and turned inward simultaneously as if the evidence of the room, of Tanya's sleeping presence in it could not quite be digested. She thought his eyes reflected her own mood, the acid, rumbling uncertainty of a body startled from sleep by an upset stomach.

—Tanya I know it's late and I probably have no business barging in here on you. It must be very late and I'm not sure I'm altogether sober. But I had to talk to you.

She wondered if she should make it easy. If she should be annoyed and protest. Give him something he could deal with. Even if it was anger.

—I don't even know how I got here. But I think I knew I was coming here all the time.

When he said *here* she was confused. Did he mean *here*, simply her apartment or did he mean more, something as absolute as the space which enclosed them, both standing as though walls and sofas and chairs had disappeared, a *here* containing the two of them and nothing else in the world. Why did he come out of the darkness demanding those few things she had set aside, why did he need to share the air she breathed.

—I must look a mess. So many things have happened. Like weeks have passed between the morning and now.

He glanced at his watch. Was he acting. Was he trying to

225

convince himself or convince her. She could tell he had been drinking, was probably still drunk. His movements were too deliberate, too dramatic for the man she knew. Yet the falseness which inflated his gestures and words made him more real to her than he had ever seemed.

—Tanya I . . .

She cut him off by asking him to sit, by sitting herself on the sofa opposite the overstuffed chair he had chosen. Because she had only turned on one table lamp, it was difficult to read the clock over the fake fireplace. The angle of the hands suggested either three or four in the morning. In one corner of the room a stripe of blue light hummed above a fish tank. Although the room was warm the blue light seemed to chill the medium through which fish were darting. Tanya shivered in a sudden pool of icy water which swirled around her ankles. She drew her long, bare legs under her body, draping her green robe over them.

—I had to come.

She wanted to say don't apologize. You're here and the damage is done. I'm wide awake in the middle of the night and you might as well get to the reason you came. But she didn't want to make it hard or make it easy on this man, Thomas Wilkerson. This man who wanted to know whether she loved him or not. As if she could love what he might be or could be or should be, all those invisible men lost behind his eyes. She didn't believe in miracles and had no reason to assume that anything called love would charge the air between them, make his flesh any less foreign, any less demanding. Beneath her in the nest of green robe her legs tingled in the first stages of numbness.

—As soon as I can get myself together. I'll make you some coffee, Thomas. Could you hand me a cigarette. They're on the table, there.

He stood beside her conscious of the whiskey smell clinging to his clothes. It took forever to get a match to work and when one caught and she dipped her face toward his cupped hands he wanted to press the cloud of hair, the fragile bones

226

of her face to his body, but he stepped back so she wouldn't brush against him. He wanted to be clean. Cleaner than he'd ever been. In the soft light it was a child's face she lifted from the match. He thought of the girl on the steps, her tight plaits opening into the bloom of fullness framing Tanya's face.

—My head's about ready to split down the middle, and I have to do something before it just explodes.

Was it theatrics again. His fingers taut against the sides of his skull as if they were all that held the hemispheres together.

—I've got to go and get the guns from Rice.

—Thomas, I don't have the slightest idea of what you're talking about. Who is Rice. What guns.

—It's so strange, even funny, I guess. How close we think we are to a person, how much we think we've shared everything and then it turns out that they don't even know your name.

—I'm not ready for riddles. But I'll make you coffee and drink some myself. Maybe you'll slow down enough so I can understand what you're talking about.

—Always a question of time. Never enough time. So you start in the middle. Then after a while you forget that you started in the middle and you assume everyone has been where you've been and things begin to pile up till one day nobody understands anything you say. Then it's too late to go back. No time to begin at the beginning.

He watched her efficient movements in the bright kitchen. He didn't try to raise his voice so it could reach her above the clatter of drawers opening, pots rattled. He didn't care if the words went beyond his murky corner; for the moment it was enough to mumble them to himself while she dawdled in the sunlight of another planet.

—You want it black and strong don't you.

The question was rhetorical and he didn't answer. He wanted to begin at the beginning. For Tanya he wanted everything to be clear. He wanted an explanation of things which would be just as tangible, just as appropriate as the cup of coffee she was going to bring him.

—You never met my mother and father, did you. You were supposed to come to dinner once.

—Yes. Something came up

—What

—I don't remember.

—Do you remember starting out. Do you remember going into their building and walking up the stairs. Do you remember a shadow in the hallway.

His voice had dropped again. If someone had been sitting on his knee, the person would have to lean toward him, straining even at that distance to pick up what he said.

Wilkerson recalled that March day thousands of years before. They had been walking in the park. The chill. The sheets of wind. Tangles of wire thin branches hazy in a mist of brilliant sunshine. He heard the tap of Littleman's cane. Saunders' loud talking and laughing mood. Off the concrete path, rags of snow littered the open spaces between black tree trunks. Willie and Saunders had been taking turns irritating one another, and Saunders' volubility was a calculated response designed to grate against the tender skin of Willie Hall's silence.

Dropping then firing cowboy style from the hip as he rose, Saunders sent a stone skipping down the pavement toward a cluster of scraggly birds bobbing at bits of greasy paper which scratched along the frozen earth. The pigeons scattered in squealy panic, the deep sigh of their flight emptying the space over Wilkerson's head. He wanted to ask Saunders why he did it. But the birds were gone, the stone gone, the blue sky had swallowed the weary clutter of wings.

Saunders could kill. The part of him which was assassin as visible to Wilkerson as it had been to Willie Hall. No reason to suppose Willie Hall ever was mistaken. Suppose Saunders' hands began to shake. The safeguard in this eventuality was Littleman's knowledge of the antagonism between the conspirators. The presence of Wilkerson a perpetual goad to

Saunders. Wilkerson constanty there to remind Saunders of the contempt he could not bear to feel for himself, of anger at those weaknesses in the teacher, which in himself would distort the symmetry of the plan. The essential ruthlessness of maneuver they would exercise against each other since each could see externalized that image of himself he struggled to destroy. All the while this infighting cemented the plan, forwarded it. Their incestuous spite a harmony in the larger rhythm of Littleman's conception.

But holes would open. Like that almost spring day in the park when ice cracked under their feet and water from the shallow depressions in the pavement darkened the sides of their shoes. You are unaware of your feet till they begin slipping out of control on the slickness beneath you. You shift your weight partially and anticipate a moment of queasy vertigo, an instant hanging in space, asking a million questions before your bones slam into the icy concrete. You hear Littleman's cane tapping the ground. Saunders tittering, the disgruntled birds behind you clucking, landing heavy with a sound like bulky overcoats flapping in the wind.

–I missed the motherfuckas. Aimed at a big, fat, gray bellied one. Way he was strutting around with his little short-legged self all puffed out sorta reminded me of somebody.

Half of the thick twig shot into the air, rising lazily end over end, then plummeting to the hard earth, a shudder and it rolls to a stop a few feet from the path. The force of the cane whipped down had snapped the dead branch, had exploded half of the wood higher than a man's head. The piece that remained on the ground quivered.

–It's not your time today. Thank whatever gods you pray to Saunders for giving you a little more time. Thank this little man and his little walking stick for satisfying themselves on that piece of wood. I give you today. I give you a little more time. Willie Hall regained his stride with a half shuffle and a hurtling shrug of his shoulders. He was again in step with the other two. Eyes glazed like a blind man, tapping the rod before him.

229

Saunders had gone too far, but Littleman allowed him to return, snapping wood instead of bone with the cane. Finally the plan had become more real than the conspirators. Littleman would not kill the plan.

And they walked the river of concrete meandering through the frozen earth, their voices icy, steam breath propelling words into the chill air. The sound inhuman as it ricocheted from the cold, stiffened trees and died in heaps around them. Wilkerson's eyes followed the bare limbs as they stretched, a delta of black tributaries stark against the steely blue. He could not call the vastness sky. It was just up. The sky had fallen, had sunk below the snow blotted ground. What he saw above was the underbelly of some immensity that dwarfed the sky. A membrane incredibly thin and blue. Vulnerable to a pinprick yet so high his imagination stretching to its limits had no more chance than the naked branches of scratching at the blue.

Wilkerson did not have to speak. Soon only Littleman's words trailed behind them, Saunders' garrulousness curbed since the cane slashed down, Saunders escaping into some world of his own, Wilkerson almost startled to see Saunders manshape beside him, the body of Saunders a hallucination since from this casually striding shell the guts and heart and brain had so palpably risen after the shattering blow.

Littleman's words enclosed in frosted bubbles, the bubbles attenuated. Oval, elipsoid, cartoon banners flapping with clumsy messages child lettered in the ballons tethered to his lips. His full beard stiff in the cold. Like if you wrapped your fists around it, the deep, cold curls would crumble, the texture of dry leaves going to dust between your hands. The man's eyes glistening, feeding on the blue, swallowing what they could not abide. He was shouting at the trees, the heavens, the snow, the last red coals in his body that he fanned by his brisk pace, the slipstream of chattered speech.

They stood beside a brown river. Mud brown, a desert the wind had whipped into infinite, identical dunes each trapping light in shredded quartz and mica flaking the sculpted sand.

230

Willie Hall had brought them to the edge. He gestured now, the cane a violent baton in the frenetic weave of his music. As far as Saunders could see, up and down and across the river from their windswept vantage point, the three men were alone in the desolate park. Perhaps the battle had already been fought, a warp in time had hurled them forward to the aftermath of the plan, the city reduced to knee high ruins around them, the blitzed trees and three shivering human shapes all of life that remained. Empty trees, empty water, the searing emptiness of blue either so hot or frozen the flesh would wither at a touch. Willie's broad back, the crushing threat in the slope of his shoulders, the slender rod, gilded silver in the sunlight. Words still flung at them like spit driven backward by the wind. The man seemed to be rising from a hole in the earth. The proportions of his torso could not be carried by the incongruous legs. Like a geyser of muscle and bone he was emerging, the pieces of a god returning after he had been torn apart and sowed in the water during a rite of fall. But the water had diminished the legs, frog's legs tucked into the trunk of a bear. The magicians had not understood the spell, the priestess who rent his flesh had been polluted. And now, prematurely risen, grotesquely risen, lured from his deep rest by the spring brilliance of the sky, the god curses the forces which crippled him.

Let it all come. Let it hang out Littleman.

Wilkerson would not have been shocked if the speaker began to flog the icy water with his cane. He would not have tried to stop the man if he plunged into the brown river. He would not have been dismayed if the three twig legs suspended Willie Hall upon the pitted surface of the water as he skated across like a delicate thread legged insect.

And so the plan seemed to roll off the trembling river and quaver through the voice of the deformed man whose eyes stared at the stark trees lining the far bank, whose back remained turned to Saunders and Wilkerson, whose message at last entered them with the shiver of life passing from the body.

When they resumed walking the transference had been complete. It was necessary to talk of smaller and smaller things. For egos to return and strike out or be singed, for the flesh to complain about the wind and temperature. It was a barren park and they had prematurely taken a spring stroll. Three ordinary men bitching about the hawk, engaging in a desultory round of the dozens, getting irritated at one another because no one could confront the common enemy of bitter weather. The plan within, fresh, untouchable already competing for the meager fire stored in the bodies' caves.

From that day growing like a fetus inside my guts. Wilkerson was annoyed at himself for the banality of the metaphor. He was childless, had created no art, yet he blandly appropriated the truth of these acts to extenuate his involvement with Littleman's plot. To call it a plot instead of a plan. Lynching/Murder. Steal/Liberate. Civilize/Enslave. Father/Fornicator. Who would do the naming?

Littleman prostrate, his beard soaked in the filthy water stagnant near the shore, the cane held in both veiny fists lashing the rust colored river. His wand buried deeper and deeper as he slithers into the ooze, the iron water shuddering closed after each blow.

The word was Lynch. Lynch a white cop. If it is done according to plan the new day must surely follow. The new dispensation, phoenix rising from the ashes of the old. But we must lay the corpse to rest. *Burn the scabby motherfucker in the city dump. Let the crows pick out its eyes. Then up in smoke.* It's got to come. It's got to come. Just waiting for somebody to crack the door. To jerk the little pinky from the hole in the dike. It's got to come.

The stone scudded along the cracked gray path. A spray of inky water at one bounce, the hiss of a sudden white veined bruise in a patch of dark ice at a second thudding collision. The final rattling slide as it lands in the midst of the birds. Stink of their dingy feathers, they hobble into the sky and for a moment you are under the stale tent of an unclean woman's billowy skirt as the pigeons pass over. You

232

see tracks in the snow. Skeletal arrowheads printed in powdery whiteness. Stylized geometric vaginas. Put a circle around the bisected V and they are peace signs.

Yet was it real that day. Was it ever real that day. The ritual at the brown river's edge. Littleman's crystalline, garbled sermon. The lynched cop swaying from the bare gallows limbs of the thousand trees surrounding us. The revelation of a single smoky streak of cloud like the disintegrating exhaust of some missile too fast and clean to be seen cutting through the blue.

If I had laughed and walked away. If Saunders lay staring at blue emptiness, his head bashed open, steam curling from his split skull. If I had pushed the iron legged man into the beckoning water.

Wilkerson surveyed the room in which he was sitting. Tanya's room. He stretched out his hands, turning them slowly, gingerly, as if too sudden a recognition could exacerbate whatever damage or familiarity he sought. These were not his father's hands. These were not words. Words could work no miracles with these shit brown hands of a school teacher. Pale, still winter yellowed hands.

He saw the hand of Andrea Palmer.

He saw the hand of Saunders curl around the plump pigeon's throat.

She said: I saw Mr. Wilkerson feeling her butt. I saw them bumping butts in that alley behind the school.

She said: His daddy done killed a man.

A stranger. Her bony two year old's arm slipped into the air. And she rose with it, tumbling head over heels, showing a wet spot on her dirty cotton drawers, spinning, in the unfamiliar medium, a fish swimming on the sand, gasping, bleeding at its frantic gills, Andrea Palmer falling after her hand, her lost bony arm.

—Who is Rice. And what guns were you talking about, have some of your kids gotten into trouble.

—No, not the kids this time. Rice is a fellow I know. A guy I've been involved with for quite a while now. But I don't really know much about him. I don't think anybody does. At least none of us. He's strange. But no stranger than the rest of us. Rice is somebody he thought he could use. A neutral person. Safe inconspicuous. No real life or thoughts of his own so he thought he could program him like you do a machine.

Tanya stood in the doorway between kitchen and living room, a steaming mug of coffee in each of her hands. Like wind or water the stronger light from the kitchen outlined her body inside the long robe. Though he had been talking to someone and the voice floating back to him from the kitchen had to belong to somebody, the figure of Tanya, framed in the doorway, elegant, slender, seemed suddenly arbitrary, an unexpected intrusion on his solitude.

–Who was programming this Rice.

–I should have said cultivating. Because that's what Littleman did to us all. He made me grow. But grow in a special way. He recognized what was already there, then made those things become what he needed. What the plan needed. Littleman is the one. I don't know why I mentioned Rice first. Why I began with Rice. Littleman did the cultivating, the programming. The plan is his. He is the reason Rice has the guns.

She was sitting again. Receding again. Why had he felt threatened by her reappearance. He knew it was coming. He was in her apartment. She had gone into the kitchen to fix him coffee. Now curled in the same rumpled pillows of the sofa she was raising the cup to her lips and though she was silent, her eyes questioned him through the veil of steam. Familiar eyes. Familiar patience and self-possession. She wouldn't interrogate him anymore, wouldn't ask what guns or who is Littleman. She would be cool. Would wait. Her lips nibbled at the edge of the cup, testing, tentative.

His smoking mug sat on a table beside him. He wouldn't even touch it until he was sure the coffee was only lukewarm. Wilkerson wondered why her lips didn't recoil from contact with the hot liquid. He recalled something he had read about

234

woman and pain. About tolerances and thresholds and bio-
logical superiority.

—You see we needed someplace to hide the cop. Just overnight really, or at most a day and a night. But the place had
to be inconspicuous. It couldn't be in a black neighborhood
and for obvious reasons we couldn't have a white man working with us. So Littleman found Rice or Rice found Littleman or maybe Littleman made up Rice, which isn't as silly as
it might sound. Anyway the plan needed a safe place to keep
the cop after we had kidnapped him and Rice is a janitor,
has his own apartment in the basement of the building where
he works. Nobody lives in his building but old white ladies
and men. Half of them don't even go outdoors anymore according to Rice. It's the last place in the city anyone looking
for guns or missing cops would come. Rice said most of the
tenants have forgotten he's in the basement. He said the
owner told him flat out to stay out of people's way. Said the
tenants didn't need to be reminded that he lived in the same
building even if he was the janitor.

—So the shotgun's there and the two hand guns. A forty-
five and a smaller pistol you can carry concealed in a pocket.
We didn't need any more firepower. One of the beauties of
the plan. Each weapon has a specific function. The shotgun
was more of a prop than anything else. Use it to intimidate
the cop while we hold him. The shotgun and the pills
Saunders got would do the trick. Of course there was the
blackjack, sack and the rope. And the knife. We had to have
those things. They were necessary. After she was dead, after
Saunders had killed her as quickly, painlessly as he could,
someone would have to use the knife. She would be dead,
and you only die once, and if the body had to be marked up
for effect it just had to be that way. Too late to be squeam-
ish. He said either you or somebody else cuts up all the meat
you eat. He said somebody kills it and cuts it up. Dead meat
is dead meat. The first time he said that I thought he was
just trying to show me how tough he was. But he meant it.
He could be that cold. He was teaching me to be the same

235

way. One dead body. What would a few strokes of a knife in its lifeless flesh mean. So we had a knife and somebody would have to do it.

He hadn't meant to tell it this way. She was sitting up straight now. Staring. He couldn't tell what was in her eyes. Not fear, he was certain. And oddly enough it wasn't shock. He had said too much and too little. It was as if a long, complicated nightmare had made him scream in his sleep and the scream had awakened someone sleeping beside him.

—I'm sorry, Tanya. You must think I'm crazy or sick or drunk. Coming in here out of nowhere. Unloading my morbid fantasies on you. Everything is tangled, connected. Images and emotions I have been living with too long. We decided we had to change things. I mean the big picture. Not a job here or a public office there, not one or two black faces floating to the top but change everything. Fundamentally. And obviously that means violence. Supreme violence. Nobody gives up power without a fight. Ruling and a sense of superiority get in the blood. You have to bleed them out. You have to turn things upside down. Topsy-turvy. You've read Fanon. He says it well. You know what I mean.

—So all of that was at stake. Everything at stake. You, me, the kids at school. My mother and father, everything. We did the only thing we could. Decided on a way to prepare a catalyst. Stage an event so traumatically symbolic that things could never be the same afterwards. Lynch a white cop. Lynch one in broad daylight and say to white people what they have been saying to us for so long.

—Littleman is a genius. A genius because the obvious is always clear to him. He has a way of seeing, a simple, un-cluttered way. He knows where to begin. He sees the simple way things begin. How the rules which lead to hopeless complications are themselves quite simple. He put the plan together. Or rather he saw the plan sitting in the middle of the chaos, sitting like a flower waiting to be plucked. He taught me to see some of what he saw. I learned slowly. Very slowly and for that reason I can't expect you to grasp much of what I'm saying now. Although I believe you would have been a quicker pupil, a better disciple, one who wouldn't have failed at the last minute.

–Tomorrow. No, not tomorrow. Just a few hours now, Littleman had prepared us to act. The woman, Sissie, was to be murdered. By the next day or so the cop would be our prisoner. On the fifth day the rally. You've probably seen the posters already. One on the school bulletin board. The usual thing, a speaker coming to tell us how to be black, proud and free. But this time an extra added attraction. Sissie's murder will be on everybody's mind. Rumors circulating. Hopefully a picture of her bloody body in the Black Dispatch. A hot day and feelings running high. The murderer produced at the rally, a white butcher pig. The rope, the sack, that's it. No place to go after that. Everything's up front.

–It's insane. If there ever was such a plan, it was nonsense and anybody who'd see it otherwise is insane. Finish your coffee and you can have the couch to sleep on if you wish. I don't know what happened tonight or who you've been talking to but what you're saying is ugly and sick. I can still salvage a few hours of sleep. I think it would be best if you did the same.

She is standing. A green blur in the shadowed room. He puts out his hand; his fingers toy momentarily with the ten feet of empty space between them and the woman.

–Dammit.

He follows her eyes to the floor where she snatches her bare toes back from the mug they have overturned.

–I'm groggy. I'm knocking things down.

From the mouth of the mug a broad, dark tongue seems to lap at the carpet. Wilkerson's hand swings back to the arm of the chair. The fish light has been humming all the time, but now he hears it.

–The funny thing is that you're absolutely wrong. And I'm one of only four people on this earth who know how wrong you are. But I'm the one who is going to make you think you're right. And anyone else who might be interested think you're right. Because I have to stop it. I have to sabotage the plan. Get the guns from Rice.

–I'm not going to clean this mess up now. Just be careful of the damp spot. Stay in the chair if you like or use the sofa. Ignore the alarm if you're not going to school tomorrow, I need it. Goodnight.

–I won't be here in the morning. I'm going to get the guns from Rice.

–Tom. Why don't you . . . shit, now . . . I'm tired. Rice and guns and Littleman and you're going to lynch somebody tonight too, I suppose. I'm sorry I have to miss it all. But don't let that bother you. You don't have to go, but if you're going, please do it now so I can put the damn chains across the door.

–Tanya, I'm sorry I got you up, I know how lame that sounds but I'm sorry. They bumped awkwardly at the door. Wilkerson hesitant, not knowing where to place his hands, how much intimacy could be squandered on the moment, how intentional the brush of her shoulder into his chest had been. The partially closed door was between them, a shield obscuring half her body when he kissed her. Flesh of her shoulder warm and solid under his fingers as one arm venturing back through the door frame rested on her body. He fluffed the hair at the nape of her neck, caressed the long bones of her arm. Image of her naked in the light sweeping from the kitchen warmed Wilkerson again. When she said stay, rest, perhaps she meant something else. Perhaps she would sleep in his arms and in the morning the world forget them both. She would help him strip the stinking clothes from his body. She would stand beside him while a hot, hot shower drenched their skin. The night chain rattled in her hands. Rattled again muted by the gray door as he stood in the empty corridor.

• • •

Rice could not sleep. Insomnia was nothing new to him. Many hot summer nights he would toss fitfully, brewing his sweat into a poison he shrank from. He was familiar with his body's flops and twitches, the exhausting search for some disposition of his limbs that would allow sleep to settle over him. But the last week had been worse than the worst nights he could remember. Sleep simply didn't exist. Instead a teasing state of semi-consciousness would let him drift off into a dream of sleep which lasted only long enough to remind him how sweet the real thing could be. The weight of the building seemed to press down on him. The Terrace Apartments, a huge square box, would teeter unsteadily on his shoulders. The building became an extension of his body, a head he could peer into, the Terrace Apartments without its roof like an architect's model to display the floor plan. His brain was honeycombed with thousands of cubicles, each in the shape of a miniature apartment. And the walls were white. A network of cold, pulsing rooms, countless white rooms absolutely empty except for the scurrying roaches. In and out of the barren rooms. The insects were gigantic. Three or four would fill one of the squares. Rice remembered mornings as a child when his mother lit the gas oven to take the chill out of the kitchen and the sudden heat would panic the insects who had gathered overnight to feast on grease stains and scraps of food.

Roaches crawling in and out of the white rooms. He wanted to smash them. With his hands, his feet, a rolled newspaper. They would pop and crunch. His mother was almost dancing. Her feet moved so fast, tapping, grinding. Her meaty arms flailing at the top of the stove, an old shoe in her hand murdering roaches, knocking the crusty burners from their moorings. She would squeal while she did it. Hating them. Hating the fury which set her frantically in motion.

But Rice didn't dare hit the roaches who made a playground of the white rooms. Their cracked, glossy shells would litter the immaculate chambers. Their black insides would stain the ceilings and floors, drip down the walls. Yet even if he could bring himself to strike at them, nothing would happen. He could see inside his skull, he could feel it

239

wobble or grit his teeth when the pressure was unbearable. Beyond this he was powerless. He couldn't change anything, could only peep through the transparent bone and watch the roaches scramble in and out.

Time was always the middle of the night. In the darkness, alone, the plan occupied his thoughts. The other conspirators preyed on him with schemes and threats, hovering around his bed the way they all had leaned over Littleman in the hospital. Some nights Rice feared he was in fact a patient in an immense asylum. His eyes would pop open from a moment's doze and he would sense the sweaty weight of restraining straps around his chest, arms and legs. For as long as a minute he would not stir, afraid to test the reality of the bonds. Then with all the blood in his body filling his head and the cords of his neck, he would burst upright into a sitting position, simultaneously thrashing both legs with the fury of a drowning man.

They came to him lying, conniving. He was their fool they thought, a weakling each could exploit. But they trusted him with the guns. How many times had he gone down on his knees and pulled the weapons from beneath his bed. The box had once held fluorescent lamps, the thick buzzing kind which were cocooned in pink tubes lining the foyer of the Terrace Apartments. Cold guns smelling of grease. Rice knew more than they thought he knew. How the metal pieces glide apart and snap together. The glint of steel. The mirror finish after you rub and rub with soft cloth. He knew the weight of the shotgun, the yawning void of its barrel. He had stroked, lubricated, penetrated to the innermost chambers of the pistol. During sleepless nights the hard, cold steel comforted him. Like a miser counting his gold in the dark, Rice would toy with the revolver, smiling to himself as he clicked bullets into the cylinder.

They had trusted him with the weapons and that meant he had the upper hand. The plan could not begin without the power he had hidden under his bed. Rice wondered how the others could be so naive. Treating him like a dog while placing their fate and the fate of the plan in his hands.

240

Rice stood naked in the black room farting once long and loud as if to test his reality against the cloying presence of the nightmare from which he was trying to awaken. With his palm he mopped sweat from his face then tentatively he patted the top of his skull. It was still there. Bushy covering, the reassuring bone. Between his legs felt steamy. Perhaps he would sit in the tub. Try to read or polish the delicate handle of the pistol.

When the thumping began, he dropped to the floor, the bed between himself and the disturbance at the door. He lay as flat as he could, fingers pressing into the linoleum as if they could dig a deeper pouch to hide his body.

Someone was still banging on the door. Rice's hand snaked into the deeper blackness beneath the bed. It seemed to move independently. It was his arm and it was resolved to do something but Rice could only watch, naked and quivering in a heap on the floor.

Someone called his name. Loud whisper through the door, as if that made any difference after all the pounding. His name. Rice. Rice. Rice.

And then another name. Wilkerson. Other hissing words then Wilkerson again.

Dark. But his fingers had often worked in the darkness, nimbly undressing the weapons. He'd better use the big one. They might all be out there.

He aimed where he thought the center of the door should be then made a fiery shambles of the darkness as he pulled the trigger.

•••

Saunders parked four blocks from Stanley's. The alarm had jarred him awake, a heavy hand unexpectedly from the darkness striking him at the base of his neck. The morning of the first day. The rendezvous with Wilco at Stanley's. The first day of a new world. He would not be late. Saunders could have driven farther down the street, taken a chance on finding an open spot nearer Stanley's but he needed to get out of the automobile, wanted to walk on his own two feet down the strip blocks. Not homesickness, he had no desire for the street to claim him once more, to share its heart and breath like the old man who wheeled a push broom and two upright aluminum trash cans nestled in a flat bed wooden cart down the sidewalk. He didn't want to be the poster plastered wood or steel mesh fronting the shops, he could not station himself at a corner or sit rigid in the naked second story windows above the storefronts and bars. He would never return, feared returning to the dead end street. Although he knew nothing had changed, he remained curious. He would flirt with the street, play games like those he did with a woman whose body no longer aroused him.

The day shift was settling in. White men with pockets full of keys were unlocking their merchandise. Saunders was disdainful of the fear in their eyes. Perhaps it was more obvious now, the sense of danger they felt, the desperate, split second searching of each black face, the meticulous weighing, like they measured out their fish and beans or gauged the value of pawned rings and watches, the calculation of profit or trouble contained in the way a black passerby walked, the way he wore his hair, where he held his hands, their stares or glares or utter disregard of the white glance momentarily settling upon them. Maybe the shopkeepers knew it was just a matter of time before everything changed. Half of the plate glass windows were bandaged or splinted. At regular intervals only glass strewn, gutted shells remained. Some storefronts were transitional. Neither ravaged with sky pouring through the roofless beams and window sockets nor preserved for business another day behind the sliding steel gates, but shadowed, impenetrable interiors, trash heaped up to the cracked gray window panes, unidentifiable clutter stretching backward into the obscurity. Abandoned to the derelicts in long patched overcoats who would emerge suddenly, blinking, sun blind from their dim nests. Later in these same caves, huddled around flashlights or lanterns, men would shoot crap throughout the night, the rattle of bones, the rhythmic incantations of the gamblers broken only by loud snores from winos sleeping at the periphery of the circle of light.

Nothing had changed, but could he enter the doorless frame, take his place inconspicuously among the gamblers in the yellow clearing surrounded by rubble, and if the dice weren't falling the way he sang them to fall would he be able to edge from the circle and become one of the huddled, oblivious mounds sleeping through the action, the night, the sunlight that could crawl no farther into the building than the sleepers willed. Could he throw the few pennies he had left into somebody's funky hat and drink the salvation wine till his wits were together enough, till he was warm and replenished, calm enough to brush himself off, prey the streets hoping some hustle brought him a stake and the stake made him welcome again squatting on one knee, dice uncurling from his fingers to stare blandly at the players in the circle, pocked skulls, black on white indifference glowing up at the gamblers, magic stare that like a magnet snatched money or scattered the pile of coins and bills building beside it.

Saunders watched three quarters of a man struggling to arrange his womanish hips on the inside window ledge of a pawn shop. Window was gaudy with rings, watches, radios, silver. The figure's head was cut off by the blackened top of the window which was background to the large gold letters of the proprietor's name. The man, white shirted, was placing on a prominent felt lined shelf a row of particularly precious items which he removed from a drawstring pouch attached to his waist. These treasures carried home each night were not to be entrusted to the steel gate, now partially collapsed, which like a jailor he had unlocked to enter his place of business. As the truncated body maneuvered awkwardly but efficiently within the gleaming window Saunders' first thought was of the vulnerability of the broad backside wobbled at the public. Then he noticed the dog, a shaggy Irish setter, too muscular and deep chested, too blunt in the jaw and forehead to be purebred, but red and formidable stretched across the door of the pawn shop.

Fish stink seeped from a window in which bloody pigs' feet daintly stretched on a couch of ice.

Fish stare, merchant stare, the eyes of the short sullen woman standing in a doorway with her mongoloid child. Two boys holding hands emerge from an entranceway squeezed between the whitewashed glass of a storefront church and a billboard plastered candy store. They are dressed in coats and hats, identical in their shabbiness. The smaller boy is sobbing as his feet touch the pavement. He jerks away from the hand of his brother, stomping forward a few heavy footed, exaggerated strides, then twisting, his face streaked with tears and snot and grime from fingers rubbed into his eyes, screaming at the vacant mask of the older boy's face, at the littered recess that had tumbled them into the street.

A cop, dressed for the moon in helmet, boots and airtight leather, glides silent as an aphid along the curb tagging the illegally parked cars and vans. Saunders had noticed his motorcycle parked farther up the block. The machine had seemed more alive without its rider. It sat serene, completed, attentive to the crackling voice that addressed it over a two way radio.

Men clustered on a corner waiting for a day's work. They would march, unchained coffles to the seedy pickup trucks that stopped at the curb. A driver would crack his window and some of the men would hear their names called, others with strong looking backs or neat work clothes or sturdy shoes would be pointed at and the bidder would shout out a price. Each morning a few would be transported to jobs around the city while the majority lingered, as content in that corner limbo as any other, glad for the company of others who must sit and wait. The groups would be swelled by passersby, by barflies and hustlers who knew that even here among the jobless a number would be played, a drink promised or shared. Some would fade into the bars or barbershops when they knew the morning trickle of trucks had ended. Saunders recognized the fat, black face of Sugar moving among the men outside Stanley's. Fat, black Sugar, every strand of shiny reddish brown hair sleeked smoothly into place in the high pompadour atop his head. Slick Sugar who made these out of work drones his special hustle. Loaning money, taking their numbers on credit, finding them jobs for a cut of the earnings. He was as together as he had always been, shuttling through the crowd on the sidewalk, his tangerine bell bottoms elegantly lapping the filthy pavement. Shugs got it. Shugs got it today. Saunders recalled the legends, the half truths and lies that clustered around the enormous black man. His connections with the dagos. The stable of white whores he kept in the city's most elegant apartment building, the cars no one ever saw because he loved to strut along the streets with the people. Shugs humping woman, man, boy anything big enough to shake its tail feathers at him, Shugs with a habit so big he had to keep fifty junkies busy in the streets dealing his shit.

Sweet Sugar would recognize Saunders immediately but never say a word. Shugs had lasted because he knew when to speak, who to notice, who to fat mouth, and who to pass without a word. Saunders had learned from Sugar. At a distance or listening to the big man's words as he had been favored with a petty errand to run for the king. King Sugar. As far as Saunders had ever wanted to go.

Sugar's laugh rolled from his belly, was chopped into deep explosive chunks by his white teeth. The laughter would prod the men, shame them. The sound would shrink them, regale them with its bottomless assurance, its coaxing roar. They must join him or they would be the object of the laughter. They must mount his laughter and let it carry them indoors to a bar stool, or to something stronger in the alley, anywhere but where they stood empty handed silently waiting.

Saunders remembered how they had laughed when his feet went out from under him, and the hot, sharp cinders had

245

rushed up to bite his skin. Sugar's laugh rolling over him. Pressing his face into the track as the feet of the other runners pounded past him. The big one. The race he had to win. Fear was being trapped, being exposed. The laughter was always there waiting to pounce on you. Not thick lipped, grinning teethed nigger laughter, not the dozens and the cheap tricks they could play on one another but the deep, ridiculing guffaw of Sugar, white as he was black, Sugar who squeezed as tight as he wanted all the black bodies he held in the palm of his hand. Whiteman's laughter that echoes through these streets like the crack of a whip behind a mule's ear.

The sound rang in Saunders' ears, stung him though he passed through an orange door and stood inside Stanley's. Stanley owned the bar and could inscribe his name in three foot orange letters along one side of his corner location, but inside his establishment he was Fats. Fats whose diabetes had prevented him from sampling his own whiskey for at least the ten years Saunders had frequented the bar.

–Fats you're not thinking about your diet.

–Oh, I'm thinking about it all right, honey. Doing plenty thinking. In the dim light Fats' puffy shape was silhouetted against the orange, purple glow of the jukebox at the far end of the bar. His legs were lost in the blackness of the bar's overhang so that to Saunders entering from the street the image of his torso seemed like a stack of truck tires crowned by a dark pumpkin wearing a stingy brim hat.

–Doing plenty thinking, all right.

–But you gonna have your coffee and rolls anyhow.

–I told that doctor I got to have some things.

–Bread and jelly and butter and cream first thing in the morning. You eat it now and you know you'll be complaining by tomorrow.

–I ain't gon wait till tomorrow. I start complaining now.

–You'll be right up there in the hospital again, eating stuff like this. They don't serve rolls and cream in there.

–You sure right, child. They don't be thinking about giving a man his rolls and coffee.

246

Both Fats and the baby faced woman serving him spoke slowly, softly, in no hurry to finish the ritual. Her arms were plump but sensuously rounded and the movements of her shoulders and hands were fluid as she set out cup and saucers and silverware that clattered delicately on the bar before the lumpish man.

Stanley in daylight the color of his coffee after he drowns it under a flood of thick cream. Easy to tell the woman behind the bar belonged to him. When balancing his bulk on the bar stool became too tiring, Stanley would slide from his perch, wheezing as he undraped his flesh and shuffled with its burden to the last booth against the wall. It was specially made, extra space had been left between table and the high backed seat of the booth to make room for the proprietor's girth. He would settle in the booth for hours at a time. Sleep and eat there while the life of the bar flowed around him.

> *My Daddy's dead*
> *My Momma's cross the sea*
> *I ain't got no body*
> *To speak nar word for me*

Saunders could not find Wilkerson's face in the purplish haze. The chickenshit nigger getting scared. Only a few shadows seemed alive in the muted light, darkened, one dimensional. Calling me this last minute. Saunders goddamned Wilkerson, the pee, smoke funk of the coffin shaped interior, the fat wheezing man and the string of soft, brown women he paid to tend his pleasures. Fats was a dead man already. Leaking out of his rubbery skin. Door marked *Ladies* wide open, a slop bucket holding it back against a wall. Saunders would have preferred taking a few more steps, steps which would bring him to a booth farther from the entrance, just beyond the edge of the bar but still two booths away from Fats' custom stall. They would need privacy. Yet moving toward the back of the bar like wading into a sewer. The smell of clogged toilets and disinfectant made him wince as he slid into the padded seat closest to him. Foul goddamn place. Needed the drink he had promised himself he wouldn't take. Why not. One or two or ten. He would be ready when it came time to do his part.

—Ain't nobody serving tables yet, my man. What can I do you for.

Saunders ordered from the bartender and watched the double shot glass of scotch splash over the bed of ice cubes in the squat tumbler.

—You sit still, baby.

She stood before him smiling. Her voice had smiled, hurrying from the end of the bar. He knew how she would have switched from behind the counter. A wide arc, hips flourishing in tow the way trailer trucks negotiate twisting mountain roads.

—I be through with Fats. He say serve my customers, now. You call me next time you ready, baby. The scent of powder, of hair freshly pressed, of elbows and ears daubed with unsubtle sweetness interrupted the stale wind from the exposed toilet as she leaned across the table into the recess where Saunders had melted. Plump breasts, long curling lashes, full lips handling words caressingly, sure of themselves around a man. Woman that made him think of slow walking, slow talking, easy access to sun, to sleep, to food and love. A southern woman. Alabama, Mississippi, Louisiana even if she ain't never been off the avenue. She would leave Fats one day and the next man could have her and believe she never been touched, waiting for him all the time.

He watched her full hips playfully switch in the path between booths and bar stools. She picked her way pretending there was barely room for her to pass, avoiding imaginary obstacles with the weave of her body down the aisle. Saunders wondered how many times a day some hand would steal from the stalls to tap her fully-packed as it teased by. The distraction was momentary. Wilco was late. Later each minute. Unexcusably sloppy. Saunders felt the bitter scotch foraging in his empty stomach. Old blues pushed from the jukebox and he heard clearly *nar a word for me*. Nar a fucking word for me. Jive yellow nigger. Old country dude crying the blues. Lost mama. Dead daddy. Wilkerson was in trouble more ways than you could shake a stick at. This day so long in coming and first thing in the morning Wilkerson hemmin' and hawin'.

Saunders recalled the women, Sissie, Lisa, the old witch. Their cave cold and wet, stinking like this room with its toilet door hanging open. He had watched the women come and go many times since. Even crept into the ruin beside theirs to listen through the thin wall. Heard Sissie talking to the cop. Heard them grunt and sigh, bounce on the titty soft springs of one of those old cots. The gray boy talking his shit and she must be believing every word, the way she does his business. Saunders had fought to keep still. He had wanted to punch through the rotten plaster and kill them both in their sweat. No humiliation would have been enough. Make the cop crawl and whine. Make the woman suck on his joint. Bring in the old crone. The girl. A real show then wipe them all from the face of the earth. But he sat still, trembling in the chill spring air. Their words, the noises of their greedy humping. Burned him that the cop did with her as he pleased. Peeling the white fish-eyed thing from his drawers, his white face puffy and bloodshot and her panting on the bed, nigger legs wide open like he's going to drive a truck of gold up between them. The cop like Fats looking for his dick inside those rolls of jelly belly. And the dumb bitches waiting, giving all they got so he'll throw them a crumb or two. His big elephant ass waddle. And the bitch he's sugaring trying to figure a way to give him some pussy through all that fat. Shugs. The cop. Stanley. So many dicks up most these bitches' ass no wonder they move around always like somebody fucking them.

His watch said 9:30. Wilkerson at least a half hour late. The Ballantine clock over the bar said 9:45. Bar time. Watered like the cheap scotch they serve in top shelf bottles. Like some nigger come in here twelve at night high as a kite yelling loud as he can J&B or Cutty. Give him iodine long as

249

it came from the right bottle. Long as everybody heard him order what he can't afford. The jive time. The hophead, lying, booze time. Early in the morning and the flies already slipping in from the street. Stanley's smelling like a fish market, sham whiskey, sham time, sham pussy shaking itself like *take some* but ain't giving nothing away cept to the high bidder.

This was the day. The beginning. How many run-throughs rehearsed in his imagination. Meticulous step by step. Yet so simple nothing could go wrong. Get the girl. Get the cop. The speech and the hanging. But Wilkerson. Where the fuck was he. With his crazy questions after all this time, this preparation, this readiness, this need. Like they were planning a picnic. The questions, the chickenshit hemmin' and hawin'.

He called Wilkerson's apartment. If the phone had been a funnel he would have spit through it. As he listened to the futile ringing, the black receiver became a club. He squeezed it, felt his knuckles sting. He cursed Wilco through his teeth, slammed the receiver like a club on Wilkerson's eggshell skull.

They had to get the whore tonight. While the girl and the old woman away. On the nights Sissie tricking the house had to be empty. The other two would be at an all night movie or in one of the little storefront churches that took turns with their nightly marathons of singing and praying. Tonight as soon as Lisa and the old bitch left he would enter. *Money for Lisa.* Come on square, insinuating like maybe he was curious about what kept his brother's nose open so long. Bullshit her if he could. Offer her enough money to tempt, but not make her suspicious. If she went for his rap, maybe she would go to his apartment. Would make everything easier. But these wise bitches know better. Don't trust anybody. Take a chance on running it down to her anyway. If not, she'll go the hard way. She would be watching him like a cat the whole time. He could tell she was the jumpy kind of bitch anyway. He would have to be careful. Get her guard down. Maybe go all the way with the sham. Go on and knock out the trim. Get the bitch with her drawers down, flat on her back. Raymond had his pick of lots of wenches. His taste was good. No sense wasting a good thing. A little trim first. He would make her groan. Get his hands up under her skinny backside. Make her shut those big eyes. Turn her on like no white pig could. Raymond was no fool. And unless the cop steady lying she got him weakening just a little too. Paddy boy don't know enough to jive a bitch. He must be half believing that shit he was talking. *I'm gonna marry you honey. I'm gonna marry and nothing gonna stop me. Just a little more time, baby. A little more time and money.* Yeah, you hustle your black ass a little longer he'll make you an honest woman. He'll be taking you to the policeman's ball, baby. Just keep spreading them legs and fattening his pocket. Love talk. Saunders had wanted to laugh out loud. Loud enough so they'd hear him through the roach rotten wall. Sure enough love. Tomorrow you both going to Hell. Maybe we throw them on the same heap at the dump.

But might as well fuck her first. See what she got that's worth seeing. If she won't go with me, I'll do it in the rat trap. On their wedding bed. Kill her before that pussy has a chance to dry. In her place easy to kill. So rotten you doing her a favor, getting her out the only way there is. Nobody will find her in the shack next door. Just the rats and bugs. When the old woman and the girl come back, they'll think she's with the cop. They both know it's only a matter of time anyway before she leaves. The cop definitely ain't marrying them. He wants their meal ticket to hisself. They'll just hope she ain't gone for good yet and wait. What else they going to do. We'll tip the cops to Sissie's whereabouts. She'll be quiet till we do. Quiet and peaceful. Little girl won't have to cry anymore listening to her mama doing tricks with that white man.

Had to be tonight. He was primed. Littleman was out of the picture. The plan couldn't wait. Littleman always said it was bigger than any one of them. He said learn to be an instrument. Learn to be dispensable if your usefulness ends. That was why Rice must go. He had been a feeble link from the beginning. He was a pocketbook they could drain. A bed to sleep in, food to eat. His basement apartment was private enough to hold the weapons and a hostage. Rice was capable of the simplest most mindless tasks. Once those were finished, he was finished. He talked too much. Would probably brag. Would have to tell some stranger of his importance once the action of the plan had been completed. His accident would be simple to arrange. No one would care or grieve. One more slightly goofy nigger found dead in a locked room. Weeks before he'd be missed. Rice was almost a hermit. How Littleman had found him was a mystery. The plan needed somebody like Rice and it was like Littleman knew this need and dreamed up somebody to fill it. Everything made sense. Every piece. And they were all pieces. Rice, Littleman, Wilkerson. And me, Leonard Saunders, a fitting piece like the rest. Maybe Littleman had dreamed them all up. Worked voodoo magic. Stolen their souls. Yet Saunders knew his own mind. Each step he took was a step he wanted to take. If the mood took him, he could sit in Stanley's all day. Drink till he passed out and when they closed the joint, ride home, sleep, wake up the next morning and go to work. He was free. Freer than he'd ever been. More free than those days hustling in the street. Hunger moved him then. And fear. If he fucked Sissie, if he choked the life out of her naked body, if he and Wilkerson ambushed the cop and held him till the lynch day, each action, each choice would be free. No man black or white controlled him. He had chosen the plan. And the plan was something new in the world. Something he was causing. Only four people on the earth even knew it was coming.

When the waitress slinked down the aisle with another drink, the first smile was broadened, was etched with nuances that suggested intimacies long shared. Bitch figures she's getting me a morning high. Which means I don't have a day job to go to, but I'm buying good whiskey. A little something going for me maybe so she doesn't want me to forget that she's out here, that she is accessible even if tied up at the moment with the hog man at the end of the bar.

Somebody playing the raggedy ass blues sound again. *Momma's cross the sea.* Damn shame they got to Littleman. Damn shame it's Wilkerson out here when the deal goes down. Saunders squished the whiskey around his gums. Remembered Clark Gable brushing his teeth with booze after shacking up with a fine bitch. Gable was free. He would smack a wrong bitch down. He would take what he wanted. Whitey's laughing at you all the time. But you can listen and learn. From the laughter even. In the movies you see what they believe. Who they think they are. Don't have to go Tomming around white folks to learn their secrets. They expose their game in Cinemascope and Technicolor just like they parade their women butt naked on the screen for anybody to see.

And Sissie. I bet she thinks she's getting a little piece of Gable or Tony Curtis all those slick gray boys when the lowlife cop sweet talking and banging her ass. Half white Wilkerson knowing more about them than they know about themselves. Books and pictures and buildings. All in his school teaching head. Trying to tell me he's into Africa. Quoting this black king and that black prince. Like I need to be told jungle bunnies all right by him too. I know who I am. I know what I have to do. When the deal goes down I know the enemy. I know who I need beside me. If he was right, he'd be here now. If he was really right, neither of us would need to be here. Littleman stone insane. Half his power is being crazy. But he's crazy smart, crazy real. I can deal with him. If his mind is set, you have to kill him to turn him back. And this fucking Wilkerson will start the day whining.

Blues song faded. Enough voices filled the room now to wrap the music into a larger swell of sound.

—Who's playing all that old timey, down home stuff. Fats, why you keep that country shit on your box. Stanley seldom answered. Like a god he stayed in his place and all inquiries addressed to him rising from the muddle of voices were rhetorical as prayers. He brooded in his corner. Absorbed by the light dancing across a diamond ring which pinched his pudgy finger. He ordered the blues records special from the distributor. Would have the waitress drop three quarters in the juke and press the buttons he memorized so no matter what else played, the up-tempo brassy rhythms, the freight train jazz, it would give way to guitar, harp, the classic lonely wail, the muted celebration.

–You got to have soul to understand blues. The waitress flung the words over her shoulder to no one in particular, telling the truth anonymously to no one but loud enough for her words to carry the length of the bar.

–Somebody's cakes got soul. Whole lot of mammyo soul.

–Sweet cakes.

Leaning into the aisle to stare past the high backed seat opposite that blocked his view Saunders saw a man from the street push open the double doors. Light blazed behind him blurring the edges of his figure, brutally flaying away half his face as he hesitated on the threshold, peering, waiting for momentary blindness to pass. Saunders was ready to shout. To jump up and grab the other's collar, drag him like a recalcitrant child to the stall.

As the figure retreated from the entrance he pulled the doors together, taking the light with him. Saunders lunged toward the open end of the booth. He could feel Wilkerson's neck in his hands, could see the ghost rising from Wilkerson's body, a puny, pasty colored ghost whose eyes were the only features left on the face, eyes slightly baffled, full of puzzlement. But Saunders' arms remained planted on the table, fingers digging into the plastic glaze, an iron bar running across his back, wrists manacled, riveted to huge stones.

Saunders could not speak. He weighed a million pounds, his skin was popping as the dry, hot pressure from his lungs expanded to bloated pockets under his eyes, in his cheeks, his forehead, nose and throat. Heavier by the instant yet all that weight precariously balanced on a pinhead. If he moved a fraction of an inch in any direction, the whole incredibly inflated structure would crash down. Seas of blood, of bile and phlegm and sickly meandering whiskey were waiting to flood from his body. Saunders remained on his feet after the door had shut. To speak would be to scream. To touch, murder. A tremor passed down through his shoulders to the clenched fists burrowing into the table. Breath left him in short nasal explosions, sheets of hard, wet air hissing between his tight lips. He could make no words, form no curses, send nothing hurtling after the pitiful shape but the molten emptiness billowing from his lungs.

He slid down into the puffy blackness of the stall. The silk weave of his lemon shirt stuck to his back's damp groove. He listened to the familiar voices. Words so familiar he half expected to see himself, pockets full, stinking fresh from a hustle, leaning elbow on the bar, foot cocked high on the silver rung of a tall stool, buying, jiving. If not himself, his brother Raymond, jaunty, sleek, the morning king. Or one of the brothers who was a stranger to him. Or a sister. The scattered Saunders clan crowded round the bar to hear the news. Or the girl. Lisa. Standing at Stanley's door. Calling for somebody in the throng.

• • •

My name is Bernice Wilkerson and I want to see my husband.

My name is Bernice Wilkerson and I want to see my husband.

My name is Bernice Wilkerson and I want to see my husband.

She formed the phrase again. It was a light going before her. It was powerful magic to roll back the stones, one by one. White faces she saw in a dream. Spots in the crowded hallway. In the courtroom. At the side door. Behind a desk.

Behind steel bars. White faces above uniforms. Above the kinds of suits her husband always talked about getting but never owned. One said he was a bondsman. He had ushered her through the knot of people outside the courtroom. He had tried to make his voice gentle and persuasive. He wanted to help her he said. She explained that she had no money that her son was bringing money. He said she should wait with him until her son arrived. No point in trying to see her husband now. She looked at the beautiful weave of his necktie. She saw he wore a diamond on his little finger and the finger dangled independent of the hand. Jerking as if its tight collar choked off the air. She would not wait for her son. She had come early to be alone with her husband. The bondsman was whispering something else but his words were lost because she was already beginning to say what she had to say to the next white face.

My name is Bernice Wilkerson and I want to see my husband. I'm too close. Too close to turn around. Too close to turn. Just can't turn. Her wrists were crossed in front of her body and the straps of her purse twisted around them making her hands droop bloodless from the leather shackles. Had the man been laughing at her. She had stated her name and business. A veil behind which she had felt almost safe. But the man at this last gate had turned his gray eyes on her and stared her nearly to tears. Not how long he had looked but how ruthlessly the coldness of his eyes had penetrated her bluff. Everything she wanted to hide suddenly exposed. She was a woman. She was widowed by the iron gates the guard could lock or unlock according to his whim. She was not standing but kneeling naked before him. His gray eyes were death. And death turned its blue liveried back on you and the last impression it left was a mocking grin.

But then he returned and opened the gate. Her husband was alone in the cell. He paced, shadowed, silent, his broad back to her, seeming to measure the limits of his cell before settling on a stone slab protruding from the concrete wall. He looked countrified. A big, brown peasant boy, his weight on his backside, splayed knees higher than the bench so his long thighs steepled toward the ceiling, shoulders hunched, head bowed now, arms dangling empty handed from bunched muscles of his back almost to the floor. The powerful arms could lift things, crush things, circle her waist twice. She was always frightened when he lifted the children and tossed them in the air.

–I'm not ready. I'm not ready to see you here crying. I'm not ready to start feeling sorry again. I sat here all night trying to get on top of this thing. Trying not to feel sorry for myself. For you and Mamie and the children. Trying to piece something together.

–I'm not going to cry. I just had to see you.

–Did you speak to Mamie.

–They wouldn't let me talk to her. They said she's too bitter now. Said I'd just upset her.

–God help her. She's all by herself now with children in the house ain't half grown yet.

–Her sister answered the phone. Mamie got three sisters and two are there to help.

–Some things I thought would never change. I was a man like Childress was a man and I figured most people don't mean much except in the eyes of one or two others close to them. And if you had that you were doing good. So I figured I was lucky. You and Childress and Mamie. I thought I was a man. Asking nothing beyond what I had. I thought some things wouldn't change. I was used to crumbs, I was used to breaking my back for nothing cause I believed some things couldn't be taken away.

–I don't want to cry. I better wait in the courtroom.

–I wonder if Mamie will be out there. And who else will be out there. I know I killed him. And I know his car is sitting where it always does on the street outside the depot. He rode me every morning. Then in the truck together. Now all of that don't even make sense. Morning after morning, just about every day of my life and now it doesn't make a damned bit of sense. And you sitting in a courtroom. And people staring up at me. And somebody will ask me if I killed a man named Childress and I won't even know what they're talking about.

Her hand touches his wrapped around the steel bar. She is not crying. She is touching his hand. She is telling herself to pray. She is telling herself be dry-eyed when they bring him into the courtroom.

• • •

Behind him the long corridor stretched empty and white. Only sound is rattle, tinkle of implements on three tiered aluminum tray he is pushing. Think of sun drenched Mexican boy, mahogany dark in peasant pajamas but without a sombrero. Sleeves and legs of belt roped costume are too short, hands and feet seem incredibly long because you begin looking for them along the thin, dark flesh, eight inches before they begin. Orderly's baggy pants and blouse about that inadequate on Anthony's gangling frame. But he pushes slowly, with dignity, eye neither right nor left through the hall to the blue doored elevator. He hears its weary response to the button he pushes. Doors will open as if for the last, exhausted time. You hope there are no stretchers which crowd you into corners. Nor the old living dead who are musk and dry leaves under stenciled sheets.

Tray clanks once, twice as wheels fall into the car which never quite meshes with floor level. Clank. Clank. If you push it in crooked like they expect all dumb sambos to do there are four Clank Clank Clank Clank. Each wheel tipsy over the edge and every eye on you to see who is being so stupid and clumsy. Some even jump or cringe when you enter with the bumping tray as if you'll dump some horrible disease on them in your clumsiness. Why niggers is lugging mops and dumping bed pans instead of doctoring is what some of your own people saying with their eyes.

She turns her pink nose up at you. But her eyes flash long enough to let you know she knows you were looking. Big butt stretching nylon. Like she is gone with a wicked swish. Too good to ride the same elevator. Car filled with her anyway. Heat perfume enough to make you dizzy. Chicks knock me out. Surely do. Telling me, no black boy, not with a ten foot pole could you touch one golden hair on my body, letting me know just how precious all that is like I don't know how fast she'd drop her drawers one of these college boys buy her a Coca-Cola.

Empty and he whistles through the slow drop of five floors.

His tray slams lightly into traffic jam of trays in the basement. Floor as usual is wet and smelly during the after dinner rush. Porter and Clement are down to their T-shirts, furiously attacking. Fast hands and otter bodies that bend swiftly, smoothly. Fingers rake, sort and stack simultaneously. When black Clement straightens up each shelf is stripped and his foot sends the enemy crashing into the dead pile. Dishwasher runs hot and noisy. Porter feeds it, dealing the dishes into rubber baskets that trundle along to heat and steam. He is at both ends of the conveyor belt, loading baskets then stacking the sweating dishes in tall piles after their sprint through a gauntlet of steam and spinning bristles. Porter and Clement both old hands. Anthony hates to see them in the changing room. Each has a locker but Anthony must hang his things on a hook. Room is barely wide enough for Anthony to pass if one of the dishwashers is standing at an open locker. They let him know they don't like to be crowded. They let him know their privileges and possessions extended far beyond simply having lockers. They never called him by his name. It was more fun to label him; a new title for each embarrassment or trick. Mr. One-shoe. Dropsy. Fifteenth Floor. Each name lasting until even they tired of laughing at the put-on. Dishwashers were Mr. Porter and Mr. Clement since twice his age and regular, long standing employees, not just some jackleg kid working after school.

Clement said: Mr. Grown-up Already Dude growin' him a moustache and beard.

Porter: Naw, you wrong. Boy just ain't washed his face.

Clement: Don't tell me. I counted the hairs. Seventeen sure nuff.

Uniforms are stacked on a table at the end of the narrow room. And since you just a boy don't be taking any the big ones. And though the big ones are themselves short in arms and legs you take pants and blouse even more inappropriate to body growing fast as weed.

—You know he wouldn't be half bad looking if he could get rid of them pussy bumps about his neck.

—He too young be thinking about cock.

—Well if he ain't thinking, his dick sure is. Shooting poison all through his system, making them ugly pussy bumps.

—Maybe you right. Young boys'll fool you bout what they gettin' into. Won't do no harm to tell 'em what he should do if he ever happen up on some trim.

—After you done, slip your hand down tween her legs. Get it nice n sticky then rub it on them bumps. If pimples ain't gone next day, I'm a lie and a grunt.

Laughter follows you up through halls. Walls ache with catching pain and screaming and blood and their chicken cackling in the hot, tight room. You are sorry for yourself, you are wasted by your own sickness, the needlepoint shivers, scabs and sores of what they know about you, the way they strip away even the skin so your rubber soled brogans quash in puddles of blood when you walk. Dying around you is nothing compared to the wounds you carry. You look away from the women's bodies carelessly or helplessly naked in the rooms off the hall. If your eyes do linger there is always some sour tangle of cloth or darkness. You are threatened and retreat.

Anthony is dreaming at his desk, history book closed, listening to the bell ringing once, twice, ten times, fashioning a song from its caroling, his bell melodious, deep toned, various until it is interrupted by the bell he was awaiting. He is a sleepwalker rising chronically at the wrong speed as the others scatter and push around him. He hears his name above the babble, strange, unexpected star in a black sky.

—Where were you this afternoon, Anthony. She is not a nurse. She doesn't do the things the med students laugh about when they talk of nurses. She is a lady. Her face is soft, a shape he is not sure of because it always melts into what she is saying. He had tried to picture her once as he sat alone in the locker room. He could not say if her eyes were brown or blue. If she was tall or if she looked up when she spoke to him. Now brown eyes look up because she is sitting. She stands and he must move back a step because she comes closer. Someday he had promised himself, weary on the bench, I will look closely and know Miss Collins has yellow hair, blue eyes, that her nose is, her height is, her legs are, her breasts are, but it was impossible for him to say, to remember any detail because just as face melted into words, her body for him was indistinguishable from what he felt about Miss Collins, her body was desire or fear or shame or yearning and these had no dimensions.

—I bet he dreaming of pussy. Hot and cold flushes. Anger. He wanted to grab black Clement, slam his hard body into the hook studded wall. It was as if they knew her. Could put their hands inside her dress. Rip all the secrets he could not even guess at.

He had said, *Fuck you, Clement,* but the word did not push him away, Clement laughed at the word and it cracked, a rotten egg dripping down the front of her dress and shock because she laughed too, laughed at the filth and the smell and Clement licking the egg white from her titties.

—Anthony I'm sure you didn't hear a word I said all afternoon. I depend on you. When you don't speak up or pay attention I feel I must be miles away from reaching the others. She half leaned on the edge of the desk, one leg suspended, the other stretched to the floor. Anthony's eyes had been lowered as she spoke. It was never to him when she was speaking. A third party was addressed, someone who fit the image her words sought, a good student who believed what she told him, who was capable of accepting the responsibilities and confidences she entrusted with him.

261

One neither black nor ugly in her presence. One who did not dream and hate and desire, one whose eyes met hers, whose hands did not tremble because cast down eyes tracked from her ankle as far as they could, up her nyloned thigh.

–I guess I'm tired, today. *One who did not lie.*

–You aren't back on that night shift at the hospital, I hope.

–No, I go after school, but still I'm tired some days. But he must not be weak in front of her. In her classroom each week they would discuss black heroes. Men who had never faltered or wavered in the face of seemingly impossible odds. From huge poster size photos they judged him. And the map of Africa with its heroes and martyrs whose names sounded like lip flipping or tom-toms.

When Miss Collins spoke it was to those black gods ranged around the room. Anthony felt like a sneak, an eavesdropper, listening to her voice, waiting for an answer from the walls.

He pushes his jiggling tray. It was really just like delivering groceries. You had a list, a wagon and everybody in a damn hurry to get what they had ordered. And you saw things. Because you were really nothing. Just the wheels under whatever anybody thought they wanted. People half dressed, undressed, your black foot on rugs you know no real black foot supposed to be. They smile or ignore you depending on how much they want what you're carrying, or how long they had to wait. Some think it's cute to know your name and call you by it. Maybe make you move a little faster, like some think they quarters grease your feet. But I wouldn't hurry for nothing. Getting there is my time. I can think and do what I want to when I'm on the way. Like you can rest a little while from ear beating and eye beating and being ordered around. My time. Like I want to get lost in it. Wander in their streets with trees and big windows and grass you got to walk around on the driveway. Homes almost as fine as where the black heroes live. Wandering these halls and faces in the wards. Seeing everything and they just see dinner coming, or a bottle of pills, or some needle to jug 'em halfway up the ass.

I push seven. Where they keep the loonies. Nobody bother me about smoking there. So I smoke. Sometimes see some weird stuff. These is crazy, but not crazy enough to be locked up. Most just lie there. Except some talk all the time to themself or every once in a while one screams loud as he can. Lot black. Like in the baby ward. I knew niggers had plenty babies, but I didn't think so many stone crazy.

Nurses here nice. Don't care if I smoke. They like to kid around. Tell me stories. Sometimes they can make the loonies do the damnedest things.

But nobody around at the moment. Night outside and over each bed a light so you can see what they doing. When nurses ain't around. Read the charts myself. Some weird shit.

The head is large, lion maned, a puffiness under the eyes and in the cheeks. Lips soft and fleshy, effeminate in their lack of definition. Eyes the flayed back of a man either sleeping or dead. The massive forehead is unmistakable, fringe of hair receding, less like baldness than a gradual assertion of the skull against shiny brown skin. The man's breathing is rumblingly nasal. But he does not sleep. Eyes are fists clenching and unclenching. Whites flash siren loud tracking blindly, blazing on nothing. Each time his eyes open the man seems startled, wide awake, remembering some crucial oversight in this world or hopelessly torn from a task in his dream. Light and darkness. Light. Darkness.

Another sound, almost like gagging, rises from his throat. Sound is chalk wounding a blackboard, traps Anthony beside the bed. The noise builds and dies in the patient's throat, struggling to be swallowed and released simultaneously. Blinking stops and the black suns orbit giddily. They see nothing and Anthony must look away from their emptiness, from the tears that collapse into the kinky beard. Then room is quiet again as rasping throat sound subsides.

Anthony backs slowly from the room. He hesitates half

in, half out of the hallway's brilliant light. His bony black wrist is a scythe as it slashes through bottles, vials, tubes, cups and glasses, all that sustains life in neat array atop the nurses' station.